HEIR OF MY INVENTION

Peter Glazebrook

CONTENTS

Heir of my Invention

By Peter Glazebrook

CHAPTER 1

I was feeling pretty good about my nice quiet academic post, right up until the moment Terry disappeared.

He was my Research Assistant, a tall Londoner in his late twenties, with thinning dark hair, a PhD in theoretical physics and an upbeat attitude to life. When he arrived that morning, he passed my office offering his usual cheery, "Morning Prof."

Shortly afterward five feet nothing of resentment called Carole stomped along the corridor. She might have greeted me, but then again it could have been one of her generic snarls. It was difficult to tell. She was of a similar age to Terry and one of the rising stars at the Daresbury particle accelerator. Her anger was mainly aimed at yours truly, who'd asked for someone to be seconded to our laboratory or, as she called it, pseudo-scientific backwater. She didn't stop to consider why her colleagues were so keen to move her to another facility. Bizarrely she got on well with the perpetually good humoured Terry.

Terry stuck his head around my door. "Fancy a cup of coffee before you set to?"

"Now you're talking my language," I replied following him into the labs. We'd knocked through a couple of rooms to form a workspace for the electrical equipment. At one end Carole was boiling a kettle.

"What are you doing today Prof," asked Terry.

"I'm writing an article about the influence of English Folklore on the theories of John Dee.

"Who's he?" asked Carole, pushing her auburn hair into a scrunchie.

"He was the nearest thing to a scientist in Elizabethan England. His big thing was that he claimed to speak to Angels," I answered.

"Pfft, did he?"

"Funnily enough only he ever saw them, so there was never any verification, but that didn't seem very important in those days. Anyway, he must have done something right. He ended up in the court of Elizabeth the First."

"Doesn't sound very scientific," snorted Carole.

I grinned, "It wasn't. He fell out of favour when natural philosophers started to adopt what we'd recognize as a scientific method. People like Francis Bacon started asking more down to earth questions such as `What can we do with this gunpowder stuff?'. Bacon's last experiment was to see if chicken stayed fresh if it was packed in ice."

"I assume it did?"

"Probably, but when he tested the idea he got pneumonia and died."

Despite herself, Carole was intrigued. "So what's all this nonsense got to do with our work?"

"Well, old John Dee had a device to help him in all this talking to heavenly beings called a scrying scope. It's this piece of obsidian." I held it up for her to see. "All those occult symbols etched on the surface were supposed to be orientated with lay lines and such like."

"Don't tell me this lashed up kit is based on a load of bollocks from the middle ages?" She gestured at the tumble of wires and electrical equipment sitting next to the neatly boxed twenty first century microwave receiver she'd brought with her.

Terry grinned, "You got it. Me and the Prof saw that the symbology used by John Dee bears an uncanny resemblance to the mathematics of quantum physics. That's what we're testing. You and I are going to prove a correlation between the two. You've set up a standard sub atomic particle detector whilst that lashed up kit, although I prefer the term bespoke, is an antenna based on our translations of the scrying scope of old John Dee himself. If we're right then they should both behave in the same way."

"Oh," she said, "Is that ..."

She stopped as Terry put a finger to his lips and winked, nodding his head towards me.

"That's obviously an in joke. I'm sure you'll tell me when

the time is right. I'm only the guy who got you the grant." Even to my ears I sounded irritated.

They exchanged a glance that could be best summed up as conspiratorial.

Terry said, "I think we've made a bit of a breakthrough."

Now I was excited. "Do you think you've actually received a signal? You're sure it's not an anomaly?"

Carole almost growled as she said, "We've been working for weeks to show that the signal isn't an artefact. Now you start picking at it before you've even heard what we have to say."

I held my hands up placatingly. "I'm sorry, but remember what happened to cold fusion. We have to be rock solid before we publish."

"Don't worry Prof, we'll check and double check. I'll find a way of proving the signal isn't some kind of reflection from the Daresbury detector," said Terry, ever the one to pour oil on troubled water.

Altering the course of the conversation he asked, "So what happened to John Dee. That's your side of things."

"That's kind of why we're here and not at Imperial College. Lizzie must have had a soft spot for him because she endowed him with an academic post at Manchester college. They moved the post to Southport in the nineteen twenties."

Carole frowned, "That would've been a very long way from London in those days. Why did she banish him up here?"

"I'm not sure really. Maybe she was worried about his influence at Court. It's difficult to assign motives to the people of that period. Their outlook on life was different to ours. Come on, let's get back to work." I replied.

In hindsight, I think that we should have given her question more consideration than we did at the time.

#

I left the room as Carole, still smarting from my question, muttered darkly about NASA specification standards for shielding.

After a couple of hours I heard Carole shout.

"Voyle get in here!"

I dashed into the lab. She was standing, white faced, in the middle of the room.

Everything seemed normal, no electrical fires or sparks. I looked at the readouts to see if anything was malfunctioning. There was nothing out of the ordinary.

"What's wrong?" I asked.

Carole stood still for a moment, then said, "He's gone."

"Who's gone?"

"Terry."

I looked around, it wasn't a big room, there was nowhere to hide. She seemed unnecessarily upset at being left minding the equipment, but in my experience, she was annoyed most of the time anyway.

"It's OK," I said, "He's probably just nipped out for some real coffee, I'm sure he wouldn't leave the experiment running if it was likely to malfunction. Are you Okay with our kit? I know it's a bit string and sealing wax but the equipment is pretty reliable."

"No, you boneheaded excuse for a scientist." She gritted her teeth with frustration, "I mean he just disappeared, from in front of me. One second he was here, the next he wasn't."

I ignored the obviously well practiced jibe. "Hey Carole, it's OK, you turn your back, and he leaves the room. The instruments will be fine."

"Shut up," she interrupted. "I know what I bloody saw, the area around him folded in on itself. Terry sort of collapsed into the portal and disappeared."

"Carole, are you alright? Has there been some kind of incident with the machinery? What do you mean by portal?"

She seemed to get a grip of herself and was quiet for a moment. "No, I'm sorry Dr Voyle. People don't just disappear. I meant that he's gone without me knowing it." She gave a short and unconvincing laugh, "I mean he's left me with all this stuff to do."

The blood had drained from Carole's face and her hand

shook as she reached for her cup of cold instant. She'd obviously had a bit of a turn. Maybe it was a migraine and Terry had left the room, possibly to get some aspirins.

"Come into my office, have a sit down and tell me what happened."

I thought that, with a bit of luck, Terry would return before she could embarrass herself anymore. I hoped he'd remember to get me a cappuccino.

We went into my office.

She sat on my swivel chair, the one seat with some padding and breathed deeply holding a cup of water. I didn't try to speak and she visibly calmed. But she still wasn't happy.

"Are you feeling a bit better?" I asked after a couple of minutes.

She nodded. Maybe it would throw you a bit if it seemed that the person you were talking to had vanished into thin air. It was easily explained of course. The mind can play some strange tricks on our perceptions.

"Perhaps it would be best if you took the rest of the day off? Don't worry, I can mind the equipment until Terry comes back."

She looked at the floor, seemingly ashamed of her outburst.

"Perhaps it would be a good idea to contact your doctor. Have you got one here?" I added.

She drew a deep breath through her nose. "I'm sorry Doctor Voyle. I think a bit of a rest will do me good."

"Don't mention it. Just get some shut eye and I'm sure you'll be right as rain tomorrow."

After she left I phoned Daresbury. Once they stopped transmitting, I'd shut down our equipment for the day. Then went back to my desk.

But Terry didn't come back. He didn't answer his home phone or his mobile. I started to worry that something really had happened to him, an accident of some kind whilst he was out, perhaps.

Meanwhile Carole called the police, her boss and the University Health and Safety officer, all of whom got the impression, severally, that Terry had either gone missing, left the country or been electrocuted. Apart, that is, from the people at Daresbury, who also called the police to report equipment being stolen, just to add to the confusion.

The next day I ended up with Carole's boss, our Health and Safety advisor and a bemused police constable standing in the laboratory whilst Carole stolidly retold her tale. It was obvious from everyone's face that they didn't believe her.

We changed our minds when, still listening to her description, we saw Terry reappear. Just as she had described, an area seemed to fold in on itself and what was left of Terry dropped to the floor.

CHAPTER 2

Terry's body hit the floor with the same dull thud as a dropped gym bag, his face and neck a mass of bloody raw flesh.

We were silent for a moment, then Carole began to hyperventilate. The constable was the first to react, bending over Terry and checking his pulse. I found out later that some apparently fatal injuries can be survived, if you get help to the person quickly enough. These weren't those kind of injuries.

The next stage would have been mouth to mouth resuscitation but there wasn't enough left to work with. The Health and Safety officer threw up and Carole started making little moaning sounds.

I put my hand on her arm and foolishly said, "It's OK, it'll be all right."

She shook my arm off and gave me a look of venomous hatred. I didn't blame her. Everything was not Okay at all. That was the last we saw of Terry. I was ushered out of the room as the police constable lifted the microphone clipped to his collar and called in the incident. He'd turned pale and said into his radio, "Ambulance needed." Pausing, he looked at Terry's body, and continued, "not urgent".

I waited in my office with Carole as someone brought us cups of tea. Paramedics pushed a trolley past the door with a shape covered in a blue blanket.

The tea was tepid by the time a uniformed constable appeared in the doorway.

"Doctor Voyle? Could you come with me please?"

She led me into the staff meeting room. Pictures of past school principals glowered down at me from the walls.

Sitting opposite she fussed over a mobile phone for a minute.

"It's all very well having technology but writing statements with a pen is a lot easier." She concentrated on the machine for a few more seconds. "Ok, that's it. Could you please tell me who you are and your role at the college? I'll need your address. Then please tell me, in your own words about the incident you witnessed this morning."

Doing as she asked I told her what happened. Her thumbs danced across the phone touch screen, only pausing when I said, "I was standing with the group when Terry's body appeared out of thin air".

"Could you repeat that for me?"

I did, then she said, "Whereabouts were you in relation to the rest of the people in the room."

"I was facing them, next to Carole, and Terry appeared behind us."

"Hmm, OK. I'll read this out to you and you can make any corrections. Is that alright?"

And that was that. Later it was explained that, however insatiable her curiosity, she was being careful to avoid leading the witness.

I imagined that a dead body popping into existence was causing something of a stir. I also had a fair idea of how the institutional mind operates. Bodies do not appear out of thin air; therefore, this was a mass hallucination. Possibly caused by the effect of excessive solvent exposure on the unstable academic mind. Having dismissed the improbable the next thing to consider would be foul play.

CHAPTER 3

The police asked me to stay around in case there was a need to clarify my statement. One of the clarifications I'd have liked, would be some explanation of how my research assistant came to be eviscerated. But I guess I was going to be disappointed about that one.

Darkness had descended by the time I came to the steps leading to my Arts and Crafts style house. The building overlooked Victoria Park. It came with the academic tenure, otherwise it would have been out of our price range. I stopped for a moment. Further down the street were a couple of rabbits sitting on their haunches, but then I realised they were too big, so mentally reclassified them as dogs, whereupon the steady gaze of the animals took on an air of surreal menace.

I reached the porch as my wife, Theresa, opened the door. She couldn't have been in long because she hadn't changed out of her suit or remove her makeup.

It must have been the stress of the day but those two animals, silhouetted by the light of a street lamp, had caused me to run up the steps. I was breathless and my heart pounded.

The first thing she said was, "What happened. Are you feeling OK?" Looking at me she put her hand to the side of my face.

"It's Terry." I said.

Theresa replied, "You poor dear, he's not left you with Growling Carole again, has he?"

"No, there was an accident and he." I had to stop, my mouth was suddenly dry. "He died."

She moved her hand to her lips, her concern suddenly serious, "Oh no, not Terry, he was so nice, what happened."

"I'm not sure, there was some kind of problem with the machinery. It was probably a malfunction and he was... Look, I don't really want to talk about it. I'm sorry, I'm dog tired, I just want to get some tea and go to bed."

"But it's safe, isn't it? I don't want you messing with the equipment. It could be dangerous if Terry or Carole got the electrics wrong. What if there's a fire or something?" she asked.

I didn't want to say what had really happened so replied, "We've isolated all of the machinery. It won't be re-activated until we're sure it's safe."

"I'll get you some tea on. Is stew Okay tonight?"

I forced a smile, "Yeah, it'll be fine."

The stew was great, normal, tasty and wholesome. I managed two mouthfuls, hiccupped, tried to hold back the tears, and failed. Theresa held me as the tensions of the day flowed out in great gulps. I realised then that I felt guilty. I was the one in charge. I'd let my team down.

We went to bed early. As we cuddled I surprised myself by falling into a deep sleep.

The next morning, I was woken by sun shining through the window. For a few seconds I had a moment of contented happiness. Then memories of the previous day crashed in on me like a tidal wave. I dressed, ate some toast and was out of the house before Theresa woke up.

The sun was shining, people drove along the road. Everyone was going about their own business. That's the thing about death, you feel like there should be a cataclysm, but the world still goes on its way.

I stopped to look at the flower beds bordering the park, they stretched into the distance. Drawing a breath to steady myself I noticed a young man in a leather jacket get out of a blue Vauxhall Viva and follow me. The car drove down the road and stopped by hitting the kerb. Ah, they knew how to make vehicles in those days. As I passed I looked in. The driver was another fit looking young man with short gelled hair. Neither of them met my gaze, even when I was staring in at the car window. Great, I was being shadowed by two of the most incompetent police officers in the world.

I dropped down to Lord Street. Who had driven round and parked on the road? You guessed it, our friend in the blue Viva.

This time I took a photo of the registration plate.

I could still get into my office. The two rooms that formed my department were part of the technical school on Lord Street and, to my surprise, Terry's office had not been sealed off with police incident tape.

A couple of guys in washable suits were poring over the equipment. I looked enquiringly at the Health and Safety advisor who was doing a very bad job of appearing blasé. In fact, he seemed more concerned than he had been by the police.

"Ah," he said almost collapsing with relief. This is Doctor Voyle, I'm sure he'll be able to answer your questions."

Would I now?

One of the newcomers held out his hand. "I'm Dave Smethurst, call me Dave, and this is Doctor Barnabus. We're from the Health and Safety Executive."

"Right, HSE. Yes, ask away. Have the police finished here?"

"I see where you're coming from. Usually we're only called in when the police are sure there's no action required under their legislation, corporate manslaughter, murder and the such like. We then need to see if there's any culpability under the Health and Safety at Work Act."

The gulping sound made by our Advisor was audible.

"But in this case they asked us to liaise with them on the technical aspects of the case. Strange place to find an outfit like this. Everyone else in the building seems a bit new age," said Call me Dave.

Ahh, this was where he broke the ice and got me to relax my guard. I said, "Originally the post, back in the day, was in Manchester. It was transferred here in the nineteen twenties. Probably something to do with the upsurge in spiritualism. My guess is that they were following the money. Southport was incredibly wealthy in the early twentieth century. My post is an endowment and is supposed to look at how some Elizabethan talked to ghosts. I guess it didn't take too much effort to alter the emphasis slightly. It fitted in with the zeitgeist of the time. What we're doing is just an extension of the way people tried to prove ghosts existed."

"Hence the, shall we say, esoteric nature of some of your equipment." Call me Dave gestured at Terry's set up.

"Like I say, we'll do anything we can to help. What do you think happened?" I replied.

Call me Dave puffed out his cheeks. "We're looking at the possibility of an electrical malfunction. With the kind of lash up you've got here there can be strange short circuits causing electrocution. For a starter you've got a lot of direct current."

"And?"

"It makes your muscles go into tetany. Your colleague could have touched a live component and been unable to let go."

"But he appeared in mid-air and fell to the ground."

"My colleague and I will get an idea of the electrical set up here."

"I just told you that he wasn't near any of the equipment," I said, trying not to sound exasperated. Meanwhile our Health and Safety Advisor was shaking his head and mouthing "No" in a manner that would have been comical in a less fraught situation.

"The details will be sorted out by the coroner. At the moment we're going to make this lot safe," continued Call me Dave.

"How are you going to do that?"

"We've cut the plugs off."

#

I extricated myself and phoned the local police station.

"Have you got some people following me?" I asked.

"We've brought HSE in to look at the equipment. They should be there."

"No, I mean some guys following me around."

"Well the HSE people can be very persistent."

"Not them. A couple of guys in leather jackets who are tailing me around the town. Every time I try and speak to them they ignore me."

"No, Doctor Voyle. We haven't got anyone following you."

"Well, you would say that wouldn't you."

I could hear the sigh. "So why did you ask? Let me assure you that we have no one detailed to follow you. If it were our people you wouldn't know they were there. Have you thought that they might be the press?"

He had a point. "What can I do about that?"

"Frankly, Doctor Voyle, not a lot. You can make a complaint if they become a nuisance, but that's about it I'm afraid."

"Thanks," I said and resisted the urge to slam the receiver down.

The Health and Safety Executive wouldn't find anything. There was no stray wire making the machine casing live. There were no radioactive emanations. The only emissions were from Daresbury and that was miles away, so the idea of a lethal radiation dose was out.

However, I had a nagging doubt concerning our work. It was certainly not something I could explain to the extremely practical engineering types from the Health and Safety Executive. It was definitely not something I could tell the police. You see, I always knew that Terry's long term goal was to tie up what we did with the modern theories of sub atomic particles. I'd always considered this as an academic exercise that might generate a few scientific papers but, I kept asking myself, what if the equipment did what it was designed to do, perfectly?

CHAPTER 4

At about five p.m. the health and safety posse came into my office.

"We'll be off. Have you got any circuit diagrams we could have?" said Call me Dave in a voice that made clear it wasn't really a question.

However, I appreciated the effort to help me save face.

"No problem, I guessed you'd want them, so I printed some out. Do you need the files, I could email them to you?"

"No, thank you. These will be fine. We'll pop in again. You won't start up the equipment again will you?"

"No, especially as you've cut the plugs off."

"We need to be very careful when there's been a fatality. It would be … unfortunate … if someone else was injured." So saying the HSE people left, and the college advisor visibly wilted.

"You need to get some rest," I said.

He nodded. "Have you heard from Carole?"

"No, she was pretty shaken up. I don't expect to hear from her for a few days."

"Okay, keep an eye on her."

I told myself not to snap at him, "I do try and look after my staff, recent events notwithstanding."

Instead I said, "Have you heard when they're releasing Terry's body?"

"In a few days. They've moved fast considering the unusual nature of his death. Are you going to the funeral?"

"I'm not sure it would be appropriate," I replied.

"Oh," was all he said as he left.

Two days later I was driving through the suburbs of London looking for a crematorium.

"Carry on along this road, it'll be on the right," said Theresa.

"I still don't think I ought to be there," I replied.

"Of course you should. Look here it is."

The car park was next to the open grassy area which formed the garden of remembrance. The place had an oddly rural atmosphere, at odds with the claustrophobic feel of the Streatham suburbs. But then I guess that was the idea.

We located the chapel and positioned ourselves at the rear. I dreaded the formalities after the service. Somehow, I felt out of place as I lined up to shake hands with Terry's parents. His mother's face turned brittle when she found out who I was. The streaks of tears in her foundation made the face look broken, reflecting the rips in her soul. I mumbled my condolences and left. Looking back I could see that Theresa, with more grace than I, lingered to hug the grief stricken woman.

"I don't know John. You should have spent more time speaking to his parents," Theresa said as we walked to the car.

"It was that look in his mother's eyes I could see that she blames me for Terry's death."

"You blame yourself. You're just seeing your own guilt reflected in other people faces. Really, John, everyone knows you're a caring person. You might not listen to other people but you wouldn't have let the experiment go ahead if you thought it was dangerous."

"But what if I missed something. What if there was an obvious fault."

"What like?"

"This is going to sound stupid, but what if we did mess around with dimensionality. What if John Dee wasn't making it all up."

"I suppose that's possible."

I smiled at her. "You'd support me anyway wouldn't you. However outlandish my ideas."

"Well, you know that I'm from ..."

"It's Okay. I understand what you're trying to do. I'll be alright, honest."

"But.."

"Come on," I interrupted, "Get us back home."

Theresa buried her nose in the A-Z, eschewing modern technology. She was unusually quiet on the journey back. The funeral must have affected her more than I thought.

\#

It was not long after I got home, that a couple of police officers turned up.

"Would you accompany us to the station Doctor Voyle?"

"What is it?" asked Theresa.

"We've just got a couple of questions."

"It's alright," I said. "There's probably a few things that need clearing up."

"But Terry's death was an accident, wasn't it?" Theresa asked.

"Of course, but …" I turned to the policeman, "What exactly do you need to know?"

"There are a couple of minor details we need to clear up."

I shrugged, there was no point in refusing and it couldn't be anything serious. Which just goes to show how wrong you can be.

As we drove away, I pointed to the blue car that was parked outside my house. This time there was a man and a woman sitting inside, both studiously looking at books.

"That car's been parked outside my house for days. Are they your people."

The driver made a "Pfft" noise.

"Who are they then."

"Probably journalists, they look amateurish enough. I mean why would you call attention to yourself by driving an antique. My Grandad had one of those."

As we drove away I could see the driver of the blue car reaching for the ignition. By the time the police car had got to the end of the street the blue vehicle hadn't moved and I could just make out the woman hitting the steering wheel.

"Yup, bloody awful at starting. Don't worry Doctor Voyle, they'll catch up with us."

"How will they know where we're going?"

"Well, my uniform's probably a bit of a giveaway."

I nodded, fair comment.

In half an hour I was sat on a hard chair in an interrogation, sorry, interview room.

Two detectives sat opposite and were taping the interrog .. well you get the idea. I'll be frank, the situation was making me nervous.

"Doctor Voyle, we've read your statement and there are a few questions we'd like you to answer," one said.

"Fire away," I replied.

"What was your relationship to Terry?"

"He is, was, my Research Assistant."

"How does that work out? I mean, I'm a lowly Detective Constable so could you enlighten me as to your academic working relationship?" This guy obviously had a bit of a chip on his shoulder. This was going to be such fun.

"I was his manager, but he had a lot of autonomy with respect to the project."

"Did you direct the work at all?"

"We worked as a team. I did a lot of the maths whilst Terry put together the equipment and formed the relationship with Daresbury."

"I understand that you didn't get on well with the rest of the team?"

"Who told you that?"

"In particular we've been told that you harboured a grudge against Terry?"

I'd had enough. "Look, I got on fine with Terry. Do you think that his death wasn't an accident? Your constable was there when he reappeared. How could I have had anything to do with it?"

"Quite a good sleight of hand there by someone. I noticed that you and Carole were partly blocking the view of his appearance." The last word illustrated with air quotes.

"I suppose you weren't aware that Terry had been dead for

several days before he was made to appear before our colleague," the detective said.

"You've got something wrong here. Terry was missing for a few hours. Go and check the computer records. People saw him around the laboratories the day he disappeared. He'll probably appear on CCTV somewhere. Have you checked that?"

The detective compressed his lips into a thin line. A bit like Human Resources do when they find that you're entitled to that pay rise after all.

He opened a manila folder. "We're going to show you some photographs. Can you tell us if you recognise any of these women?"

"Aren't you going to caution me?"

"I don't think that's necessary at this stage."

This stage? I didn't like the sound of that one little bit.

They put pictures of various youngsters down in front of me. The images were of bright looking people in their twenties. A few were obviously holiday snaps. Others looked like graduation photographs, the subjects smiling proudly at the camera. I stopped at one, a dark haired girl.

Tapping the photograph I said, "This is Natalie, she used to work with my wife. I think she got another job a year or so ago."

"Do you know her well?"

"Not really. I think I saw her once or twice at work events. She lives with her Mum somewhere in Birkdale."

"Where were you on May 25th?"

I pulled out my phone and called up the calendar. "Hold on, normally I have a good memory for these things, but I just want to check. That was exam paper moderation day. We were there until 8 pm when I went home. My wife can vouch for me then."

"What about the 30th?"

"I was at a conference in Salisbury."

"Do you have a dog?"

"Pardon?"

As if he had infinite patience that was being tested, the detective repeated the question.

"No, we're both at work and ..."

"Have you ever worked at a zoo; maybe as a volunteer?"

"What? No. If you don't mind me saying this is getting a bit surreal. What's going on? Is this anything to do with Terry's death?"

He looked annoyed. Like I'd got the answers wrong. "That's all. Thank you for your time Doctor Voyle. We'll be in touch if we have any more questions."

With that, I was shown out of the police station. It was a modern building on the outskirts of the town, inconveniently far away from the bus routes.

It had started to rain. I looked around. There was the blue Viva. Sod it. I walked over, knocked on the side window and said loudly, "Any chance of a lift home? You're going there anyway, and it'll be easier to track me if I'm actually sitting in your car with you."

CHAPTER 5

They took me home, they of the blue classic car. Didn't say a word. Just reached over and opened a door. Then drove me to my house and sat there, looking at me as I walked to my front door.

I felt unsettled. The detective was obviously disappointed that I had alibis. I seriously hoped it spoilt his day.

As I logged onto my terminal the next morning the phone rang.

"Hi, Is that Doctor Voyle? This is Carole's line manager from Daresbury. I want to check that Carole's Ok?"

"She's not come in today. I've had an email to say she's staying at home."

"Has she got anyone to talk to?"

"She's on her own. The place is about half a mile away."

"How's she taking it?"

"Not bad considering. She was close to Terry, the guy who was killed. Funny really, they were like chalk and cheese. Nothing romantic, that is to say I don't think so. But then it wasn't any of my business."

"Forgive me for saying this. But how are you taking it?"

"I'm fine, tough as old boots."

"It's just the way you talk. It's a bit like you're running through a slightly different conversation inside your head."

"I appreciate your concern, I'm fine. I'll just keep an eye out for Carole. Try and involve her in things. Bring her out of herself."

"Sounds ... good. Call me if you need anything."

He rang off. Bloomin' cheek. Talking to myself indeed. Still, it was a good idea for Carole to take a few more days off. Even if there hadn't been a romantic attachment, she'd worked very closely with Terry.

I couldn't settle. Looking at the computer screen just made me fidget. Coffee didn't help, not unexpected I suppose, so

I worked through my day as best I could.

The Health and Safety people had come back to run some more tests. I popped my head round the door.

"Do you guys need anything?"

Call me Dave said, "No, we're fine."

He and his colleague went back to tracing circuits. It was like looking at scientists, patiently working their way through things. If they found something that could explain what happened to Terry, well, good luck to them.

There was a newcomer. He wore a grey suit that wasn't machine washable. His tie had burgundy and blue diagonal stripes so he'd either served in the Guards, or gone to a grammar school in Birmingham. Both of which can give you a chip on your shoulder.

He held out his hand, "My name's John Smith, I represent the Environment Agency. You must be Doctor Voyle?"

"Yes," I replied, "if you need anything just call."

"It would be helpful if you could give an account of what happened."

I sighed and recounted the events as I saw them, again.

Smith pursed his lips, "So you're saying that Terry appeared in mid-air."

"Yes,"

"Well away from the equipment."

"Absolutely."

"And at that point he was injured?"

"Yup."

"Was there much blood?"

I opened my mouth, closed it again, then asked. "How much is a lot?"

"Gushing forth old man, absolutely splashing about."

After hesitating a moment I replied, "I don't think so, he just fell and lay there."

"Just the classic soggy wet thud was it?" said Smith in an almost jolly manner.

One of the HSE people made a tsk noise.

Smith smirked, "Don't worry about them. They hear a lot of made up stories about how people get injured. Yours is just a bit more outlandish than most."

"Have you thought about whether this incident is actually anything to do with the Environment Agency?" snarled Call me Dave, irked by Smith's attitude.

"We're worried about radiation affecting members of the public and so forth," answered Smith, waving his hand.

Personally I think I preferred the HSE people, they seemed more professional than Smith. However, he didn't seem to have the unconscious mental block that everyone else had about Terry's body popping into existence in mid-air, even if his interest was ghoulish.

Another man entered. This newcomer stood in a corner, not doing anything, just taking it all in. I nodded to him, because he was rudely ignored by everyone else, and he stared at me with raised eyebrows. I wondered which agency he was with.

Smith asked, "Could you tell me about the X-ray emissions?"

One of the other inspectors stared fixedly at the instrument he was examining, whilst Call me Dave looked at Smith with incredulity.

"There aren't any," I said carefully.

Call me Dave said, "This operates in the Ku band. There wouldn't be any X-rays. And it's a receiver not a transmitter."

Smith nodded sagely, seemingly not embarrassed by his gaff. Makes you wonder what the regulators are coming to these days.

To break the embarrassment, I turned to the newcomer and held out my hand.

"Hi, I'm John Voyle."

He didn't reply, and the room was silent for a moment. But now I had everyone's full attention.

Smith said, "Who are you talking to?"

I pointed to the newcomer, "Him."

Call me Dave had gone back to his work. The other was red faced.

Only Smith didn't react. He just said, "Interesting. We must discuss this later."

The person they were all so studiously ignoring still didn't say anything, so I backed out of the room.

The guy followed me, and I got a good look at him. He was, well, a bit off. His jacket was a little too long for a suit. It had too many buttons and was paired with a waist coat that looked like silk, with a red and blue pattern. His shirt collar was unfashionably long, and he had a paisley cravat. He looked like a Goth arts student who had dredged the most conservative items from his wardrobe to attend a dinner dance.

"Doctor Voyle, hello," he said with a half-smile; shaking my hand, he continued, "My name is Wells and I need to speak to you."

"I'm sorry", I said, "I've got a lot on at the moment and it really isn't convenient." Mentally adding, because my colleague has just died and I'm not talking to anyone else without a lawyer being present.

He looked closely at me and waved his hand in a slightly dismissive fashion.

"Are you a journalist?" I said.

"I am not a journalist. Please, follow me," he replied walking towards the exit.

I stood still and after a few steps he stopped and turned back.

"Fascinating," he said, holding his head to one side in a bird like manner, examining me closely. "Don't you feel compelled to follow me?"

Bemused I said, "Not in the slightest. Should I?"

"Well, frankly, yes you should. Will you come with me anyway?"

"If you're a journalist you're wasting your time. I'm not telling you anything."

"On the contrary. I need to tell you some things. What

happened to your colleague, it doesn't feel right to you does it?"

"It feels wrong to everyone," I replied.

"I mean none of the explanations make sense to you, do they? You feel something is missing."

He had a point. If he was a journalist, he was showing an impressive ability to play mind games. But then maybe that's what makes a good journalist.

"OK, let's go. But I should warn you that we'll be followed," I said.

"Don't worry about that."

As we passed through reception one of the blue car people looked up from the newspaper he was reading. He started to stand up, but Wells walked past him giving that little wave of his hand. My follower returned to his seat and resumed catching up on the day's news as we exited on to Lord Street.

We walked along the wide pavement and turned down an alley next to one of the more gothic creations lining the thoroughfare. He unlocked a door set into the wall of the building and we ascended two sets of stairs. At the top was a single door that led into a Victorian hallway, all William Morris wallpaper and dark stained woodwork. To the left was a lounge decorated in the style of the early 20th century. Everything looked authentic. Normally when people put together something like this there's some kind of anachronism, but this was perfect. It didn't look shabby either. These really were excellent reproductions. We were on the third floor looking out over the traffic. People strolled along the wide pavement occasionally stopping to look into shop windows. I felt a moment of dislocation, it all seemed so normal.

"Please, take a seat, I expect you have a few questions?" Wells said.

"Let's think," I replied, "How did you get into the building? Why were you in my laboratory? Why did everyone seem to ignore you and how did you stop a person following me who's shown great tenacity in that respect?"

"Anything else?"

"Yes, what do you know about the accident in my lab? In short, what the hell's going on?"

"I think that I can start to answer your questions by dealing with the one about your experiments first."

"What's that?" I asked.

"That the work you and your associate ..."

"Terry,' I interrupted, "His name was Terry."

"Indeed, I apologise," he continued, "Terry and yourself appear to have been very successful in your work."

"But we were trying to establish a relationship between ancient alchemical maths and quantum physics. Quite frankly, it's bullshit," I said.

I know what you're going to say. Academics aren't supposed to say that kind of thing about their own work, or indeed anyone else's; but I was having a very trying day. I was also starting to get a bit frightened because I was wondering, even though it seemed outlandish, whether we had been successful. If so, exactly what had we unleashed.

He looked at me, steadily. "Ah, actually it isn't, as you put it, `bullshit'. In fact, you succeeded very well. What would you say if I told you that you were totally correct in your assumptions; that, at some point, physics and the mental manipulation of matter become one and the same."

This was getting a bit much. "I would say you were talking nonsense. Look; are you trying to tell me that we were doing magic?"

"No", he replied, "However, it is possible to manipulate items at, what you call, the quantum level, by focussing mental energy to affect matter. Where I come from, we can control matter using our minds, although I can't do it very effectively here."

I drew in a breath to explain what I thought about this using clear and colloquial language, when I stopped, because a whiskey bottle and two glasses lifted themselves from a side board and drifted silently onto the table. I stared at them stupidly.

"Drink?" he said, with something of a self-satisfied smirk. He poured us a couple of glasses.

"So, you can do magic. I take it you can also make yourself invisible."

He nodded. "To all intents and purposes."

"Are you a wizard or something?" I asked.

"Good lord, no! What a ridiculous idea. No, no, no, I'm just a visitor from another dimension," he answered.

"Oh, that's all right then. For a moment there I thought you were going to say something really outlandish."

"Let me explain," he said. "You must be aware of theories of parallel universes, yes?"

"Of course," I said, "The theory is that there are an infinite number of universes that exist side by side. Anyone reading New Scientist knows that. I always thought that you could just drift between the nearer ones and you would never know you had. There might be a slight difference but nothing worth noticing, like when you thought you'd put your keys down somewhere and they're unexpectedly somewhere else."

"No," he said. "It's not really like that. The universes aren't side by side, they're sort of jumbled up. Adjacent universes, and I don't really want to use that term because it's a bit more complicated than that, can have different physical laws. So, if one moves to another universe the physical laws might be different, leading to radically different worlds. Take my universe as an example, the gravitational constant is 7 x 10 to the minus 11."

"Hold on," I said, "That's wrong."

"Not wrong, different," he replied, "So where I come from John Dee's experiments led to a technology based on the mental control of physical materials. Moving the bottle and glasses is simple in my universe but here it's exhausting because the fundamental physics is different.

"I had to concentrate very hard to affect perceptions of people back at your college. And yet it had no effect on you.

I'm guessing that you spent a lot of time close to that machine you've been putting together in your laboratory?"

"Well, I had; wait a minute, how do you know what we were doing?"

"Dr Voyle, I travel between dimensions. The operation of a device that affects dimensional barriers is a bit like a fire engine siren going off in my ear. I took the opportunity to find out what you and your colleagues were up to."

"So, what happens to your physics when you come here?"

"As I said, I can still manipulate items. As my body adapts to this universe those abilities become less pronounced."

"If that's so, then there's no point in people from other universes coming here. As soon as they arrive, they're subjected to our physical laws and they cannot do their stuff. Hence, we're not swamped with magicians, wizards and such like," I said, feeling I was starting to get the hang of the thing.

"Fundamentally you're right, but we actually come here more than you think. We are still able to do our 'stuff' as you call it. Just not as well as where we came from. But my universe is comparatively close to yours. There are some very strange, and really quite dangerous places, just a sub atomic particle away," Wells said.

I felt he had hit on something there. "Exactly how dangerous?"

He paused, "Probably enough to give rise to a lot of your myths and legends."

"What, fairies, elves, little Red Riding Hood?" I asked.

"Not in the way you portray them in your stories. Those tales have been corrupted by time and imagination, but yes, some of the nastier creatures in folklore probably derive from actual meetings recounted by the survivors."

"What do you mean 'survivors'?"

"Some of the other dimensions can be very dangerous."

"Did we create a weak point between universes that poor Terry got sucked through? Perhaps to some place inimical to our kind of life?"

Wells looked uncomfortable. "Possibly," he said, "I rather suspect that you have created a fairly permanent trans dimensional weakness. If so, it would be easier for people and things to move between other universes and this one. The people in my universe would like to seal you off and leave you to stew, as it were. But your experiments have created instabilities that have promulgated themselves through several dimensions. In fact, your amateurish bungling has created chaos."

"So, people like you could sort of fall into this universe and vice versa. Terry might have fallen out of this dimension and ended up somewhere that caused those injuries to him. Maybe there are places where chemical bonding is different, and he sort of fell apart," I said.

Wells replied, "I'm not sure. Moving between universes takes skill but to be honest I just don't know what happened." He drew breath. "Now listen, we have a common interest here. I have no contacts. My people haven't even had a permanent presence here for a while."

I looked round the room. "About 100 years?" I guessed.

He pursed his lips and nodded, "Yes, approximately."

That explained the decor and furniture. This wasn't a reproduction Art Deco room. It was just what was in fashion last time they decorated.

Wells said, "Come to me at any time. Myself or a colleague will always be here. We have some knowledge of other dimensions and how to travel between them. But be careful about who you take into your confidence."

"You mean in case it's someone like you from yet another universe?"

He ushered me to the door, hesitated for a moment on the threshold and said, "People like me are going to be the least of your problems."

"That's cheerful."

"I'll walk with you for a while. I feel the need for some fresh air. Do you live far?"

"Rotten Row?"

"Really?"

"It's named after the road in London."

"Where's that?"

"It's our capital city. You should visit."

"I don't think so. I'm quite happy here. Nice buildings." He gestured at the frontages above the arcades. "To my mind they seem too elaborate."

"You've got a point. The great and the good came to live in Southport at the end of the Nineteenth century. They were attracted by some peculiar building regulations and unpolluted air," I answered.

I looked at the building frontages. The unrestrained architectural exuberance was normally a source of amusement. But in the present circumstances the creations took on a gothic menace.

"Why can't you detect Carole?" I asked.

"Who?"

"There's someone else who was working on the project."

"Things get a bit mixed up. I can detect you, then there were others, but they dip in and out of my perception."

So maybe his antennae weren't as highly tuned as I thought. We turned up towards the promenade and the pier.

"I ought to give you a tour some time. Second longest pier in England," I proclaimed.

"What's it's purpose?"

"It's so you can pretend you're on a ship, taking in the sea air."

Wells shuddered. "How ghastly."

"Look on the bright side. Half of it is landlocked now."

Wells said "There are things you don't understand. To be honest you have no idea about most things. But worry, things will become clearer."

"You mean don't worry."

"I know what I mean," replied Wells, darkly. He walked back down Neville street, the lion gargoyles guarding the sweet shops glared down at him.

Near the end of the promenade I reached the flower beds. There was another one of those rabbits that seem to inhabit all green spaces, even grassed areas in the middle of cities. This one didn't scamper away as I approached. It sat on its haunches and looked at me. Close up it was quite big, unfeasibly big in fact; about five feet tall.

The animal engendered that sort of unease you get when something normal is out of place. As I walked past, it turned its head to look at me.

"We need to talk," it said.

CHAPTER 6

Now it's not every day that a rabbit stops to pass the time of day, so I halted and stared. It remained stationary for a few seconds, then hopped a bit closer. As I looked, the animal jumped in and out of focus. I found myself squinting.

"Are you a rabbit?" I asked.

The animal looked irritated, "No, I'm an elephant! What do I look like? A giraffe perhaps? Look can we stop messing about and go somewhere where we can talk in private."

"I'm sorry, it's just a little unusual to be accosted by a talking rabbit," I replied thinking, why not just go with it? I looked around and there was a rain shelter a few metres away. I pointed and said, "In there?"

"Okay. My friend needs to come with us. Sergei, would you accompany us please?"

Another rabbit came out from the shrubbery. This one looked a lot bigger and frankly, a bit nasty. It resembled an overgrown Rottweiler with steroid abuse issues. The general air of menace was not helped by a scar across its muzzle and what looked a sword strapped to its back. I took an involuntary step backwards but the first, and now I realised comparatively cute looking, rabbit put a friendly paw on my arm and led me to the shelter.

It was a nice solid British seaside construction made of cast iron. The benches faced the points of the compass, enabling hardy holidaymakers to have a nice sit protected from the prevailing wind. I sat on a bench and the first rabbit hopped up next to me. When Sergei squatted on the other side, we were nearly face to muzzle.

"Are you from another dimension?" I asked.

"Do you know many talking rabbits?"

"Well, no," I admitted.

"So, make an educated guess," said Rabbit One, "My name is Adam, and this is my friend Sergei."

"Is it Russian?" I asked, then realised what a stupid question it was to ask of a creature from another dimension.

"What is Russian?" asked Sergei in a heavy East European accent.

Adam made an impatient noise and said, "Can we concentrate on what's important here? Sergei and I are what you might call ambassadors, maybe traders. We find ourselves somewhat more …" he seemed to search for a word, "… more real in this dimension than we're used to."

The rabbit continued, "Your magic seems to have changed things somewhat and you are pivotal to what is happening. We can sense an aura around you and we think you're going to be very important." It wagged a finger at me whilst it's paw seemed to blend between something furry and a human hand.

I was about to point out that we had just been carrying out an academic exercise when I realised the futility of saying anything. I was having a conversation with a talking rabbit just after having a nice civilised drink with a magician. I may as well take this all at face value and hope I wasn't being detained somewhere under the Mental Health Act. Still, the bracing sea air seemed real enough. I told myself that was why I began to shiver.

I sighed, "What do you want me to … what do you mean by aura?"

"I mean," Adam said, "That from our point of view you are standing out like a mountain in a savannah or like a fire in a forest. My guess is that you've been doing magic and it has affected you somehow."

"OK, what do you need me to do?"

"In the short term," Adam said, "We would like you to stay alive."

"Da, keep living," said Sergei from four inches behind my head, causing me to start.

"Well, what, why wouldn't I keep living?"

"If we can find you others can," said Adam enigmatically.

"What others?" I asked.

Adam and Sergei looked at each other.

"Probably best if you keep an eye open," said Adam, "We'll stick around, but we need to get used to being here." It produced a carrot seemingly from nowhere. "We will stay with you. I suggest that Sergei takes the night shift and I will be with you during the day."

"But you're a talking rabbit, don't you think that it might cause some comment?"

"Well, it doesn't where we come from," said Adam. "Let's see how it goes."

We walked towards my house. People who saw us didn't seem unduly bothered. I mean, why would they? I was just walking along with a large rabbit and a monster rabbit. When I mentioned this, Sergei growled, and Adam said he didn't like being called a monster. Apparently he was just big boned.

In the spirit of scientific experimentation, I went into the supermarket with them. We stood in the middle of the fresh veg aisle. The shoppers didn't pay us any attention.

To illustrate the point, Adam approached a middle aged woman who was browsing the fruit and veg.

"Give the cute Bunny a carrot," it simpered. She looked confused for a moment. Then she placed a carrot in the animal's paw.

"Here you are little cutie," she said. It came back over to us, munching the booty. Sergei went over to another lady.

"Give cute little bunny carrot," it growled. This time the woman looked a lot less sure and held the vegetable out to him at arm's length. Sergei came back looking a bit disgruntled. It obviously thought it was being given unfair treatment.

I accosted the first lady and said, "Excuse me, did you just give something to a large rabbit."

She hesitated for a moment, "Yes, of course I did," she replied smiling.

I wasn't expecting that. She seemed quite at home with the idea of a massive talking rabbit.

"Umm, did you find anything unusual in that? I mean, a

giant rabbit who can speak, in a supermarket?"

Again, she looked blank for a moment, then said, "What rabbit? what are you talking about?" and walked away, eyeing me suspiciously.

I picked up a mixed bag of vegetables and went to the checkout. Adam looked with interest at my credit card.

"What's that?" it asked.

"It's a method of paying called a credit card,"

"Hmm," it said. "I must get one."

We continued back to my house. I opened the door and Adam and Sergei came in with me.

"Dear," I called out, "I've brought some friends home."

Theresa came into the hallway and stopped dead.

There was an awkward silence and I was about to say something when Adam stepped forward and proffered its paw.

"Hallo, glad to meet you."

Theresa did a double take then invited them in. Adam and Sergei stayed in the kitchen whilst we cooked. They squatted munching on carrots and lettuce, wrinkling their noses when we had meat. I am sure I heard Sergei mutter something about filthy carnivores under its breath before it went out through the front door.

We settled down in the lounge and I noticed that Adam sat next to Theresa, who started stroking its huge rabbit ears in an absent minded way. I asked Adam about something that was starting to bother me.

"Adam," what did you mean when you said..."

I stopped because the animal was looking at me vacantly.

"Adam," I repeated a bit more forcefully. It shook itself and became more awake. "What did you mean when you said that I stand out. There was another person involved in these experiments, a lady called Carole, can you see her like you can see me?"

"We can only see you," the rabbit said.

There was a tap on the front door. Adam said "OK, we need to leave now. Sergei's seen someone coming."

"But why can't you see Carole?" I asked because I kept thinking about what had happened to Terry.

The rabbit shrugged, quite a trick for a creature with no shoulders, hopped down off the sofa and went to the front door. I let it out and it joined Sergei who was doing an impression of a stone statue in the porch, looking exactly like something standing guard. I made up my mind, I pulled on my shoes and decided to go back to the lab. I needed to get Carole's phone number from the records and see that she was all right. I told Adam and Sergei and they decided to stay with me. Then I had a sudden thought.

"Is my wife safe?"

The rabbit shrugged, "I don't think anyone is safe," it said, "Probably as safe as anyone else; will she be going out tonight?"

"No, she'll just settle in front of the television. Why isn't she phoning someone at this very minute? It's like she just accepted I walked through the door with a talking bloody rabbit."

"Frankly, I don't know," said Adam. "It seems to just happen; you're the first person to actually react to us as if we're unusual. Maybe she's used to seeing strange people."

I began, "Well, she does work in a Refugee Advice Bureau …" Then I remembered the two Health and Safety guys. "Shit, I need to get back to the lab. Besides which I need to track down Carole."

"Why do you need to go to where you work?" said Adam.

"Because those Health and Safety guys could shut us down."

"Ah, they're going to kill you are they? Well, we can't allow that to happen."

"No, no," I said, "but…"

Adam waved its paws dismissively, "Then they're a distraction."

"No, they're going to shut my lab down."

"Is that dangerous?"

"That depends on how wound up I get."

We started to walk towards town, Adam tutting at my obstinacy.

A brown Austin parked behind us whilst a familiar blue car pulled in front blocking the pavement. It mounted the curb and bumped into a lamppost which caused it to come to a standstill. Three people jumped out of the vehicle and adopted menacing poses. I couldn't really say why they were menacing, because all they did was stand there. Maybe they'd been on a special threatening stance course.

Adam and Sergei tensed and stopped walking. They looked at each other for a moment and bounded across the road, hopped across the carefully tended flower beds, jumped over the hedge and were lost to sight, dodging round the bushes in the park.

Then who should get out through the passenger door but Mr Smith. The Environment Agency man who knew nothing about environmental science.

CHAPTER 7

Smith looked around and pulled a disappointed face. I must admit I'd always thought the Environment Agency came with beards and clipboards. Not groups of muscular people with short haircuts and unsmiling demeanours.

"All right Lieutenant, you can stand your people down. And please get someone to sort out the brakes on that car. It's embarrassing," Smith said.

Since when did people from the Environment Agency have military titles?

Just then Adam popped up from behind a hedge, put its paws in its ears and blew a raspberry. Sergei appeared further along and waved its paws theatrically. Both animals then set off in different directions. Sergei bounded off towards the darker more densely overgrown areas that bordered the sand dunes. Adam shot off towards the shopping areas and the supermarket we'd visited earlier.

Smith nodded and, without orders, a buddy team set off after each animal. Either they could see the rabbits, in the same way I could, or the rabbits wanted to be seen. I wondered if Smith realised this.

Smith advanced towards me, his hand outstretched.

"Dr Voyle. So nice to meet you again." He could see me scanning the undergrowth.

"Don't worry about those chaps, they won't shoot the animals unless it's absolutely necessary," Smith said.

"Can you, and these people with you, see those rabbits?"

"Yes, why?"

"No reason." I replied, wanting to ascertain what else he knew.

He tutted, obviously impatient that we were going off at an unimportant tangent.

"I wondered if we could ask you some questions."

"Let me guess," I replied, "You're from another dimension

and I've disrupted the fabric of reality and I'm in great danger."

I did not take the proffered hand.

"Look," I continued as he opened his mouth to speak. "One of my staff has died in very strange circumstances and an increasingly bizarre series of individuals, including remarkably street savvy rodents, are appearing like the chorus of a Greek tragedy to warn me of mayhem and destruction. What are you, the spirit of Christmas bloody future?"

When I paused for breath he commented sarcastically, "We probably won't need the water boarding to get you to talk then. I should tell you that I'm from the Home Office, not the Environment Agency."

"Gosh! Really? Is that why you know sod all about the Environment?"

"I can see you're upset. Perhaps we could we go somewhere to discuss this, ahh, situation."

He indicated a nearby car.

"I need to get to the office and phone one of my staff; if all these people and … things are right, then Carol's also in danger," I said.

He looked away and I felt sick. "I've just been monitoring the police radio traffic, they've found the body of another woman on the outskirts of town."

"Another?"

"Yes, I should have mentioned that. Anyway, the officers involved are, understandably, somewhat distressed. Reports are a bit garbled, but there seem to be some unusual aspects to the incident. Also, we have some preliminary post mortem results on your colleague." I flinched, but he continued, "You are going to have to face up to it; this is an unpleasant situation. You don't need to worry about the Health and Safety people We've told them that your colleague died from natural causes."

"Did he?" I asked.

"Don't be ridiculous. Great chunks of flesh were ripped from him. Come on, let's go to my office."

As he led me to his car I asked, "So are you one of these

shadowy government units beloved of conspiracy theorists?"

He pursed his lips, "My military support was the nearest unit that had urban surveillance training and last week I was analysing Russian economic documents, but other than that, you're essentially correct."

"So why are you driving round in vehicles that would have a vintage car dealer salivate?"

"I was told there was a car pool. These are what I found when I arrived. A local firm had the contract to maintain them."

"They're in good condition apart from the iffy brakes. But why such old vehicles?" I asked.

"You'll see."

We drove away from the town centre to a big building that used to be a hydrotherapy hotel. It had been requisitioned to house troops during World War Two. After the war the government forgot to give it back and used it as a home for various executive departments. I'd always wondered why they were situated in a resort, apart from senior managers getting to live by the seaside.

Smith took us in through a back door that needed a lick of paint but sported a modern swipe card lock. He switched on traditional fluorescent lights that flickered a few times before they lit up. We walked along a corridor painted in nineteen fifties institutional green paint and into an office with nineteen forties dial telephones and metal desks. There were maps and maritime charts on the wall.

He gestured to a metal framed seat with worn seventies floral polyester covers. I sat down, and he went to a table by the wall and switched on an electric kettle. He turned to me.

"This place hasn't been used for years. It was kept in readiness, along with some vehicles. Nothing has been updated."

"It looks like the photos from where my Dad worked in the seventies."

"Tell me what happened today?" he said.

I gave him the story detail by detail. I didn't care that it sounded insane and outlandish. Smith didn't show any surprise, just asked me if I wanted sugar.

"So, Mr Wells, and these creatures that appear to be rabbits, have freely conversed with you?" Smith said.

"Yes, I told you so."

"Were they speaking English?"

I suddenly saw what he meant and couldn't understand why I'd not considered it before. How the hell does a creature from another dimension speak English?

"Frankly I was more concerned about what was going on. It's all quite unusual for me you know."

"Doctor Voyle, you need to understand that we may be dealing with entities that have telepathic powers. It is entirely possible that these creatures, that appear to you as rabbits, are manipulating, possibly unconsciously, how you perceive them."

I went on the offensive. "Now, tell me about what you know, or I will not cooperate, and you do not get to speak to Wells or the ... the rabbits."

"OK, you need to prepare yourself. Your colleague who died in the laboratory suffered terrible injuries to his soft tissues, but he was also exsanguinated, he had lost about fifty percent of the blood in his body. They found a woman's corpse earlier this evening. We don't think it was your other colleague, Carole, but we still need to check. A preliminary examination of the body suggests similarities to the injuries sustained by Terry. Next to her was some kind of animal, also dead. The animal isn't like anything on earth. It seems to be some kind of chimera with canine, reptilian and human characteristics, but we're still at an early stage of investigation. Initial observations by one of our attending doctors suggest that this creature is so far removed from how mammals evolved on this planet that comparisons become meaningless."

"Two points: are any of the things that Wells told me true, and why are you not surprised about anything that I've told you?" I asked.

"We have no reason as yet to doubt the beings you

have encountered so far. I'm not surprised because I've read up extensively on the notes left by my predecessors and, consequently, I can tell you that we've encountered similar entities before, but only on a small scale. However, look at the map behind you."

I looked at the charts. They showed the defence lines from World War Two: a system of bunkers and fortified buildings on the coast and along the Leeds to Liverpool canal. They'd been built in a hurry during 1940 in case of a German invasion. I pointed this out, local history being an interest of mine.

"Look at it again. Describe what you see." Smith said.

I shrugged. "There was a chain of defences along the river Alt that separated Liverpool from the agricultural land of the Lancashire plain. Then the defence line continued as a series of jury-rigged bunkers along the canal."

"Go on."

"It's well documented. The defences effectively box in the area of Southport and the coastal towns. They built the fortifications because the long flat beaches and wide fields were ideal for landing ships and troop carrying gliders."

"You've not seen it yet have you?"

Mystified I continued, "It was a lashed together defence set up at the beginning of the war. Everyone forgot about it after V.E. day. I don't understand?"

"You know, occasionally there were incursions here," Smith replied.

"Really? I didn't think the Germans had ever landed in Britain. It's not in any of the history books."

Then the penny dropped. "The defences box in Southport and the surrounding area. It not only protects against an army landing on the beach. These fortifications would also stop something coming from Southport itself. Is that why they're so far inland?"

The full implication struck me, "Wait a minute, that means people knew what the scrying scope could do. Has this happened before?"

Smith said, "This was more contingency planning. It seems that historically the use of a primitive version of your apparatus caused incidents. In the past they were put down to supernatural events. In subsequent decades a more rational, if farfetched explanation was sought, similar to the research you carried out. This time I think you've magnified the effect and really blown the lid off the tin."

"Blown the lid off the tin? You know I've spoken to rabbits that make more sense than you."

Smith opened a cupboard extracting some coffee and long life milk. "You said your rabbit friend thought it felt more real than it was used to. My hypothesis is that things, beings, have crossed over from other dimensions but were never stable here. In fact, it used to happen all the time, giving rise to a lot of our myths and legends. After all, if John Dee developed a system of maths that enabled trans–dimensional travel, then transfer could go both ways. Your more advanced work might have changed things, weakened the barriers between worlds, and, if Wells is correct, it might be happening across several dimensions. However, what interests me is the focus on yourself. These denizens from other versions of Earth seem to be drawn to you in particular."

"It sounded like Wells and his kind have been coming here for ages. I was in his apartment and it was like one of those museum houses where every room is made up to reflect a different historical era, He said that our visitors would lose stability, become more like us." I said.

"Perhaps you're right. But our immediate problem is that something is killing people, so let's concentrate on that."

"How many people have died?" I asked.

"Why do you ask?"

"Because I was pulled in by a couple of coppers and given the third degree. They showed me pictures of young people and asked me where I was on certain dates. I'm not an expert on police procedure, but even I can put two and two together."

"You think this is connected to the incident with your

colleague?" said Smith.

"There's a good chance. The population of this town is only eighty thousand. Young people don't go missing on that kind of scale."

"I'll talk to my police contacts."

He handed me a mug of instant coffee in a George VI coronation mug. I felt like a time traveller.

"You're not from another dimension, are you?" I asked, taking in my surroundings.

"Very droll," he laughed, "I can see that all this must be a bit disorientating for you."

"Are you aware that beings from other dimensions are able to make themselves disappear?"

"Our records seem to indicate that this can be the case."

"When I was with those two big rabbits, no one could see them. So, why did they make themselves visible to your people?" I asked.

I have to admit to a certain amount of satisfaction when the implications sank in and a worried look descended on him.

As I took another sip of coffee, his phone rang. He answered and stood listening for a while, then replied, "Thank you lieutenant. Please see to the arrangements and ensure your people get some rest."

He pinched the bridge of his nose and took a few moments to collect himself. Then he turned to me.

"Lieutenant Knowles just reported in on the progress in apprehending your lagomorphine friends. It appears the bigger one drew her people into the sand dunes to the south of the town. They followed it into the area and got split up. It attacked one of them, who sustained disabling but not serious injuries. The smaller one drew them into the shops, where it attacked them. Shots were fired. In the melee which ensued the rabbit rendered one of the troops unconscious. He then made off with the man's weapon."

"Impressive, so now the rabbits have guns and you've got one of your troops injured. Why didn't you just try and talk to them?" I asked.

Just then there was the sound of a heavy diesel engine outside. We looked out of the window as a wheeled excavator swung inexpertly into the car park. Sergei was driving. Adam was hanging off the cab and waved perkily up at us.

I opened the window and Adam shouted up, "Are you going to open the door, or do we need to make our own?"

I couldn't help but smile to myself. Not least because I could almost hear Smith grinding his teeth.

I turned to him, "We may as well face it that these two are going to stick to me like glue. Stop trying to get rid of them. They might be able to help us."

"They may well be the problem," he replied getting, I thought, overly exasperated. He should have tried having my day.

"They probably just want to get things back to normal like we do. Wells certainly gives that impression," I said.

"All right then," he replied with ill grace and went to open the door. He came back with Adam who said that Sergei was keeping guard.

"These gun things are fun, aren't they?" was Adam's opening remark.

"Have you not encountered firearms before?" I asked.

"Of course, we have quite an arsenal, but I thought I'd wind everyone up."

All things considered, Smith kept his temper quite well.

"You just injured someone," Smith said.

"Actually, we wanted to make a point. Don't hunt us, ever," Adam said to Smith.

"Makes sense," I said, "Rabbits will have a peculiar terror of being hunted. They are a prey species after all. They probably have a bit of a chip on their shoulder."

Adam craned his neck to look.

"No, not an actual chip. Never mind. It's just a saying."

"Oh, that's alright then. What were you saying?" the rabbit replied.

"Perhaps we can work together?" I said in what I hoped was a conciliatory tone. "Let's try and figure out how serious the situation is and see if there's any way of controlling it."

"Very well," said Smith, "We could work together. You might have insights I lack. But now I think it is time to get some rest."

"We could go and see Mr Wells," I said.

"Seems like a good idea. Where's he based?" said Smith.

"Didn't you have me followed yesterday?"

"Yes, but we lost sight of you when you left the building," said Smith.

"But I only went across the street and Wells was with me. For heaven's sake, he dresses like a Goth, you couldn't have missed us." A thought struck me, "He influenced your chap. I was there, I saw it. So, he either rendered me invisible or controlled the actions of the person following us."

"God, this just gets better and better," Smith said.

"Look, we need Wells' cooperation. Any heavy stuff and he'll just make himself invisible or whatever he did yesterday and we won't see him again."

"Very well, we'll visit him tomorrow and I'll find out if the police have anything on what happened to your colleagues. Lieutenant Knowles is my military liaison. I'll get her team briefed and prepared for eleven hundred hours."

"I just said that we don't want any heavy stuff. If a load of troops come along it will probably be counterproductive."

Just then Sergei came in. Smith and I looked at him aghast. He had a piece of cord round his neck with what looked like a couple of ears threaded on to it.

Adam sensed the change in mood, and jerked his head indicating that Sergei should leave, which he did with ill grace.

"Sergei comes from a rough area," he said.

I turned to Smith. "Ok, I think I quite like the idea of a military escort now you come to mention it."

CHAPTER 8

The next morning I found Carole pacing the laboratory. The strain was beginning to show. Her face was drawn, the lines of age visible and she'd lost weight. There were grey strands in her hair that I hadn't noticed previously.

"Carole, have you told the police that I didn't get on with Terry."

She looked at me coldly. "I said you didn't get on with the staff. You don't, and I hold you responsible for Terry's death."

"But I didn't do anything."

"Exactly, you just let him blunder around taking his exploration too far."

"You mean taking his experiments too far? That's not fair. I reviewed the project every week."

"Well, what if he'd gone further than you thought? What if he'd started to look at trans-dimensional travel?"

"But I've only just considered the possibility of moving between dimensions myself. How was I to know?"

"You should have bloody well asked!" she shouted and ran out.

I looked at my watch. It was time to meet Smith.

Adam came into the room, hesitated and raised his muzzle.

"There's another one like you. I can feel it."

"That would be Carole."

"There's something wrong with the other one."

"I expect so. She's been under a lot of strain. I'm not sure she's behaving rationally."

"No, she flares more than you. Lots of fire."

"You're not making sense," I said, feeling disorientated as, in a moment of clarity, I remembered I was communicating with a talking rabbit.

"I can't explain. Something is very wrong," Adam said.

"I'll try and have Smith assign some people to her. Come

on. You can tell him when we meet."

We started to make our way out of the building. Adam stopped.

"The flare's gone."

"Gone where?"

"I don't know. It's just not there anymore."

I ran back to the office. Carole was nowhere to be found. Her laptop wasn't on her desk. My phone pinged. It was a text saying she'd gone home. It was reassuring that Adam's inability to detect her presence wasn't that she'd been sucked into another dimension, but merely got on a bus to go home.

If the rabbit's perception was limited in range, it meant I had less of a target painted on my back as far as denizens from other dimensions were concerned. Of course that only applied if I were correct, I didn't consider any alternative.

CHAPTER 9

I was running late now, so walked out of the building picking up Adam on the way. He had ensconced himself next to the receptionist who was hand feeding him bits of salad. I told him I would wait outside whilst he finished, then stood on the steps wondering when Adam had changed in my mind from "it" to "he".

Adam came out. Apparently, Sergei was off on business, but it was unclear as to what this entailed. It was one of those things that you didn't like to ask about.

Smith was waiting near Wells' residence.

"Nice day for it. This really is a lovely street," he drew a deep breath and beamed.

"Yes, it is," I replied, briskly.

"Apparently Napoleon lived here for a while,"

I did a double take.

"Napoleon?"

"Well, his grandson. Napoleon the third. He modelled the wide boulevards in Paris on this road."

"That's very interesting, but is it relevant?" I asked.

Looking around I could make out 10 short aggressive looking types. They were all characterised by desert boots, T shirts and various types of loose-fitting leather and denim jackets. I wondered if they were trained that way or whether they naturally gravitated towards a uniform.

"Yes, amazing what you find out about places."

"Are you trying to make me feel relaxed?" I asked, "Because it isn't working."

"The irony is that this street is wide because it flooded on a regular basis, so they built on the higher ground. What I'm trying to say is that you should try to gauge exactly what this chap wants. Find out why he wants to help you."

"Look beyond the obvious?"

"Exactly, well done," Smith replied heartily.

The officer I recognised from yesterday approached; she had regulation length mid brown hair, a round face and compact build. I hoped she didn't have a Napoleon complex to fit in with the style of the street.

"You the silly sod who's caused all this then?" she said. Well, that answered that question.

I resisted the urge to make a sarcastic response. OK, I thought, she's let me know who's in charge. Let's hope she didn't continue in the same vein.

"Yes, but I'm also the best chance we have of stopping it," I said.

She harrumphed.

Time for me to build some bridges. "I'm very sorry about your colleague."

She narrowed her eyes, "Bit of a scrap but we'll be OK. You just do what you're told and try not to get eaten. It'll look bad on my record." Tough hombres these military types, somebody had lost their ears.

"Enough foreplay," drawled Smith who obviously found the civilian baiting a bit irritating.

"Yes Sir," said Lieutenant Knowles, "Jones and Evans will run close protection for you in the building. We'll wait out here. If there are any problems, we'll come running."

"Right then" said Smith, "Let's get on with it. Will you do the honours Dr Voyle?"

I led Smith, Adam and the two escorts up to the door and, feeling a bit self-conscious, knocked. A few moments later the door opened. A tall, aesthetic looking blonde young man stood smiling at us.

"Hello, we're here to see Mr Wells. This is Mr Smith who is a representative of our government." I gestured down at Adam. "This is ahh, a denizen of another dimension called Adam, and these are ..." I'd forgotten their names already.

"Evans and Jones," one of them said.

"Come in then," said the blonde young man, standing to one side.

Then, as Evans and Jones came to the threshold, he put up a hand. "But not you two. I'm afraid we don't allow firearms in the building."

Jones sneered and went to push past but could not get beyond the threshold. Evans found the same and they started trying to shoulder their way through an invisible barrier. Before things could develop further, Smith told them to wait outside and we all trooped up the stairs, along the hall and into the lounge.

"Thank you, Tom," said Wells as he rose from an Art Deco armchair to meet us. "Could you make us some tea please?"

The blonde young man, Tom, left the room and Wells gestured to us to sit. Adam plonked himself next to me on a sofa.

Smith asked, "Why won't you let my men into your building? I assume you did actively stop them coming in?"

Wells said, "Tom did actually, I fear it may have taken it out of him a bit, but you see, we are what you would call pacifists. We do not accept violence in any form. You're lucky we let the lagomorphoid in."

Adam looked offended but said nothing. I tried not to be distracted by wondering how I could tell a rabbit looked offended.

Smith said, "I can bring you up to date on what's happened so far. We have incursions by various denizens from far off places. These are due to Dr Voyle's ill thought out experiments. Two people are dead. Frankly we don't have a lot to go on. We're still having our casualties autopsied and the veterinary school is examining a creature found next to one of the victims. We know that Dr Voyle seems to be important to several inhabitants of other dimensions, so we can assume that whatever caused the deaths will have a similar attraction to him."

Comforting.

Wells replied, "We're having similar problems. You people had better hope that what you did isn't causing trouble on some of the more aggressive worlds. Is the anomaly localised to this area?"

"I was wondering that myself," said Smith. "In my records there's a reference to a Fine Jane. She seems to have been consulted in the past. Does the name mean anything to you?"

Wells shook his head.

"It does to me," I piped up.

They both looked at me as if the table had just spoken.

"Do you know Fine Jane? I thought you'd told me about all of the interdimensional entities you'd had contact with," queried Smith.

"It's not a person, it's a place. Fine Jane's a name for a pumping station that's part of the local land drainage system. It can be accessed from the Cheshire Lines walking path. You could go there tomorrow. It would be a nice walk for you all. So, who is Fine Jane?" I replied.

Smith said, "The question would be better framed as what, not who. Apparently, she's some kind of aquatic being."

Just then Tom came in with a tea tray and served everyone. We drank from traditional teacups and he'd used leaf tea, not tea bags. It was like visiting a maiden aunt who'd not made it out of nineteen seventies.

Tom seemed a gentle soul, but he was sweating and looked a bit feverish.

"Are you feeling ill?" I asked.

"Sorry, putting up a barrier like that would have been child's play where I come from. It's so difficult here." With a little smile he offered Adam a carrot, which the rabbit munched on happily.

Smith spoke to me over the rim of his teacup. "We'll need you to come with us Dr Voyle."

"Oh good," I said. "Things have been working so well."

"Don't worry," he replied. "Lieutenant Knowles and her people will be with you."

"Ahh good, tough special forces types who have been seen off by a couple of rabbits," I said.

Adam nudged me. "Don't worry, I'll be there. Unfortunately, Sergei has business."

"What sort of business could he possibly have?" I asked.

"Bit of this and that," replied Adam.

Wells looked worried and, as there didn't seem a lot more to say, we took our leave.

As we left, Wells took me by the arm and said quietly, "You need to be careful in your dealings with the lagomorphoids. For the sake of simplicity, let's call them the rabbits. They seem well adapted to your world but that's an illusion. It is possible they may be naive, emotionally immature even. They don't have the experience of this world that you have."

"I'll try and remember that. Listen. There could be some briefings with the police and so on. You could slip in unnoticed and it would save you getting all of your information second hand from me," I suggested.

He nodded, and I turned to go.

"Oh, I forgot to mention," Wells said, "I'm sure you've already thought of this but the people you really need to fear may be from your own world. Some of them might think that the best way of dealing with this problem is to get rid of the person who caused it."

Before I could register my dismay, he continued, patting me companionably on the arm, "Well, goodbye and feel free to drop in at any time."

"Thanks, I feel much better."

I left the building to find Knowles and Smith in urgent whispered conversation. I don't think these military types liked being unable to accompany us into Wells' building. To be fair, if anything had happened it would have been interesting to hear Knowles trying to explain to her senior officers that she couldn't get her men through an open door.

As we crossed the street, Lieutenant Knowles and one of her troops fell in beside me.

The soldier was a deceptively slight woman called Amber. I didn't bother to ask if it was her real name because it was becoming almost embarrassingly obvious that their monikers were all aliases. Her face was a mass of bruises, so she'd obviously got the sharp end of whatever had gone on when they had tried to capture Adam and Sergei.

I fell back a little so that we were out of Knowles' line of sight. There was something about the way everyone was describing the incident that was bothering me.

"I heard it got a bit rough last night," I said.

"Could have been worse," said Amber

"So which group were you in, the guys who had a dust up in the supermarket?"

"No, we ended up in the woods with the big bastard."

"Hmm, yes," I said, this was the bit I wanted to ask about before they all clammed up. "I understand someone was quite badly injured?"

"Sorry? There was just me and Pink and she's … ", she stopped speaking as Knowles virtually barged between us and glared at her with what I took to be a "don't talk to the civilians" look.

"It's very insensitive to talk to my people about last night. They might be very upset," she said and strode away.

I waited until we got closer to the college and invited Smith and Knowles to come in with me. Amber and Evans wandered off and no doubt would ensconce themselves in a cafe. I thought of it as their arriving-too-late-to-be-of-help distance. The three of us went up to my office and I found a walkers' map of the area.

I began, "Drainage ditches crisscross the flood plain of the river Alt. Water is constantly pumped from the ground level into the river which is itself raised several metres above the level of the surrounding land."

"Like in the Netherlands?" asked Knowles

"Exactly, there's even a place called Up Holland nearer to Wigan."

"Could we focus on the matter in hand please," ordered Smith.

"Sorry. Fine Jane refers to one of the pumping stations that move the water round the system of ditches."

"You're saying something lives in a ditch next to a field? It's going to be quite small then," said Knowles.

"Remember this area would normally be marsh. The pumping stations have to shift quite a bit of water and the larger ditches are the width of canals. It's quite possible that an aquatic entity could live there. Have you any idea what we are looking for?"

"Not really," replied Smith, "The records just refer to a being living in the area. It must have been there for some time. I got the impression it was some kind of aquatic organism, so you're correct in your assumption."

"What like a Loch Ness monster? Maybe some kind of reptile?" I didn't like the way this was going.

Smith shrugged. "I had Knowles send some people there earlier on today. They walked around the area but didn't see anyone, or anything, unusual. That's why we need to take you with us. You seem to have an attraction for our visitors. Maybe you'll generate more interest from this organism as well as others."

He pointedly looked at Adam who was doing his perky Beatrix Potter character routine. So, the rabbit obviously wanted Smith to see him.

"You know I really don't like this whole tethered goat role you're so keen for me to adopt," I said

"One last thing. Carry this with you."

He passed me a cell phone.

"I've already got a phone," I said.

"This one has a panic button. Lots of people who have to deal with the public carry them, health inspectors and the like. If you hit the button on this one, it will alert Knowles' people."

"How will they know where I am?"

"It has a GPS facility. So, if the worst happens, they'll be able to find your body." He grinned, and I realised he'd made his first joke.

"You're hilarious."

Smith continued, "As well as that I would be a lot happier if Lieutenant Knowles' people stayed near you. An extension of the armed escort they already provide. I know you don't want anyone close by, but I insist that they keep a watch outside of your house."

"I appreciate that, but for all we know whatever killed Terry just appeared out of thin air and snatched him. Have you had any more information about the person who's been killed. I assume you're talking about the incident where an animal was found next to the body?"

I could see his indecision. It must be endemic with these civil service types to try and keep everything confidential.

Smith made up his mind. "I contacted the police. They've had reports of young women going missing. That's probably why they interviewed you. I'm still trying to get the details from the Police HQ. The attack you refer to was the only one captured on CCTV. The creature found next to the body is being analysed at the Liverpool Veterinary School. Given the unusual nature of the creature, we thought they would be the best placed to give us a steer on it. Although animals seem to be remarkably anthropomorphic these days." He glared at Adam.

"You know that you're going to have to keep me in the loop on this. If I have some kind of connection to interdimensional beings, then I need to know everything you know," I said.

"Fine," Smith said, "If you're that keen you can come to the police briefing. I'll say that you're a civilian expert. But the meeting is going to include details of the autopsy. I hope you have a strong stomach."

Well, I walked straight into that one.

CHAPTER 10

I went home early and we passed a normal evening: ate a meal, watched TV and then bed. Of course, this depends on your definition of normal. It was now customary for us to have an oversized talking rabbit in the house. Theresa insisted on sitting next to Adam on the sofa. I asked her if anything was out of the ordinary, as she stroked Adam's ears.

She replied, "Of course silly, we have a house guest." There was no indication in her manner that anything actually unusual was happening.

The next day I rose, showered, shaved, brushed my teeth and then had breakfast of toast and coffee. Meanwhile, Theresa tutted over Adam grooming himself in the kitchen. She shooed him into the shower cubicle, not outside I noticed, but in our bathroom. A few minutes later he came out looking a bit bedraggled but cheered up when Theresa wrapped him in a towel and fed him some lettuce.

I took the precaution of preparing my walking gear, which included some thermals and water proof clothing. Smith must have been waiting for Theresa to go to work because he pulled up to the house a few minutes after she'd left. We travelled in his Vauxhall and as we turned into the next street, two more ancient vehicles pulled in behind us. I guessed that was Knowles and the heavy mob.

We drove out of Southport along the Coastal Road. A fast single carriage way that follows the path of the, now defunct, Cheshire Lines railway.

The convoy turned onto the dual carriageway that passes the Woodvale aerodrome, the last of the World War Two emergency built airfields.

Looking at the place with my new perspective, I realised that it was well placed to fly in airborne troops should, for example, you wished to contain an influx of monsters from another dimension. It was an aspect of strategic planning often overlooked by BBC documentaries.

Halfway along the dual carriageway I tapped the driver's shoulder. "Turn left here."

She pulled onto one of the narrow single track roads that cross the area known locally as the "Moss".

"This was the flood plain of the River Alt. You can see what I mean about drainage," I said.

Knowles grunted non-committedly.

"They grow a lot of carrots," I said to Adam, who was much impressed.

Then I realised I was talking so much because I was nervous.

Our car pulled off into an area where a track branched from the road. It allowed utility vehicles to get to the drainage canals and pumping stations.

We got out of the cars and Knowles' people formed up. They were wearing a variety of civvies and like me they had dressed up warm. There was a cold January wind blowing. At the order to try and look natural, they milled about and then started strolling down the path, looking as natural as a spray tan on a Scotsman. Smith, Adam and I followed. Adam put a paw on my arm and held me back a couple of paces, then passed me an orange tubular bag, looking a lot like a carrot. It was about 8- 10 inches long and was filled with heavy small beads.

"I always find this a great comfort in times of trouble," he said and patted me on the arm before continuing. I put it in my pocket. A lead shot filled carrot, whatever next.

The troops fanned out as we reached the drainage canal. The actual waterway was bounded on each side by raised earth embankments.

I turned to Smith, "What do we do now?"

He was about to answer when two people came walking along the path. A typical middle-class couple with waterproofs, walking boots and a determination to enjoy themselves despite the cold. They stepped to one side, giving us plenty of room. This was because Knowles' people stood out like a sore thumb.

Not least amongst their breaches of normal rambler etiquette was that they were looking in different directions to scan the surrounding area. As opposed to nodding and saying, "Good morning," or even just chatting amongst themselves.

Then, one of the troops, Evans was his rubbish pseudonym, nudged Knowles, pointed towards the horizon and hissed, "Boss, over there."

Across the moss a flock of avians took to the air. They were just dots at this distance. The creatures flew over a copse. This enabled me to get a sense of perspective and I realised what had alarmed Evans. These things were huge.

Knowles was taking no chances. She barked an order and the troops took cover by throwing themselves on the sloped grassy side of the embankment, drawing automatic pistols as they did so.

A soldier called Pink took hold of my coat and pulled me down. Our eyes met, and I felt her grip tighten protectively around my shoulders. Of course, she'd had experience of mixing it with creatures from other dimensions.

Our momentary reverie was interrupted by the double click as the slide of an automatic pistol chambered a round. A sound they dub into all bad adventure films when someone draws a gun.

I looked behind us. Adam had crouched behind a concrete trapezoid shape that stopped people driving vehicles down the path. He was aiming a pistol in a twin … pawed grip. Pink also saw this and her hold on me became less insistent.

We could hear the strange guttural cries of the creatures now as they formed into loose V shaped formations. Everyone readied their weapons.

But, as the creatures came closer, the cries resolved into a honking sound and I realised that they were geese.

The walking couple were still there looking at us with bemused apprehension. Everyone stood up and sheepishly holstered their pistols.

Knowles looked at her watch and said crisply, "Well done

everyone, excellent reaction times."

She turned to the walkers, "We're just having a civil contingencies exercise."

They didn't look particularly convinced, and hurried away.

"Well, that wasn't at all embarrassing," said Smith, "let's get down to the water."

This proved easier said than done; the sides of the drainage canal being close to vertical. I didn't fancy being trapped at the base of a slippery bank if something like the Loch Ness monster suddenly reared out of the water. Knowles said her people would keep hold of me and drag me out if things went South, but I was not to be persuaded.

We walked along the bank until we came across a path down to the water. It was a small slipway for boats. I approached the edge of the water and crouched down. After a bit I put my hand in the water and swirled it around a bit. Then stepped back because I'd seen those wildlife films where the crocodile leaps out of the water and drags the antelope to its grisly doom. We waited and waited. Then we waited some more.

After 30 minutes I turned to the others and gave a shrug. It was obvious that nothing was going to happen.

They were all staring past me and the hairs on my neck stood on end. Slowly I rotated my shoulder, then my head, whilst my body tried to lean backwards. A woman's face was inches from my own. Yelping, I fell on my bottom, then composed myself and knelt on the ground so my face was level with hers. I looked at her for a few seconds. She appeared to be in her early twenties with a pert nose and a smile, that if you pushed me, I would have called mischievous. The top half of her body was out of the water and she was naked. Okay in St Tropez but bizarre in the single degree temperatures of the British winter.

"So, you're the one causing all the fuss, are you?" she said, speaking with a BBC accent that carried a hint of disapproval.

I cleared my throat, "Ah, ahem, are you Fine Jane by any chance?"

From the bank above me and Adam said, "He asks stupidly obvious questions while his mind gets up to speed. It can take a while."

I noticed that for all his nonchalance, he had the presence of mind to draw his gun while everyone else stared, slack jawed, at the woman.

"You may as well call me that. Is this a social call? Have you, perchance, some live fish on you?" she said, looking hopefully over my shoulder at the group surrounding me.

"Erm, well, no, not as such, you see we didn't quite know what to expect."

"Give you a clue," she said and swished a tail through the water. The tail flukes were horizontal and moved up and down like those of a dolphin. There were no scales but a smooth skin, again just like a cetacean. So, obviously a mammal, although that much was obvious from the upper part of her body. To avoid giving offence, I tried to maintain eye contact and not let my gaze drift.

I felt myself blushing as I said, "Right, mermaid, OK. I'm sorry we didn't quite know what the social etiquette was in these situations. Should we have brought you some fish?"

"Well, it would have been polite to bring a gift as you are visiting my home and I don't eat chocolates. But I shall put it down to your gaucheness," she replied, raising her nose in the air, half turning her face away with a touch of haughtiness. But it was the pose of a young woman playing the part of a queen. She spoilt the regal image by looking sideways at me to see what my reaction was.

"I apologise. Excuse me for asking," I said as curiosity got the better of me, "But what is a mermaid doing living in these drainage canals instead of the sea?"

"I was stranded when they raised the river Alt up to its present level. My only path to the sea was blocked off. It was very sad, I've been so lonely," she said with tears falling down her cheeks.

"What do you eat?" This was really interesting.

"Small meagre fish, insects and crustacea that I sift from the silt." She was really looking quite miserable now.

Smith had obviously had enough small talk. He knelt beside me and said, "Now look here, we need..."

He did not get to finish the sentence because Fine Jane interrupted him and said, "You are a very rude man." Then slyly, "I bet you would just love to come with me for a swim."

She began to sing. I couldn't make out the words, but it seemed to be a melancholy song of love and loss. I could feel myself drawn to the water. I turned my head. Smith had a look of rapture on his face and was shuffling forwards. Now, everyone knows that mermaids lure seafarers to their doom by singing, so I thought I ought to do something about it. I took the carrot from my pocket and twisted my wrist so that it slapped Smith in the face. Of course, it would have been a mild blow were it not for the core of lead shot, which meant he fell backwards with blood pouring from his nose.

As he lay cursing, I stepped away and looked at everyone else. Pink was pulling back Knowles and the one I knew as Evans. Adam had thrown himself at the legs of the nearest man, then fired his pistol in the air several times. This seemed to shock everyone else out of their reverie.

Fine Jane's main focus had been Smith, so the others were only mildly intoxicated. They shook their heads as if surfacing from a deep sleep.

"Is everything that comes through those bloody portals lethal?" I shouted, mainly to myself. Give me a break, things were a bit tense.

Adam nudged my leg. "I'm not," he said, winsomely. The effect was slightly spoilt by the smoke drifting from the muzzle of his automatic, which now pointed back at Fine Jane.

She set her face in a coquettish expression and said, "Can't blame a girl for trying."

I approached her a bit more carefully this time.

Something was out of place.

"Why did you do that? There aren't any records of unexplained drowning here, so why try and pull one of us in the water. Why now?"

"He's a nasty boorish man, I don't show myself to everyone you know. Also, I wanted to see what you were made of."

She lifted both hands towards me. I noticed she had long curved claw like nails, perfect for holding on to struggling fish. Or, a timid little part of my mind pointed out, hapless university lecturers as they drowned.

"I think we can help each other," I said, leaning back slightly and keeping an eye on those hands. "Would you like to go back to the sea? We could make that happen, but you would have to do something for us."

"Back to the sea, to my home? Oh yes! Anything!" she replied slightly breathlessly.

"Have you noticed things changing for visitors such as yourself?"

"Yes, indeed. I feel more," she considered for a moment, "more real."

That was the second time I'd heard that description of the changes wrought by our experiments.

"Can you find out how far this change extends?" I asked.

"Of course, I can travel all along my domain. I can sense where there's a change. It will take me until the next half moon. How will I find you? We don't use the same names for places."

I hadn't thought of that, so improvised. "I'll come back here so you can find me. You can sense when I'm near. It'll be the day after the next full moon. But I don't want to see anyone hurt, do you understand?"

"Oh, don't be so silly," she said with a theatrical wave of the hand, "I've never hurt anyone, and no one is likely to get in the water with me when it's so cold."

"Do people ever get in the water with you?"

She giggled, "You'd be surprised what young men get up

to when they want to cool off in the summer heat."

Obviously, things were not as boring in the countryside as I had previously supposed. I backed away.

"Bye bye," she said, waving, and disappeared into the water. The last we saw was the curve of a dorsal fin as she dived.

CHAPTER 11

The autopsy, or scientific meeting if you are of a squeamish disposition, was scheduled for later in the week. The days seemed interminable. I tried to concentrate, but every time I looked around all I could see was a cosy little burrow that I'd created. A place where I could hide from the world. Now that world was forcing itself in on me, big time.

I phoned Smith, "Have you got anywhere with getting Carole some protection?"

"Doctor Voyle," he sighed, "I have a section of ten people. They've made numerous attempts to contact your colleague, but she seems very elusive."

"I'm betting she's moving around. Even the people from other dimensions are having difficulty tracking her."

"It may well be a good strategy on her part. You must understand that I can't force people to accept protection."

"But she's in much the same position as me."

"Look on the bright side. From my point of view, it means that I have a backup in case anything happens to you," Smith said.

"You're so comforting. I bet your kids sleep well after you tell them a bedtime story."

"Like tops, Doctor Voyle, although funnily enough my wife usually puts them to bed. Goodbye."

I was about to phone Theresa, then realised I just wanted to talk to people. Instead, I got on with some filing. Having managed to put the third year comparative physics essays in order my firm intention was to mark them. But then Carole appeared.

Some rest had done her the power of good. The stress lines had gone, and she looked quite perky. Having her grey hair tinted probably helped her morale. So much for grieving for Terry, I thought sourly. Then realised that kind of thinking meant the poor girl couldn't win whatever she did.

"You're back to normal then?" she said. I told myself I was imagining her sneer.

"If you can call visiting a mermaid normal, then you would be correct. How are you?"

"Fine, why wouldn't I be!"

"OK sorry. Smith wanted to get in contact with you."

"Well, I don't want to be in contact with him. I'm going back to Daresbury for a few days, then plan to take a couple of weeks off."

"Sure, that's OK."

"I wasn't asking your permission. I'm telling you."

She turned and stomped out of the room passing Pink and someone called Jones.

"Is she alright?" asked Pink.

"I think this situation has got to her and she won't admit it."

"I'll go and have a word," Pink said turning to follow Carole.

I was left with Jones, who seemed to have a habitual frown.

"You alright?" he said.

"Yes, I'm having a bit of trouble sleeping though."

"That's Okay then," he replied and turned to leave.

"Before you go. I just wanted to ask about Pink. Has she recovered from her encounters in the park?"

"Look mate, I was doing something useful before we got called here and all this weird shit started to happen. I'm not talking behind my mucker's back." With that, he walked out.

Putting the exam papers back in the filing cabinet, I wondered if I needed to improve my social skills.

There was one thing I could do to remedy the situation. Namely, get Carole more involved.

I rang the land line number that Smith had given me. His switchboard hadn't been upgraded when the rest of the network had, in the nineteen eighties. There was a clicking on the line as the twenty first century interfaced with the mid twentieth, then an interminable set of rings before the handset was lifted.

"Yes? What is it?" I thought these civil service types were supposed to be trained in phone etiquette.

"Smith, it's John."

"John who?"

"John Voyle."

"Oh yes, Voyle. What is it? I was briefing a Permanent Under-Secretary."

"I've had an idea."

"Last time you did that, you tore a hole in the fabric of reality. Please, stop having ideas. No good ever comes of them."

"You're miffed because I tapped you on the nose."

"Doctor Voyle, you smashed me in the face with a lead cosh. Forgive me if I'm a little upset."

"I saved your life. Look, why don't we bring Carole along to the Police briefing."

"Because Carole never stays in one place long enough to talk to. On the other hand, she hates you, so she can't be all bad. Do you know how I can get in contact with her?" Smith said.

"She's having a heart to heart with one of Knowles' security people. The one with the code name Pink."

"I'll see if I can get Pink to persuade her. Anything else?"

"Why don't the security people like me? They resent being here."

"They were involved in an operation to rescue a high profile kidnap victim somewhere in Kosovo. A politician's daughter, lovely girl by all accounts. Then they were pulled out to provide security in this operation. They think it's all a fairy story that you've made up," Smith said.

"You believe me, don't they listen to you?"

"Not really, and neither does the Permanent Under-Secretary so if you'll excuse me, I must go and try to persuade a civil service mandarin that all the nightmare bits of fairy stories might come true."

"Tricky."

"Not necessarily. He has to deal with politicians. Good

bye. Someone will pick you up tomorrow."

CHAPTER 12

Smith was as good as his word, or threat, depending on how you looked at it. On the set date he collected me. He still had a sticking plaster over the bridge of his nose, but the bruising was starting to subside.

"I've saved your life with that," I said gesturing at his face, "no need to thank me." I heard Adam sniggering next to me, "And you can shut up."

"Who are you talking to?" said Smith. Either, Adam was not impinging on his consciousness, or he was being really difficult.

"No one, let's go," I said, resigned to my future role as the nutter who speaks to himself.

The briefing was at the University in Liverpool. We were met by a plain clothes policeman. He was a senior rank, if his made to measure suit was any indication. We were led down labyrinthine corridors to a meeting room. Knowles was there and a couple of guys in police uniform. They had the 'leader of men' attitude that characterises everyone above a certain pay grade in any organisation, regardless of their competence.

It was disturbingly like a faculty meeting. I got a cup of tea from an urn, adding sugar and small plastic tubs of semi-skimmed milk. Carole was sitting with Pink. The two had a rapport that I hoped would calm Carole. She did indeed require soothing because I realised that she hadn't seen Adam before. She sat open mouthed, then started whispering urgently to Pink who patted her hand, quietly reassuring her.

Adam sidled up to me. "The other one. Something is very wrong."

I whispered out of the side of my mouth, "She's like me. That's why she can see you."

Adam tried to say something, but a couple of people were looking at me, so I ignored him, smiled, and sat down.

When everyone was seated around the institutional

conference table, the chairman went through the formalities of introductions. I let most pass me by but registered Larsson, the pathologist, and Johnson, the zoologist.

Larsson presented first. He had photographs of the body as it was found. They were in black and white, which seemed a pointless anachronism until I realised what I was looking at, then became grateful. His description was clinical and concise. Basically, the young woman had been eaten. I confess I had been expecting something more along the lines of an American police procedural with esoteric forensic clues. But then we didn't need to look far for a suspect as it was found next to the victim.

The police were up next with a video of what had happened. The woman was walking across a car park, talking on a mobile phone. We could also see a creature lope across the tarmac towards her. The animal was taller than the woman, I would have had it at just under 6 feet. It was bipedal with the sort of thin muscularity you see in chimpanzees. Compared to a human, the arms and legs were long and bent, almost as if it wanted to walk on all fours, but was forced to stand on its hind legs. Despite that, it moved with a predator like fluidity. It had a nightmarish face. Imagine a photo of a human, where an image analysis program has extruded the mouth and nose into an animal like muzzle.

The woman should have seen the creature because it was right in front of her, but she didn't seem to notice. She just continued to walk straight towards it, talking away on her phone as if she hadn't a care in the world. She even seemed to be smiling.

When the creature was about three or four metres away, she stopped dead. She didn't react for a moment, then dropped the phone and turned to run. But it was too late. The creature lunged forward, wrapped its forearms around the woman and buried its muzzle into her neck. She struggled, then went limp. I don't know what happened next because I looked away. I could see from everyone else's faces that I'd made the correct decision. When I glanced back at the screen the creature was lying on the ground, spasming, next to the thing that had been the young woman.

Johnson was the zoologist. He'd stared at the video with detached interest, which made me take an instant dislike to him.

He cleared his throat. "You asked me for my opinion of the nature of the creature in the video. I have its body in my laboratory and I can now give you my preliminary findings."

He cleared his throat again in an irritatingly portentous manner.

"Ahem, this creature is unusual in several ways. Firstly, the manner of its death. It, ahem, fed on the victim which appears to have poisoned the animal. Also, by the time it came to me, it was starting to decompose."

"How long was it before you analysed the carcass?" asked someone in a police uniform sporting unnecessary amounts of silver on the epaulettes.

"A good point," continued Johnson, "The level of decomposition looked to be in the order of two to three weeks, but I examined the body within a couple of days of the attack. I'm unable to explain this. Once in our possession bodily decomposition proceeded at a normal rate. It's as if the rate of putrefaction accelerated when it died and then slowed.

"We'd been briefed that this creature is not native to this world. Initially, as you can imagine, I was sceptical. However, my investigations do support this conclusion. So, the manner of the creature's death, namely, that it was poisoned by feeding on the victim, indicates that this world is an inimical environment to the organism."

Larsson commented, "I take it that we can draw some conclusions as to the creature's intelligence from the fact that it ate something poisonous."

This got him a laugh, I couldn't tell if it was a release of tension or that people didn't believe what they were hearing.

I put my hand up, "Perhaps we resemble its normal prey?"

Johnson looked irritated. "Possibly but I'd rather we didn't conjecture at this point. But, to continue. I would like to talk about the physiology of the creature. It is not similar to any organism on this planet. To start with, it's venomous. Did you notice the way it attacked the young lady? The first action seems to be to hold the victim and introduce venom into a major blood vessel leading to the brain. These are located in the neck. This is much more efficient than any venomous animal on our planet as it causes unconsciousness in seconds."

"The creature looks mammalian. Are there any venomous mammals?" asked Larsson.

"There are a few venomous mammals on earth, but they are the exception. The slow loris in South East Asia absorbs venoms from its insect prey. The loris subsequently exudes the poison in its saliva.

"Shrews are another example. They are very small mammals and have venom to disable their quarry. The poisons do not kill the prey but stop it moving, so the shrew can set up a cache of living food to sustain it through the winter. But, as I say these animals are unusual."

"So not a mammal then?" continued Larsson. I resisted the impulse to tell him to shut up. Who the hell cared what it was.

"I repeat, the animal seems to be a chimera. For example, this organism has very specialised teeth, they are like hypodermic needles. We only see that in the most advanced snakes. The rest of the dentition is adapted to butcher its prey, as we find in mammals. This creature is superbly designed to hunt. However, I haven't yet come to the most surprising part. It's blind but has an extraordinarily well-developed olfactory system."

"Olfact what?" asked someone.

"It means a very well-developed sense of smell. Better than that of a dog. I have come to some conclusions about its native environment. It will live somewhere where there is limited visibility. This also accounts for the development of venom. If prey are difficult to come by, you do not want them to get away. From the creature's point of view, it needs to disable its quarry quickly and efficiently because the victim is going to be difficult to find if it runs off."

"Why?" asked someone.

"I just told you, it's blind. Snakes use the same strategy. They can't run after their prey so use a venom to disable its neurological functions. Some snake venoms even have opiate analogues so the prey doesn't even want to run away. My mapping of the amino acid structure of the proteins in the creature's venom suggest that it is not toxic as such. It paralyses it's prey."

"You mean the victims are alive and conscious as they're being eaten?" asked Smith.

"I'm afraid so."

There was an uncomfortable silence.

"Joking aside, how intelligent is it?" said one of the police high ups.

Johnson replied, "Well, I've tried to map the brain functions of this organism compared to earth mammals. If I'm correct, it has limited conceptual ability."

"Why didn't the victim..." began Smith.

One of the police officers interrupted, "She was a young woman with a name. She was probably close to her Dad and kept a picture of him and her brother on her desk. I suggest you show more respect."

Smith broke the ensuing silence, "I apologise," he said and turned to a plain clothed policeman, "What was her name?"

"Diane," he replied.

Smith continued, "Why didn't Diane see her attacker, the creature showed up on camera."

"For Heaven's sake Smith. We know why," I said, "It's for the same reason that we're ignoring the elephant in the room. These creatures are perfectly visible, but you have to want to see them. They can affect our perceptions." Turning my head I said, "Isn't that right?"

There was a crunching noise, and everyone looked in the same direction as me. The part of the table that everyone, up until now, had as part of their peripheral vision. The part of the table they hadn't wanted to look at.

Adam sat there gazing with interest at proceedings. "Everyone OK?" he asked taking another bite of carrot.

Wells was sitting next to him and added, "Any chance of a cup of tea?"

After this, things got a bit hectic for a minute. Words like prosecution and Official Secrets Act were bandied about. That was before people realised the futility of trying to threaten someone who could just become invisible.

Smith eventually pulled rank on everyone and calmed them down. Someone went and fetched Wells his cup of tea, upon which we all realised we could do with a cuppa. I noticed that we all got plastic cups, but someone had dug out a porcelain cup and saucer for Wells. Just goes to show that posh people do get better treatment, even when they're from another dimension.

One of the police high ups said, "Doctor, er, Voyle, is it? Were you aware of the presence of these two, ahh, people?"

"One's a rabbit," I replied.

He closed his eyes for a moment, with the air of one who is being very patient, but might not be in the near future. "Please answer the question."

"Absolutely, it's what you might call my USP, the ability to see visitors from other dimensions. I've sat here, a bit bemused, whilst the rest of you had, from my perspective, studiously ignored Adam and Wells. It's a form of selective attention. They can somehow manipulate your perceptions to con your brain into concentrating on everything else except them."

Carole said to me, "You could see them though, couldn't you?"

"Yes, I just said so. I wanted to see what everyone else's reaction would be."

"It's interesting that they can do the same things that the

creature could do. I wonder if they are linked somehow?" she said.

I was taken aback. Up until now her attitude towards me had been of outright hatred. This seemed, whilst not friendly, at least constructive.

So, I didn't see it coming.

She continued, "If so, then you could be in league with these two and the creatures. I'm not certain who can be trusted."

I spluttered that she could see the rabbit but the damage was done and the police types looked at me with suspicion, thanks 'Friend'.

Smith asked, "Why are you and Carole not affected?"

I replied, "If you asked me to speculate, I would say it's because she and I were very near to the apparatus when it was operating."

Some of the group, including Knowles, wanted to start up the kit in the near vicinity of her people to 'perception proof' them. I objected to this, partly on the basis that one of the three people operating the apparatus was dead, but mainly because it had already weakened the barriers between dimensions. Further use could break those down even further and possibly destroy the whole of reality as we know it.

They soon dropped the idea.

CHAPTER 13

I asked Smith if we could have a further meeting with Johnson. Initially the majority wanted to join in, but, when I explained I needed to talk about fairy tales and legends, everyone else went off to plot and plan. I couldn't really blame them. They hadn't interacted with organisms from other dimensions. Although I would have thought that a talking rabbit showing up at the meeting might have given them cause to stop and think. But no, they could not quite grasp what was going on and were determined to look for human killers.

Johnson himself did not want to talk to us but Smith strong-armed him, so he grumpily sat at our table. I gained a new respect for Knowles who sat with us and did not join the 'let's ignore the facts group'. Pink joined us along with Carole. Adam and Wells kept close.

"Mr Johnson, I realise that this is a bit unusual for you, but we are encountering some bizarre circumstances," I said.

Wells joined in, "Let me illustrate the situation. Adam is not the most unusual person in the room."

As he finished speaking, a cup and saucer rose in the air and drifted towards his outstretched hand. We waited, finally Johnson managed to close his mouth.

Having broken the ice, I felt we could get down to business.

"These people, such as Mr Wells and the rabbit, are from other dimensions. Our hypothesis is that they've been visiting us for as long as we've been on the planet. So, I want to ask you a couple of questions. The first is, what happened to the organism you examined? It doesn't seem as happy in this dimension as our friends here."

Johnson thought for a moment, "Well it died pretty quickly. Part way through its attack on Diane it shows signs of distress, ceased to feed and after a short while collapsed. When it came to me it had started to decompose. It is as though time was running faster for it than us, so it had started to rot faster. It also appears that we are, well, poisonous to it."

"So why does it seem so keen on feeding on us?"

"Frankly I have no idea," Johnson replied.

Larsson chipped in. "We looked at the bodies and it was difficult to examine victim two, I mean Diane, because of the level of disfigurement, but we could put together enough of the neck area to see the puncture holes made during the initial stage of the attack."

"What about Terry? Was he killed by a similar creature?" I asked.

"When we examined Terry, we found the same type of puncture wounds. A toxicological examination showed that they had very pretty much the same poisons in their bloodstreams. So, it seems that the attacks were carried out by similar organisms."

"Similar or identical," I pressed.

Johnson took over, "We can't say for sure, but if they are not the same attacker type, then they are very closely related species. We did a DNA test on the creature. The DNA has homology, sorry, similarities, with the DNA of dogs, snakes and humans. The creature was a chimera."

Knowles made an impatient noise.

Johnson continued, "Put simply, it's like the creature has bits of each, sort of mixed up. Basically, we have no idea what it is.

"Wherever this creature came from, it is as though there are some conditions there that have pushed evolution down a rather strange path, well, strange to us."

"I've got to say you're losing me here. I watch David Attenborough documentaries as avidly as the next person, but this is way over my head," said Knowles.

Johnson cleared his throat. "I'm probably not explaining myself very well. In this world creatures follow evolutionary pathways. Their genome alters over time as the forces of evolution favour one DNA change rather than another. The bizarre thing is that the creature seems to have a sort of pick and mix of the DNA of the various organisms. That just doesn't happen."

Smith said, "Very well, we'll have to accept that our adversaries don't follow the rules of biology on this world. But we need to find a way to combat them. Our working hypothesis is that entities such as this gave rise to some of our myths and legends. This creature seems to have some of the characteristics of a vampire. In mythology vampires are killed off in various ways. Could this help find a way to neutralise the damn things?"

"Really," said Johnson, "I hardly think that we can speculate too much in that direction."

"What about garlic?" suggested Knowles.

Johnson drew breath to dismiss such pseudo-science then stopped, "I suppose that as we are dealing with a creature that relies on its sense of smell to track its prey, then spraying around a lot of garlic would confuse them. It's possible that garlic could mask your smell and stop them tracking you. But they would be able to follow the garlic trail subsequently. Why, do you think you're especially vulnerable to attack by these organisms, Ha, Ha."

"Yes. They are, trust me on this," interrupted Smith.

"I'm not sure I would like to stake my life on spraying around a bit of garlic smell," Johnson said.

"Well I might have to," I replied.

"Shit, I hate garlic," said Knowles, "but we can pack a CS gas canister or thunder flash with some packs of garlic paste or powder. When it goes off there'll be a cloud of stinking garlic out to about 10 feet, possibly further.

"Assuming it works, and you don't end up as breakfast for some trans dimensional carnivore, you'll stink like nobody's business. If you can slow the thing down, my people can deal with it." She nudged me, "Of course, it might just give you a tasty seasoning. Want us to put a bit of salt and pepper in it?"

"You're a real comedian."

"We aim to please," Knowles said.

"Probably best to use paste, you want to get the aromatics into the air," said Johnson, who was getting into the swing of things.

It was at this point that Carole leaned over and whispered something in Smith's ear. Then, she stood up and left the room.

"What about all that stake through the heart business?" I asked.

Showing an unexpected sense of the dramatic, Knowles laid a chunky looking automatic pistol on the table, "Don't worry about killing it. It's what we specialise in."

I wanted to make the most out of having an expert, so I continued, "If the stories about vampires have some basis in reality. The myths where they come in under the door as mist and what not are down to them being pretty much invisible to us unless you are, well, far closer to them than is healthy. We've worked out that they are susceptible to having their sense of smell overloaded. What else are vampires famous for?"

"If you get bitten by one you turn into a vampire," said Smith, "Were there any signs of changes in the victims?"

"None whatsoever," said Johnson, "That part of the myth might be pure fantasy. But the people we're talking about were attacked and died almost immediately. I suppose it's possible," he considered for a moment, "no, it's too outlandish."

"You've got the remains of a chimeric vampire in your cold room. I think you can indulge in some speculative hypotheses," encouraged Smith.

"I've got no evidence for this but, let's consider viruses. They sequester the apparatus of cells to make more copies of the infectious agent. If a virus, or analogue, was sophisticated enough it could get the whole organism to change into something else. But this is pure fantasy. No viruses like that exist. Viruses just make more viruses."

He paused for a moment. "But then, a couple of days ago I didn't believe vampires existed."

Smith said, "The one advantage we have is that Dr Voyle seems to have an attraction for creatures from other dimensions. They will turn up wherever he is."

Knowles said, "So, all we have to do is use my friend Voyle here as bait, wait until an invisible ferocious carnivore turns up, hope it has the same reaction to garlic as my Grandad and blow the bugger's head off."

She turned to me and grinned, "Is your life insurance up to date?"

CHAPTER 14

When the meeting had finished Smith took me to one side.

"I need you to come with me. Some of our scientists have had these results for a while. Could you shake off your friends from other dimensions?"

"I can try. But what about Carole?"

"She can't be forced to help. It's just you I'm afraid."

"OK. I'll try. When do you want to go?"

"Immediately, time is of the essence."

"Should work out OK. Adam has gone off in a huff. He doesn't like Carole for some reason," I said.

"Well, she's not exactly reliable."

Smith led me out to his car. Adam appeared and looked quizzically at me.

"The other one is gone," he said.

"Could you have a look around?"

"I mean she is not here."

"Yes, I know but could you have a scout around then go back to my house. I'm not going to be back until late tonight. Oh, and make sure Wells is OK."

"Wells can look after himself. Sergei is looking after Mrs Theresa. I can come with you," said Adam.

"I don't want you to."

Adam sniffed disdainfully and raised his muzzle in a 'be like that then,' manner.

A couple of people from the meeting regarded me as if I had just confirmed their suspicions as to my state of mind.

"When people look at me talking to Adam they just see someone speaking to himself. I must seem loopy," I said.

Smith replied, "You seem crazy to me and I've accepted the presence of people who are, to all intents and purposes, invisible. Get in the car. You can phone your wife as we travel."

Smith had traded in the old Vauxhall, with the dodgy

brakes, for a more modern SUV. It was black with tinted windows.

"Not exactly inconspicuous is it?" I said.

He sighed, "It's the car pool people. It's what they think spies drive."

"Aren't you a spook?"

"Good lord no. I'm just a functionary at M.O.D. To be honest I don't think my elders and betters take this situation seriously."

"But you do?"

"Yes. I've read the files."

We drove in silence as the car headed eastwards on the M62. Signs for the M6 flashed up and we drove south.

"What do you think of our visitors from other dimensions?" I asked.

"You've got more experience of them than I have. We really can't fathom their motivations because they're completely alien," Smith replied.

"Have you thought about the day we met? Those rabbits chose to have a dust up with Knowles' people. Why did they do that instead of becoming invisible?" I said.

"I've no idea. We don't even know how many people from other dimensions live in the area. Do they just adapt to our dimension? Assimilate as it were?" said Smith.

"If so, they're pretty innocuous. Mind you, people from Southport are a bit left field."

We'd passed Birmingham and were headed for the Southwest. I realised I could do with a chance to stretch my legs.

"Any chance of stopping for a cup of coffee and a toilet break?"

Smith pulled off at the next service station. As he got out of the car the side seam of his jacket billowed to reveal a holstered pistol.

Not a spook? My arse.

Our destination was not the Chemical Defence Establishment, as I had expected, but a small outfit called

Henderson Pharmaceuticals. Part of the C.D.E. site had been turned into a science park and Henderson's occupied a new concrete and glass building. Although it was a commercial organisation, there was tight security. After signing in, we had to hand over all communication devices. I noticed that no one batted an eyelid when Smith deposited his pistol. He then had a word with a uniformed official who took me to one side and put a form in front of me. It was the Official Secrets Act. In for a penny, I thought, as I signed.

As I stood up, I said to Smith, "What have I committed to?"

"Frankly, nothing. People are bound by the Act anyway. I think the idea is to focus one's mind. Back in the day even the tea lady had to sign it. I suppose it just reminds you that you're about to be briefed on some very secret material."

We were met by a woman in her thirties who escorted us into an atrium and bought us coffee from a franchise stall. Somehow the bright modern building didn't fit in with my idea of a secret establishment. I expected low wooden Nissen huts on a windswept hillside. I mentioned this and was reminded that we were in the twenty first century.

We were ushered into the sort of identikit meeting rooms that people the world over try and avoid. The woman left us, and we were introduced to a variety of people whose dress code varied from a suit, like Smith, through to someone wearing a tee shirt with a DNA joke on it that only I seemed to find funny. We were waiting for a Professor Winter to arrive.

The lady who'd escorted us re-entered the room, put a folder down at the unoccupied space at the head of the table and said, "Sorry, should have introduced myself. I'm Julia Winter. I always like to meet visitors in person. Shall we get started?"

Various presentations covered a lot of what we'd already seen at the Liverpool University meeting and I was grateful for the coffee. Then Julia stood up and moved to the screen.

"It appears that various people have come to a conclusion about how we could neutralise the threat posed by the organisms that have been attacking people in the North West. I understand one of Dr Voyles's staff has also suggested it."

Smith leant in my direction, "Carole spoke to me after the meeting. I have to say I found her very impressive. Julia's team are used to coming up with solutions to tight timescales. They thought up the one we're going to hear about whilst we were driving down, yet Carole intuited the same concept after a single briefing."

Julia politely waited and continued, "We're dealing with what one might call an invasive species, albeit one that's a bit more serious than Himalayan Balsam."

The one with the witty tee shirt put his hand up and said, "Himalayan Balsam is driving out native species all over the country."

Before I could stop myself, I replied, "Yes, but it doesn't eat people, does it?"

At that point we had a short lesson in why Julia was head of a research group.

"Let's not get side-tracked. We have a species that originates in a trans-dimensional space and is inimical to humans. I want to hand over to James who's come up with an idea," she said.

Mr Witty Tee Shirt stood up and gave me a wink. It's always the hippies you have to watch.

"Analysis of this creature shows that smell is the primary sense by which it hunts. This is actually not as peculiar as you might suppose. Experiments have shown that if a dog is given a track of footprints associated with a scent, they will follow the track. However, if the footprints and scent diverge, the dogs will follow the scent not the footprints. To canines their olfactory sensory input is more important to them than their visual sense. So we needed a way to disrupt the sense of smell of your creature. Mr Smith gave us some vital information."

Smith acknowledged the invitation to speak by inclining his head and addressed the group. "We have reason to believe that that these creatures would find the smell of garlic especially troublesome, for reasons that I won't go into."

"Like vampires," laughed one of the team, who went quiet as Smith and I fixed him with a cold stare.

Witty Tee Shirt continued unabashed. "We've engineered a plasmid, that's a small section of DNA, to express Allicin, which is what gives garlic it's odour. If we introduce this into one of the creatures it will attach to a cold virus analogue. The virus will replicate, and the creatures nasal passages will be suffused with the odour of garlic."

"Do we have to treat each one. We don't know how many of these things we'll be facing," said Smith.

"Not at all. It's infectious. As the virus spreads through the population, eventually every one of these strange animals will be affected. The effect can be imagined if one were to think of every human becoming blind. The target organisms will be unable to hunt, job done. Any questions?

I asked, "How long will this effect last?"

"Forever," said Witty Tee Shirt, looking at me as if I was a four year old.

"Won't they starve?"

Julia said, "Absolutely. You have to accept that this will disrupt the ecosystem for these creatures. We were told this is a situation of national security. Extreme measures were authorised."

I thought about Terry's face.

"OK, fine by me."

Smith then asked a question that I hadn't thought about but which, as it turned out, was quite important.

"Have you given any thought as to how we are going to introduce the plasmid into the nasal passages of these creatures?"

Mr Witty Tee Shirt looked at the floor. Julia shifted uncomfortably in her seat.

She said, "We thought that the easiest way would be to inject a victim with the plasmid just prior to an attack."

Even I could see an obvious flaw to this plan, "We don't

know who is going to be on the menu or when."

"Ideally it would be someone who we knew would be in the firing line."

"But there's only me and Carole that ..."

"Quite," said Julia.

So, this was why they'd brought me down here.

"How long will it take you to cook up the potion," I asked.

"At least a couple of weeks. A few years ago, we wouldn't have known where to start. But with recent advances we can literally work miracles."

"I'm so glad."

Witty Tee Shirt leaned towards me and said, "Try not to get eaten before the plasmids are ready. I'd hate for this to be a waste of effort."

I replied colloquially.

"I don't think that sort of language is called for," said Julia.

Smith led me out before things escalated.

CHAPTER 15

As we drove back, I broke an uncomfortable silence.

"Did you know what they were planning?"

"No. Although it makes sense. Let's face it, these entities will be hunting you anyway. We've got nothing to lose by dosing you up."

"So you can feed me to some hellish creature?"

"Just a quick nip. That's all it'll take to introduce the plasmid. Then the DNA will insert itself into one of their common cold analogue viruses. Problem solved. The creatures will be snuffling allicin," Smith said.

"Quick nip! Have you seen the size of the teeth on those things? A quick nip will have my arm off. And don't forget they've started drawing the victims into their own dimension."

"Listen Doctor Voyle, every effort will be made to protect you. We don't want you to be captured by one of these creatures. What if there are more intelligent denizens in their dimension? If they got hold of you, they would have access to your knowledge. All this business with the plasmids is a backup."

"What about Carole? Are you going to inject her?"

"It seems that Carole has disappeared again."

"So, let me get this straight: she turns up, suggests some scheme to get me eaten by the creature from the Black Lagoon, then disappears. Has it occurred to you that she might, just conceivably, not like me very much?"

"There is an alternative. Knowles suggested we mount an expedition to the creatures' dimension. She proposed using veterinary tranquilliser darts filled with a plasmid solution. We'd only have to get a dart into one of them and the virus will spread through the whole population. Does that sound a better option?"

Sulking now, I said, "You could've told me that at the beginning."

"Yes, sorry. Should've mentioned it. Shall we stop off for a

coffee and sandwich at the next services?"
He drove on with a self-satisfied smile.

CHAPTER 16

Smith dropped me off at his lair. I was greeted by Adam and Sergei, who seemed to think that going anywhere without them was the height of folly. I pointed out that I'd been accompanied by Smith, which they seemed to think was ... well, you get the idea.

Deciding that I'd had enough of work, mainly because the college was locked up. I began to walk home accompanied by Adam.

"Can you see any of Knowles' people?" I asked.

"Nope," said Adam.

Sergei didn't reply. He just kept walking in front, falling back and repeating the process until I got a headache.

"I expect you were a bit worried when I disappeared," I said.

"No, we saw you drive away in a car with that strange Mr Smith. We do notice these things," said Adam sagely.

"I mean that it must have worried you when you couldn't sense me being around."

The rabbit looked at me quizzically.

"I could always feel that you were around. I told you. You are like a beacon. It just gets a bit dimmer when you're far away. Although I'm surprised that it isn't the same when you are closer - you being a bit dim at the best of times."

I decided to ignore the bait. "Can you detect Carole?"

"We can when she's here," Adam replied.

"You mean you can't detect her now?"

"Nope. Totally gone away. She went away yesterday. I tried to tell you. Really Voyley, you should pay more attention."

"You mean she's dead or been taken to another dimension."

"Indeed."

"But why didn't you tell anyone."

"I did. I told you," Adam said.

"Couldn't you see that I'd misunderstood?" I replied.

"Not really," Adam said with remorseless logic.

" ..." I couldn't think of a reply so phoned Smith.

"Doctor Voyle, missing me already?"

"I've just spoken to the rabbits."

"I find it so amusing when you say that."

"Shut up and listen. Have you been drinking?" I said.

"It's been a long day," Smith replied.

"Carole is gone."

"To Daresbury. You phoned up to tell me that?"

I drew a deep breath, "The rabbits can't detect her presence. I thought their perception was limited by distance. It isn't. So, if they can't detect her, it means that she's either dead or not in this dimension."

"I'll get on to the police. They might not believe what's going on, but they'll pay attention when I invoke the Home Secretary. We'll try and find her. Get back home. I'll make sure your escort is on its way. Hunker down," Smith ordered.

All of a sudden, he didn't seem so relaxed.

#

The next day I was up early. I hadn't slept that well. Looking outside there were another couple of Knowles' guard dogs. These two were Evans and Jones. Presumably a Welshman was thinking up the code names.

"Our Lieutenant thought it would be best if you went to work," said Evans.

"That will keep you moving around. They think it will make you a more difficult target, Adam said, nodding his approval. A gesture lost on Evans as the Rabbit was hiding his presence.

"Also, we got you this," said Evans.

He handed me a small aerosol. I looked nonplussed.

"It's a modified pepper spray that's full of garlic stuff. Hold it in your fist and put your thumb under the shield. Then you aim by pointing your arm. That way you won't spray yourself in the face."

"Thanks, what about a gun?" I said, pocketing the spray.

"Sorry mate. If you had a gun, you'd be more of a danger to yourself than anyone else. Stick to garlic spray. Although there is something else you could do after you use the spray."

"What's that?"

"Run like hell. Leave us to do the shooting. We're professionals," Evans said.

"Me and Sergei are talented amateurs," Adam added.

"Really! I'm sure you'll be very useful," I said.

"There's no need to be sarcastic. We can't all have PhDs," Evans said huffily, re-joining his companion.

Sometimes it seemed that life would be a lot easier if everyone could see Adam and Sergei.

Smith was waiting for me in my office.

"Was the escort OK?" he asked.

"Yes, they gave me a garlic spray and everything."

"They'll stick closer to you from now on. The police are searching, but we must work on the assumption that Carole has been seized by one of the ..." He took a deep breath, "one of the vampire creatures. Sorry, I can't get used to saying it."

"The rabbits are always nearby," I said.

Smith looked around. Then started as Adam made himself visible.

"Are you really sure you can trust them?"

"Hopefully the rabbits will be able to see inter-dimensional beings, even if Knowles people and I can't."

"Your escort are the best troops around."

"I know, but Knowles' soldiers just won't see these creatures. The first indication they'll get of an attack is me screaming. Let's face it, someone from another dimension could walk straight past them, possibly blowing a raspberry, and they wouldn't know."

"Very well. It's not like I can do much about it. You may as well try and carry on your life as normal, well, as much as possible."

CHAPTER 17

Some of the younger staff, in a well-intentioned attempt to cheer me up, organised an outing to one of Southport's night clubs.

"Lovely," I shouted to one of the students, "Dark and noisy. It's just what one needs after a traumatic incident."

But they meant well. I couldn't help noticing Adam's behaviour. He was dancing on a table, paws in the air, whilst women of various ages boogied round him like he was a pile of handbags at a seventies disco. So, they must've been aware of him on some level. I wondered about formulating a research project.

Meanwhile, Sergei was in close conversation with several dodgy looking characters in a corner. They were hunched over their glasses and looking over their shoulders like villains in a Dickens novel.

As such evenings go, it was a great success. I kept relatively sober so ended up with one of my male students tearfully telling me about an unrequited love for a colleague. The object of his desire was a nice looking girl who took her essays very seriously. I did the pep talk one always gives and told him to follow his heart. They were last seen leaving the club in a close embrace. I had finally done some good in the world.

Sergei finished whatever nefarious business he had and some of the rowdier elements looked like they were making fun of him. Probably saying he had big ears. Could they see him, did they even realise what they were looking at?

Adam suddenly stopped dancing and appeared next to me whilst his admiring harem giggled.

"Get out," he said with an urgency I hadn't encountered before.

"What?"

"Leave, now!"

I reckoned that if Adam was worried, then something was going to happen that the average man in the street would classify as B.A.D. Moving towards the exit, I realised I couldn't abandon my students. A full scale evacuation was called for. Now, what would get pissed millennials out of a nightclub … got it.

I shouted to those nearest, "Come on, I'll buy everyone some nosh."

"Spoil sport," said one of my students.

"And cocktails!"

That got their attention. They started to grab their compatriots.

Going over to Knowles' people I said, "Get everyone you can out of here, now."

They studiously looked away from me like I was going to decide I was mistaken to think they were following me.

"Don't piss about," I hissed, "Everything in here's about to go south. You don't want me telling Smith and your officer that you didn't help." That got **their** attention.

The group milling around outside was a mismatched assortment including some middle aged ladies who'd taken a liking to the rabbits, even if they couldn't quite remember who they'd spent the evening with.

There was a sense of tension, palpable, like the static in the air before a thunderstorm.

The group was beginning to relax, thinking to themselves that they'd got spooked, even feeling slightly foolish.

The lessening of tension was followed by the sound of crashing, characteristic of a party really taking a turn for the worse. The racket was enlivened with the occasional scream. The bouncer on the door rushed in and came out backwards, propelled by someone who had been thrown face first through the exit.

One of Knowles' men half ushered, and half threw some of my students out whilst the other was effectively blocking the door with someone he was beating the living daylights out of.

Then both of them waded in. I almost expected cartoon bubbles to appear with exclamation marks and words like 'bash'. After a few moments they re-joined us looking dishevelled. One had a nosebleed and the other a split lip. It was also the happiest I'd seen any of my escort contingent since they'd joined me.

Adam peered back through the entrance, "Hmm, Sergei's going to be busy for a while."

Dramatic convention would have had someone crashing through a window to lie groaning at our feet at this point. But modern safety glass, being as strong as it is, meant there was a less dramatic thud as someone hit a window and bounced back into the melee within.

One of Adam's harem spoke up, "Oh poor little Sergei. He's so cute and they're picking on him. That's not fair." At which point she actually stamped her foot, which I thought was something people only did in books.

Now the words 'Sergei' and 'cute' were not ones that would normally associate themselves in my mind. I tried to think how I would describe a 12 stone bundle of muscle bound homicidal rage topped by bunny ears, and the word cute would still not come into my head

Alarmingly, the harem looked like they were psyching themselves up to go back in. In what universe do a bunch of women, of various ages, charge into a horrendous bar fight? It wasn't as if we were living in Newcastle.

Adam looked thoughtful again, and then said, "You're right it is dreadfully unfair."

He paused to think.

"But they did bring it on themselves. Let's go for Margaritas!" he finished throwing wide his paws.

Now, I know for a fact that some of these people were not big drinkers but, as they were all still under his influence, they all shouted, "Yay Margaritas."

Adam turned to me, looking a bit alarmed and said, "I just heard someone mention them. What's a Margarita? It's not dangerous is it?" I told him not to worry; it was a potent alcoholic drink.

I wanted to leave them to it, but Adam would not let me go home on my own, so I joined them in a cocktail bar. The night became a bit of a blur, until the cold night air hit me on the way home.

I heard someone say, "No you don't, this way. Oops, watch those steps now. Come on, up you go," It was one of Knowles people. He was holding my arm and hammering on the door, as I fumbled for my keys.

Adam was lying on his back singing some bright little song about the sun rising over the lettuce patch.

Another voice said, "I bet Pink will be sorry she missed this." It was the other chap standing next to me.

"Takes all kinds." I shook off their hands and they grabbed me as I slumped.

A light came on over the door and Theresa was in front of me wearing a dressing gown.

"Hallo Love. Me and Adam and some of ... everyone ... We've have been out."

"Do you want us to bring him in? He's a bit the worse for wear."

"No, thank you. It was very kind of you to escort him home. I'll take it from here." Theresa guided me over the threshold and Adam followed, tripping over the doorstep.

"Where've you been. Sergei came back hours ago and looks like he's been in a car crash. I was worried sick."

Adam pulled out a pistol, looked at it blearily. He gently put it on the hall table before lurching forward and passing out.

"He's been drinking," I pointed out.

"Let's get you into the lounge. God you're in a state."

She guided me onto a nice comfy chair and put a blanket over my legs. And then, thoughtfully, brought a bucket. My eyes closed as she stood in front of me with her head to one side.

"It's all a bit new to you isn't it."

That was true, I'd not had so much to drink in years.

CHAPTER 18

The next day I awoke feeling like something had crawled into my mouth and died. I staggered upstairs and showered.

Downstairs Theresa scowled. "You made a right exhibition of yourself last night. I'm late for work."

Adam came in and gave her a forlorn look.

"Oh dear, aren't you well? Here, have a cuddle." The rabbit rested his head on her breast then slunk off to the lounge.

"Why did you leave Sergei. He's obviously been in a fight. Where were you?"

I wanted to explain that Sergei didn't need any help, but the banging in my skull made coherent thought impossible. I shook my head sadly and drank some water. Fortunately it felt like it was staying down.

To add insult to injury Sergei sauntered into the kitchen, grabbed a couple of carrots and hopped off. He'd lost his normal coiled spring demeanour. If anything he looked relaxed.

"I'm off to work. Do you think you can get through the day?" asked Theresa.

"Sorry."

She harrumphed past me and, seizing her jacket, slammed the front door as she left.

Adam and I left the house. There was a different close protection team on shift. This one was Pink and a guy whose cover name I hadn't learned, but was probably some primary colour. They knew my routine now so went ahead of us and turned down Scarisbrick Avenue.

Adam looked askance, "Don't like it."

I glanced along the alley. It was narrow to the point of looking medieval, even having enclosed wooden balconies extending over the road.

"Don't worry, no one's going to dump their night soil on our heads." I said, trying to dispel the claustrophobic atmosphere that the narrow space engendered.

"Come on," I said in the best jovial voice I could muster. I should have listened to him.

Pink and her companion had reached Lord Street whilst Adam and I lagged behind and hadn't reached the intersection with West Street.

As I ambled down the slope the rabbit pushed me and shouted, "Run." My peripheral vision caught a figure charging towards us, so I took off towards the soldiers, who I suddenly thought of as my bodyguards.

Behind me I heard three bangs followed by a yelp, but I was moving too fast to take it in. Pink was running back up the passage with arms outstretched to catch me and, bizarrely, a huge grin.

Her colleague was chasing her. His pistol was drawn as he shouted, "Shoot him!"

I had just reached the crossroads of West Street, Pink was still a good four metres away, when I cannoned into two police constables who were rushing towards the sound of the shots. We met in an untidy tangle as the creature chasing me careened off a wall leaving a bloody print. It was a paw with an opposable thumb.

The animal stopped, looked at us and then at Pink who also halted and stared, not having seen the foe before. As we formed a sort of frozen tableau I got a good look at the creature. It resembled the result of a genetic recombination project to join a human with dog and snake. It was a face only a hardened wildlife TV presenter could love. We were only still for a couple of seconds, then the creature was off, running away along West Street, presumably not liking the odds.

One policeman held on to me, or maybe I held onto him, whilst the other chased after the creature. Fortunately for the copper, he stood no chance of catching up as it made its escape, bouncing off the roof of a car.

Just to be on the safe side, with what I thought was great presence of mind I said to my constable, "Tell him to watch out, it has a gun."

I didn't fancy the policeman's chances if he tangled with the creature.

The copper with me started urgently speaking into the radio clipped to his stab proof vest. Pink showed him some identification and conversation ensued about making statements, whilst I took the opportunity to walk back up the road towards the Promenade.

Adam was propped against a wall nursing his left arm. I looked behind me and surreptitiously picked up his pistol, tucking it into my rear waistband, under my jacket. I fervently hoped it didn't discharge and take bits of me with it.

I then carefully picked Adam up and, hoping my back wouldn't give out, walked down the road to the little group who'd only just realised I'd left.

The constable who'd so heroically but, fortunately fruitlessly, pursued the attacking creature had joined the group.

"Bloody sod just disappeared," he gasped, bending forwards.

Again, there was an air of dislocation, as if their minds wouldn't quite accept what they had seen.

The copper continued, "That bastard could run for England and I lost him. He was some kind of free runner bouncing around like a rubber ball."

Of course you lost it, I thought. Once it got ahead of you it would affect your perceptions and become invisible.

I wanted to stay and see what their description sounded like, but I had an injured rabbit to attend to.

"I need to get him to a doctor," I said nodding down at Adam in my arms.

The constables looked at me, "You mean a vet?"

"Yes, sure," I answered," Just find the nearest will you, please?"

Pink came to my rescue. "Family pet, he's very attached to it. We'll guarantee his safety and come in to make statements when your Inspector calls my C.O."

With some reluctance the constables let us go and

directed us to a vet's practice. Pink's colleague helped me carry Adam into the Victorian gridwork of roads on the landward side of the main street.

Panting, we traversed the waiting room, the receptionist not having time for more than a, "You can't go in there", as we clattered into the surgery.

A man looked up from a perky Labrador, who was enjoying the attention.

"Excuse me?"

"I'm sorry," I said, "But we've got an injured rabbit."

"R.T.A." Clarified my helper.

"It's an emergency, please could you help us out?"

"He's Voyle and I'm Green. Really need your help mate."

"Right, ah, I'm Tony, one of the practice vet's. Just put the poor little ... poor chap down there will you." He made a harassed gesture towards a clinically shiny table.

"I'll be with you in a couple of minutes, could you please take Ruffles back into the waiting room." Having divested himself of the dog he gave us his full attention.

"Gosh, he's really is a big rabbit isn't he. I don't think I've seen this breed before. What seems to be the problem."

"Like we said Guv, hit by a car. We think it's his arm."

The vet looked up.

"His foreleg. He's hurt his foreleg," corrected Green.

"Poor little guy. He's the kid's favourite pet. They'll be devastated if anything happened to him," I played to the crowd, stroking Adams ears.

Adam groggily opened his eyes, "Where am I. Where's my gun?"

"Ahh bless," I added.

Tony stopped dead. "Did that rabbit just speak?" he asked.

"Don't be ridiculous," I said keeping my voice deadpan, "Rabbits can't speak."

He continued his examination.

"What about concussion," I asked.

"We can't tell with animals unless it's really bad," he

replied.

"What do you do if it's a human?"

"I don't know, I'm a vet, not a doctor!"

"What would you do if you were a doctor."

"I think you'd ascertain if they were compos mentis. You see if they can answer some simple questions."

I leaned closer to Adam who opened his eyes. "How many fingers am I holding up," I asked, showing him my hand.

"Four fingers and a thumb," Adam answered. "Can I get up now?"

Tony drew breath, then shook his head. "I'll just strap up the limb, it's merely a sprained shoulder."

An hour later I was supporting Adam as we walked back to my house. The rabbit was grumpy because I wouldn't let him have any painkillers, but if physical laws were different where he came from, then his physiological response to pharmaceuticals could be altered. I didn't want to risk killing him with an aspirin.

We walked through the front door and Adam suddenly developed a pronounced limp and woebegone expression. Theresa, coming into the hallway, gave me an accusing look.

"What have you done to Adam?" she said installing him on the lounge sofa.

She then turned on me. "What happened?"

I toyed with the idea of explaining that a shapeshifting carnivorous nightmare from another dimension had attempted to devour me and Adam had been injured when he threw himself in its path.

"There was a car accident. He ran into the road. There was nothing I could do," I lied.

"Go and get dinner on," she ordered, "And get some carrots for Adam."

Fair enough, he had saved my life. Although later I realised that I'd just missed something very important.

I wondered about my supposed bodyguard's words "Shoot him". It would have been more helpful if he'd specified the creature as the target, unless it wasn't.

I'd thought Pink had a soft spot for me. This seemed to confirm it, as she'd been prepared to ignore her orders and put her life on the line.

I certainly had lots to think about as I peeled and julienned the organic carrots that my besotted wife would feed to Adam.

CHAPTER 19

Theresa left for work and I was alone with Adam. It gave me a chance to give him back his gun and clarify what happened.

He clicked on the safety catch saying, "I could hear the thing coming, then, when it appeared, I shot off about three rounds before it swiped me aside. It was strong and fast."

"But you shot it, are you sure you hit it?"

Adam looked at me, "I know what I'm doing. Of course I didn't miss it. All that 'good, these gun things' was for Mr Smith's benefit. Sergei and I can defend ourselves. It's a dangerous world out there."

"Well it certainly is when you're around. Where did you learn about guns?"

"Here and there. We've been around for a while but, as I keep saying, we were never as," he paused, "never as grounded before. It's difficult to explain. We're more solid."

"Are you the first of your species to come here?"

"There's a story where Me and Sergei come from that a couple of us formed a close relationship with someone before. But she must have been a bit unusual. We always hope we'll meet someone else like Beatrix. She's a bit of a legend in our dimension."

I decided I could wait to find out about the effect of interdimensional beings on children's authors at another time.

"Adam, I'm worried about Theresa. What if something happens to her? Could you stick close to her for a bit?"

"Well, Okay but I'm going to get Sergei to stay with you then."

"Sergei? The carrot fixated homicidal psychopath?" I queried.

"He's not that bad, I'm sure he's not very obsessed with carrots. Well, not for a rabbit anyway. I'll get him over. But he won't be happy. He's in the middle of some business negotiations."

I thought this would be a good time to broach something that had been bothering me, "What do you and Sergei do for money? I mean how do you get to buy all this stuff?"

Adam thought for a moment, "Well, generally we just take what we need. But we do a lot of bartering and I've started getting credit cards now you've showed me what they are."

"How do you get the money to pay the bills."

"What are bills?" he said looking nonplussed. I decided not to press this, but obviously there was a very disconcerted debt collection department somewhere.

Then I had an unpleasant thought, "What address do you give them?"

He laughed, "I don't give them this one, that would be silly."

I breathed a sigh of relief.

"No, I give them Mr Smith's. You know, that big building where we first met him. Is that funny?" Adam said.

"No, not at all."

"It's just you started laughing."

"Don't worry about it."

"I don't see what's funny."

"You mentioned business. What other business is Sergei doing?" Goodness only knows what trouble they were causing. The credit cards were probably the tip of an iceberg.

Adam didn't say anything.

"Come on," I repeated, "cough."

"Ahem."

"Funny. Now tell me what's going on."

Adam looked shifty, "I'm not sure what he's doing is strictly legal."

"Nothing you do is strictly legal, in fact most of it is completely illegal."

"Import mainly," Adam said evasively.

"What sort of import, not guns?"

"No, no, nothing like that."

"Any small packages, powders or anything?" I asked.

"Really, no, we don't get involved in anything nefarious. Apart from guns for our own use of course. Mind you, now you come to mention it, I bet lots of people would like to have guns."

I needed to nip this idea in the bud. "No, you two are not going to start importing guns."

"What about exporting?"

"No! not that either," I said, putting off the moment when he found out about the exports from our armaments industry. God, this was like telling your children the facts of life.

"Well, you don't need to worry," Adam said, patting my hand in a reassuring way, that completely failed in its intent, "We help people. We facilitate getting people from abroad into this country."

This couldn't be good.

"What sort of people from abroad?" I asked.

"They're young ladies. We have to reassure them a lot because they get very scared. But I am sure it's Okay because Sergei's friends look after them."

"What, those gangster types who were in the nightclub! Have you lost your mind? There is nothing that bunch are doing that isn't illegal and probably causing a huge amount of human misery."

"I suppose they're a bit rough, but Sergei says they're all right."

"Sergei cuts people's ears off and wears them as a necklace. I don't think you can use him as a barometer of moral rectitude," I said, sharply.

"But he will look after you. If he says he'll keep you safe, then you will be kept safe."

"What about everyone else round me?"

"Ahh, that might be a bit trickier, but he means well. Come on, give him a chance," Adam said with a winsome look.

I relented, "OK, but we need to talk about this work that you two are doing for the gangsters."

So, with Adam convalescing, I ended up with a somewhat

dangerous companion in the shape of Sergei. I have to say I wasn't completely comfortable with the idea. Sergei was very different from Adam. Not for him the being lovingly fed root vegetables by besotted humans.

No, Sergei was to be found in the student gym impressing people with his ability to bench press huge weights, even if afterwards they had difficulty describing the short guy with big ears. Then you would ask them what it was about those big ears and they would look a bit nonplussed, then mumble something about not being racist and move on.

That wasn't so bad, but Sergei had zero powers of discrimination. Take Vera, a nice lady who had taken partial retirement when she had reached sixty five a couple of years previously. The elderly matron had adopted the anachronistic role of tea lady. It was probably more for the company rather than the money, but, unfortunately for her, she did enter offices unannounced.

She managed to get out a cheery, "Hello, luvvie, I've brought you a nice cappuccino," before she found herself thrown against a wall with a dagger held at her throat. I have to be frank with you, she was a bit shaken up because ladies of a certain age aren't used to such treatment.

Fortunately, she wasn't badly bruised. I sat her down and after a while she calmed herself and ended up with only a hazy recollection of 'the boisterous Rottweiler that you ought to have better control over'.

Needless to say, I was not at all happy. I pointed out to Sergei that little old ladies seldom posed a threat to life and limb, but this didn't seem to cut much ice with him.

"She shouldn't have come creeping in through the door. That's very suspicious," he growled.

"But she was wearing an apron and was carrying coffee."

"How did I know she was just going to give you a cup of coffee. She could have been an assassin." He lowered his muzzle to the coffee splashed across my desk and sniffed.

There was no reasoning with him. Even when he wasn't

causing mayhem, he was irritating. When I was trying to write emails, I couldn't concentrate for the scratching noise as Sergei trimmed his claws with his much loved combination dagger and knuckle duster. The noise just set my teeth on edge.

After a couple of days, I couldn't cope anymore. I sent him out of the building and just hoped he wouldn't kill anyone too close to the College. He wasn't keen on the idea because Adam had ordered him to guard me, but I persuaded him that the two special forces people following me would be on hand. He remained unconvinced, considering them to be a bit weedy and not nearly tough enough. However, he eventually agreed to leave me alone and hopped off, in a stomping manner, to check with Adam.

CHAPTER 20

As Sergei left, I breathed a sigh of relief and settled down to prepare a lecture on the synergy between folk tales and archaeological finds. However, I had barely covered the introduction when Wells entered.

I looked up from my work, "Were you just waiting outside doing your invisible act?"

"I must confess I was, but we need to talk. I've been thinking about your predicament, so I wandered into Mr Smith's offices and had a word with him. It seems he's liaising with the police, so was able to tell me about some worrying developments. There've been reports of several disappearances, here and in the next town."

"We know this. The police questioned me about it after Terry was killed. I expect they're worried that someone will say there's a serial killer on the loose."

"What's a serial killer?" Wells asked.

"It's someone who is compelled to murder other people. They do so because they think it's fun."

"Seriously, you murder other people for fun?"

"No, not everyone. Some people have a kind of mental illness which means they can't feel empathy for others. We call it psychopathy."

He looked at me with complete disgust and said, "Just when I think you people can't get any worse, you come up with some new depravity to show me how wrong I can be. Do you think there are connections between these people who disappeared?"

I replied, "Smith told me that they don't fit the profile of those who commonly go missing, no home problems, no drug addictions, they just disappear and are reported to the police by their families. A lot of them are young women. I think we can safely assume they are victims."

"Something isn't right," Wells said. "Why did a creature

attack someone here, and poison itself, when other victims have, presumably, been drawn into the other dimension."

"Maybe not all of the creatures have learned the behaviour. They aren't that clever. It also means that Terry wasn't the first victim. He must have been breaking down the barriers between dimensions for a while."

Changing tack Wells said, "I want to talk to you about something else as well. I'm developing a hypothesis about the creatures that shift between dimensions. I want you to help me out with a little experiment. Just for a short period I wonder if I could take you through to my dimension. You see I would like to, Oww! what the hell do you think you're doing!"

This last bit because I had activated a small device powered by a carbon dioxide cylinder that sprayed garlic powder over him.

He glared at me from reddened eyes, "I repeat, what do you think you're doing. What is this? Garlic?"

"How do I know that you're not one of these vampires?"

Wells cocked his head to one side and gave me a look that eloquently said, "stupid boy".

But he explained to me anyway. "Dr Voyle, I don't look like one of the creatures we've seen. If I were a vampire, I don't think I would be asking you to accompany me in such polite terms, do you?"

Then he considered for a moment, "However, I think you are right to be cautious. Especially if my ideas are correct. Now, come on."

He grabbed my arm and there was a disorientating feeling. A bit like when you are feeling really sea sick and suddenly turn your head.

A glowing portal appeared and we stepped through.

I dropped to my knees and retched. Next to me Wells had kept upright, but his eyes were closed and he was breathing deeply.

"You get used to it after a while, or so I'm told," he said.

"How long have you been making the journey."

"About 20 years" he replied.

"Someone's lying to you."

"I worked that out when I was still experiencing nausea with every jump after the first year."

"It's like seasickness. People say it gets better, but I've never found it to."

"We don't go on the sea, so I wouldn't know."

"Where are we?"

"A relatively benign dimension where you can test your abilities."

"How benign?"

"Don't eat anything." Wells paused to think, "And don't touch anything. I'm going to attempt to get us to move between this world and mine. This place has the advantage that time passes here at the same speed as in my world."

"Does time pass at a different speed in your dimension?"

"Indeed. I spend a few days in your domain and months have passed at home."

"Does that mean that when you go home everyone has aged?"

"Exactly. That is why I try and minimise the amount of time I spend in your world."

I said, "It's like in a fairy tale. You know, someone lives with the fairies for a couple of weeks and comes back to find a hundred years has passed."

"I refer to my original comments about your world's legends being based on some kind of factual event."

"Have your people colonised this world?"

"No, why would we?"

"Because it's there."

Wells sighed, "Doctor Voyle, in my world I am considered positively reckless. Tom is almost ostracised for his complete lack of caution."

"You seem quite circumspect to me?"

"That's because you're judging me by the standards of your society. Where Tom and I come from, people are much,

much, more risk averse."

"Why?"

"We have our reasons. Now, I'm going to lift an object using what you refer to as telekinesis. Try and feel, with your mind, what's going on."

Nonplussed, I waited. Wells looked at a fallen branch. It rose in the air and hung there.

"Can you feel what's going on?"

It seemed pointless, but, I sensed something. Like the intention to move your arm before flexing a muscle. The branch dropped lower, then rose upwards again. The sensation was stronger this time.

"Yes, I see what you mean," I said.

"Try it yourself."

I looked at the branch and imagined that I was going to wrap my hand round it and tense my biceps and ... the piece of wood trembled.

"Oh, well done, Doctor Voyle. That really is very good. I suspect the phenomenon that's causing the weakening of the barriers between worlds is enabling you to take on the characteristics of this dimension at an accelerated rate."

"Compared to who?"

Wells said, "We've had visitors from your world before. As I say they did not adapt as fast as you."

"Because I'm clever?"

"No, because you have unwittingly been teetering on the edge of different dimensions for a while due to your ill thought-out experiments; which might still bring doom to us all."

"Sorry. So, people who go to other dimensions, take on the characteristics of that place?"

"Precisely. You are developing telekinetic abilities. My own view is that people have been slipping into other dimensions for centuries, seeding the dimensionality with humans, so to speak. Those unwitting pioneers have been moulded by the physics of the new universe they inhabited," Wells explained.

"The first records we have are from John Dee, who used his scrying scope to talk to angels. Those were your lot, weren't they?" I asked.

"I believe so. You must remember that for us this is ancient history. Time moves a lot faster here. It's possible that this person you spoke of actually facilitated humans appearing in our world. Try again with the object."

Concentrating again, feeling the branch in my mind, I caused it to shift a little more. The stick rose slightly, trembling in the air, then sank down.

"Well done, Dr Voyle. Very well done."

"I feel exhausted."

"That's only temporary. Rest a moment and we'll try opening portals to other worlds," Wells said.

"Should we? There are some nasty things in other dimensions."

"You are wise to be cautious. However, I've been doing this for many years. Do the same exercise. Feel for the shape as I create it and we won't go far wrong. OK, here we go."

The light shimmered, and a portal opened. We walked through. There was a nauseating lurch and we found ourselves standing in a meadow.

"Is this your world?"

"Indeed. Did you detect anything?"

"I think I did. In my mind, like a key fitting a lock."

"I'll take us back and you can try."

We returned to the clearing. I felt in my mind for that key fitting into a lock. Almost there. It wasn't quite the same, but I was sure it was good enough.

A portal opened and there was a white light and intolerable heat. I shielded my eyes, lost my concentration and the portal closed. Grass smouldered.

"I think a little more precision is called for," said Wells, checking his jacket to make sure there were no burn marks.

He opened the portal again a couple of times. I felt I had mastered it now. The difference was becoming more obvious with repetition. Reaching out, the key fitted the lock, and a portal opened.

"Shall we?" Wells gestured.

We stepped forward and were in the meadow again.

"Well done!" he said. I tried it a couple of times.

"I think I can detect the key for the world where the vampires come from," I said.

Wells put a cautionary hand on my arm. "Perhaps we should leave that for now. Maybe you could try it when you have some heavily armed people with you?"

"You have a point."

"Would you like to meet my family? I confess I've organised a little picnic. We should see them soon."

"Of course, I'd be flattered. Perhaps I should tell Theresa I'll be back late."

"There's no need. Remember time runs faster here."

We walked across the meadow. Wild flowers peppered the grassland with colours that England hadn't seen since the development of industrialised agriculture. But then maybe Wells' people didn't have a burgeoning population to feed.

Rounding an overgrown hedge, we came across his family. A grey haired woman in late middle age was seated on a picnic blanket with an open hamper. Sitting next to her, was a younger lady of about Wells' age. That they were mother and daughter was obvious from their facial similarities. The younger woman sprang up and ran towards us, her auburn hair hanging loose about her shoulders.

Flinging her arms around Wells she shouted, "Father! Welcome back, we've missed you so much."

The older woman raised herself, literally rose to her feet, without bracing her arms on anything. The benefits of telekinesis, I realised.

"Welcome back," she said, with tears in her eyes. "I see you've brought a visitor."

"This is Dr Voyle. He's from the technical world. I'm helping him with a slight problem." The older woman turned to me and wiped her eyes. She held out her hand.

"So pleased you could come. Do join us. You can call me Rosemary and this is our daughter, Emilia." She gestured to the blanket. I waited while everyone else sat down and tried to avoid getting between Wells and his family.

"How long have you been away?" I asked him.

"A few weeks on this visit. I return here most nights. That is, as time passes in your world. I get to spend a few days here each night."

"A bit like being a sea captain?" I proffered.

Both women blanched.

Wells hurriedly said, "I'm sorry Doctor Voyle, please remember that our ways are different. Being a sailor here is ..."

Rosemary finished the sentence, "Thoughtless, irresponsible and thoroughly reprehensible is what it is."

Emelia said, "They don't make you go to sea, do they?"

I was confused, "I'm sure there's no question of Mr Wells going to sea."

"Wells is my first name," he said out of the corner of his mouth.

"Sorry, in my world being a sailor is a respectable profession. It's really very safe. Ships rarely sink. The crew are usually rescued in the unlikely event that a ship founders. It's safer that being on an airplane and air travel is safer than driving."

"Airplane?" Wells' daughter queried.

"Yes, a flying machine." One look at the faces of the two women was enough to tell me that I'd made a mistake.

"I've never used one. You must believe that, I take no risks when I'm over there," said Wells.

"Never mind, let's eat," said Wells' wife, briskly.

She opened a picnic hamper. Or I should say the picnic hamper opened. Plates floated through the air in a fashion I found disconcerting. Equally strange was the way the foodstuffs were transported. It was like being in a slow motion food fight where all of the comestibles ended up in the correct places on the tableware.

There was a momentary sense of embarrassment when they realised that I would need utensils, but I settled to eating with my fingers.

The food was familiar but with unexpected twists. Like mushy pea pasties in Malta or Arancini in Italy. There were minced beef pies with herbs and dried fruit, fish balls and soft cheese pasties. I'd relaxed after eating sandwiches of dried meat, so the banana and honey version was unexpected.

I noticed that everyone avoided watching me eat, although Emilia threw the occasionally glance, a mixture of interest and disgust on her face. Thinking it through I realised that to them the thought of actually handling food would seem insanitary.

In order to distract them I asked Wells wife some questions. "What sort of things do you procure in my world?" I asked.

"My husband trades for the items that we don't make here, medicines, technical equipment, chemicals for euthanasia and so on," Rosemary said in a prim voice.

I was about to comment on the euthanasia chemicals, but Wells caught my eye and I closed my mouth. It was the matter of fact way she'd said it, sitting in a meadow with the sun highlighting the colours of the flowers. Somehow it made the place seem more alien than the mental powers on display.

Wells said, "There aren't many people who will run the risks of your world, so only a few of us act as merchants. Tom is the first new person in many years willing to go to your dimension."

Wells' daughter clapped her hands saying, "He's so dashing and handsome. I don't think he's scared of anything."

"To us he seems a timid and gentle soul," I replied.

Wells' wife sniffed her disapproval, "That young man shows such a reckless disregard for danger that it verges on mental illness."

"A little like me then?" said Wells.

"I might have had a weakness for dashing young men in my day. It doesn't mean I condone such behaviour," said Mrs Wells with that air of coquettish disapproval that only ladies of a certain age seem to be able to carry off.

Wells' daughter bombarded me with questions. She was intrigued, in a horrified way, by the idea that we had to move everything physically.

But, as I answered her questions, I learned as much about her society as she learned about mine. Whilst, to me, the concept of telekinesis would offer scope to achieve great things, it seemed that their telepathic powers had somehow limited their scope for advancement. When I told her about our space travel, she could hardly believe me, and I think she thought I was pulling her leg when I talked about men walking on the moon. It was then that the conversation went south.

"Really Doctor Voyle, I can't believe that people could be transported to celestial bodies," said Emilia.

"Space travel was a spin off from the development of ballistic missiles. We found that rockets could be used to overcome Earth's gravity. It all started with research during the Second World War."

"Did you say war?" asked Emilia. There was something about the tone of her voice and the look on Rosemary's face that should have warned me, but I hadn't yet realised the enormity of the cultural gap between us.

"Do you have many such..." Rosemary paused, searching for the right words, "conflicts?"

Wells said, "I'm sure Doctor Voyle has answered enough questions. I've kept him long enough from his family."

"You wage war on each other? And we let Daddy go there?" said Emilia.

"Now really, you shouldn't worry about such things," said Wells.

But Mother and Daughter had turned white, immediately clearing away the picnic. I expected Emilia to be angry with me as a representative of a civilisation that put her father in danger.

I wasn't prepared for the look she gave me as Wells led me back across the field.

It was one of disgust.

CHAPTER 21

Wells said, "Right, Doctor Voyle, I'm going to teach you how to navigate us back to your dimension."

I felt nervous, which wasn't helped by the pallor Wells developed. But, having met his family, I'd got an insight into his background and culture. It dawned on me just how frightening the uncertainty was for him, and also his courage in actually letting me open trans-dimensional portals.

"Are you really sure about this? I've nearly roasted us once. What if I put us into the vampire's world?"

He said, "Nevertheless you must learn. If it helps I will take us to your world. I want you to analyse what you're feeling." So saying, he grabbed my shoulder and opened a portal. Stepping through, we returned to my office.

As waves of nausea passed over me, I tried to remember the experience as he's opened the portal. It was purely a mental phenomenon. Imagine running your fingers along the ridges of a Yale key, then fitting that mental image into a lock and twisting to open a door.

He opened a portal from my office returning us to his dimension.

"You try, just copy what I did." Wells said.

I felt for the that pattern again, like pushing a key into a lock. Yes, it was there. If I could just find it and try to move it… The wave of nausea was massive this time, but a doorway opened to my world. We stepped through into my office.

"Well done. You're an able pupil. You can now find your way to several dimensions. It's just like magic," he smirked.

"The nausea's getting worse."

"A result of passing through several portals in a short space of time. Rest a little and it'll pass."

Just then Smith came in with Knowles. "Oh, sorry, I thought you'd gone out. We were just going to …"

"Rifle through my stuff?" I finished for him. "Well, you do

that, I'm going home. Tell me if you find anything interesting."

"Good idea, you look absolutely awful. Have you got a stomach upset?" said Smith.

"Could be something I ate." Even as I said it, the nausea was starting to wear off, but I thought it was a good idea to let Smith and Knowles have a rummage. Get it out of their system.

Wells and I walked out of the room.

Knowles came to the doorway. "I'll send a couple of people with you," she said.

"Would that be so they can shoot me at the first sign of trouble?"

Knowles scowled, "Do you want to end up like the woman in the car park? There are worse things than being shot by my people."

Fair comment, but I'd rather not be dead at all.

I walked through the Memorial Gardens and crossed over Lord Street. Tomorrow I would go and see if Fine Jane the mermaid had come up with anything. Assuming she wanted to talk to me.

Wells went in the opposite direction to meet Tom. I cut up along Neville Street. The presence of people made me feel safer. I had no doubt that Knowles's people would be behind me, but they hadn't been particularly helpful last time. The only one whose default position was not to prematurely put me out of my misery was the one called Pink.

I turned onto the Promenade, which ran alongside the gardens, then cut across a supermarket car park. I reached my house without being accosted by denizens from another dimension or being attacked by something out of a nightmare. So, quite a good day really.

I walked up the steps to my house and let myself in, calling out as I entered. Theresa replied, and I went into the lounge. I should have guessed what I would see. Theresa was sitting on the sofa with Adam resting his head on her lap. She stroked his ears and he had a dreamy look. Sitting next to them was our next door neighbour.

"Hallo everyone, are the kids in the garden?" I asked.

"Yes, and Sergei's looking after them," said Theresa.

My blood ran cold. Sergei. Necklace made out of people's ears Sergei. I heard a scream from outside and rushed to the open French window. I was ready to do my hero to the rescue act, although given what Sergei was like, I didn't fancy my chances.

Outside, Sergei was bounding gently with my neighbour's son sitting on his back. The daughter, who was aged about four, was chasing after them and the scream I'd heard, was the squeal of delight she gave when she had grabbed one of his ears. Sergei stopped and faced her. She reached up and gently ran her finger along the scar on his muzzle. I could vaguely hear her ask what it was, but I couldn't catch his reply.

I did hear her say, "Poor Mr Bunny."

Sergei shook his head, so his ears stood up again, and nuzzled her.

The boy shouted, "Giddy up!" and to more excited squeals of laughter, they were off again. I noticed that whenever the boy started to slip, Sergei crouched down, so the child sort of rolled to the floor instead of falling.

I backed quietly into the room. This was not the Sergei I knew about. I thought that as far as he was concerned, we were just another bunch of carnivores. Well, I suppose we like the young of other species, puppies and kittens. If we adopted the characteristics of other dimensions as a result of contact with them, then we could expect this to apply to visitors to ours.

I beckoned and Adam followed me into the kitchen. He had an expectant look, so I got a carrot out of the fridge. He munched happily whilst I made a cup of tea.

We sat in companionable silence as we heard Theresa saying goodbye to the visitors, her voice muted by the kitchen door.

"I need your help tomorrow. I'm going to talk to the mermaid again and I want you to come with me."

"No problem, you need a bodyguard?" queried Adam.

"Yes, but I don't want anyone else to know. So, let's try and shake off our soldiers. Without killing anyone. Especially without Sergei killing anyone."

"Why do you need a bodyguard?" asked Theresa. I hadn't seen her come to the door.

"Just a figure of speech. Talking to myself. Silly really."

Then I realised what she'd said. I looked at her.

"I didn't mention a bodyguard," I said.

"No. That's what the rabbit said. How long were you going to keep it from me that there were a couple of entities from another dimension here?"

There was an awkward silence.

Theresa sighed. "Please love, close your mouth. It makes you look stupid and I know you aren't."

"You can see Adam and Sergei? Properly see them?"

"I always have. I'm guessing they have some way of, what's the term, blending in?"

"But, what, who. How can you see them?" I said.

"I am here you know."

"Shut up Adam," I said.

Theresa took a deep breath. "Really dear, you're quite naive. One cannot work in a refugee advice bureau in Southport without being able to interact with people. Especially people with, shall we say, visa issues."

"I thought that people from other dimensions were rare. I mean, surely we'd know about them?"

"There does seem to have been a lot more activity recently. It's not something to do with you is it?"

Defiantly on dodgy ground here. "It's possible that Terry and Carole ..."

"Don't forget all the work you did, Voyley."

"Thanks Adam. Yes. They and I did some experiments that appear to have weakened the barriers between dimensions. As a result, something rather nasty came through. Hence the guys parked outside the house all night. They're Government agents."

"When were you going to tell me any of this?" Theresa said in a quiet voice.

"When the time was right. I just wasn't sure when that would be." Then something struck me, "There always seem to be quite a lot of odd people in this town. Maybe they're all from different dimensions. What about Angry Elvira at the fish and chip shop? She's definitely weird."

Theresa looked at me a pityingly, "No dear, Elvira's just from Latvia. She escaped the Soviets, has a degree in mathematics and could only find work serving up fast food."

"Pity, it would have explained a lot. So why did you let Sergei play with children?"

"He seems harmless enough," Theresa said.

"Rough diamond, that's Sergei."

"Shut up Adam," I said.

Theresa sat at the kitchen table and said, "Just get some dinner on. It's turning into a long day."

CHAPTER 22

The next day I did not tell Smith, or anyone else, what was going on. I walked to the town centre and bought the freshest fish I could find, packed on ice in a polystyrene box.

Followed by a bemused team of Knowles' people, I returned to the house and got in a car with Adam and Sergei. Adam had removed the cast from his arm. They had holdalls carrying God knows what.

We set off followed by a couple of soldiers. One driving, the other talking into a radio. I expected to get a good talking to myself when I got back. We followed the same route as before. I walked down to the slipway where I'd met Fine Jane previously. There were no embarrassing incidents this time.

When questioned about the content of the holdalls, Adam said, "I thought we could do with a bit of extra firepower after what happened in town."

He pulled a bulky weapon out of the bag. The stock was sawn down and the foregrip was oversized and wider than the barrel, which, to my inexperienced eye looked like an army surplus anti-tank gun.

He said, "It's a semi-automatic shot gun with a cut down barrel. Five rounds as fast as you can pull the trigger. At short range, it's like an elephant gun."

"How do you know what an elephant is, let alone an elephant gun?" I asked.

"It's what the man in America said when we bought it. We tried it out and it put a hole the size of Sergei's head in a door."

"That isn't a figure of speech is it."

Adam sniggered, "No, he put his head through the hole to apologise to the family in the next room."

My old friends Jones and Evans came down the path shouting incomprehensible orders in the "we're in charge and you're in trouble" tone of voice so beloved by the military.

"Shut up, you'll scare the mermaid," I said. That brought

the two up short, as did Adam swinging his shotgun round to cover them. Sergei, who had bounded off when he retrieved his gun, did the same from the bank above.

"We've got orders not to let you communicate with the creature until Mr Smith and the C.O. turn up."

"Well, they can catch up with me."

I opened the cool box and took out a small cod which I dangled over the water shouting, "Fine Jane, can you hear me. Come on, I've got a fish."

Just before I started to feel foolish, Fine Jane rose from the water creating barely a ripple.

"Do I look like a dolphin?" she said gazing at the fish I was dangling over the water. "Maybe you'd like me to do a back flip and leap from the water to snatch it from your hand?"

I pulled my arm back and sat down. "I'm sorry. I meant no offence. I just wanted to get your attention. Would you like a fish?"

"Ooh yes please!" she said, and I handed her the fish which she dismembered and ate with some delicacy, considering she was using her teeth.

"I wondered if you had any luck in establishing the extent of the weaknesses between dimensions," I said.

She pointed southwards and replied, "It goes as far as I can swim in that direction."

"Jones, take a bearing, make yourself useful," I said hoping the soldiers had a compass with them.

"What about in other directions?" I continued.

She pointed inland towards the east, and said, "A couple of leagues that way. Then it started to taper off."

"How far is a league?" I asked with little hope that she would know.

"A league's about 3 miles. It's supposed to be how far you can walk in an hour," said the one called Evans.

We all turned our eyes on him, "What? My dad used to teach Geography!"

I jerked my head back to Fine Jane.

"You don't like taking your eyes off me. Still don't trust me, do you?"

Of course I didn't trust her. She was a talking marine mammal.

"Fancy another fish?" I replied evasively.

"Don't mind if I do," she said, taking the fish and devouring it as before. I handed her the cool box.

"The fish are packed in ice. If you close the lid after you take one out, they should stay fresh for a day or so."

"Ta," she said allowing the box to float beside her.

I asked, "Can you move between dimensions? Everyone else seems able to."

"I don't know, I've been here for so long. I'm not sure I could find my way back home."

"Don't try it. If there's one thing I've learnt in recent weeks, it's that you can land up in some very nasty places if you move between dimensions when you can't navigate properly."

She smiled warmly. "You care what happens to me. How sweet!" she said, clapping her hands together and spraying me with fish juice.

Her gaze became intense, "What about your promise?" she said.

"I **will** remember. We'll find a way of getting you back to the sea when all this is over."

"Silly man, this will never be over."

"I promise I'll return you to the sea. And one day I'll find a way of getting you back to your world. It's just we haven't started exploring other dimensions yet."

"Maybe I like it here," Fine Jane said, with a flirtatious flick of her hair.

"Incorrigible," I replied.

Adam nudged me, "Car coming, a big 4x4. Just turned off the main road."

I turned to Fine Jane, "I've got to go now. I'll come and talk to you again."

As I walked up the bank she called, "Good luck, remember

you can only come back if you're alive."

God, I wished people would stop saying things like that.

CHAPTER 23

In a novel Fine Jane would dive elegantly into the depths. In reality I could see the pale shape of her upper body near the surface. The drainage canals just weren't that deep.

"Make yourselves scarce boys," I said, as the vehicles drew up.

The rabbits hopped off a few feet and sat on the grass, seeming to discuss the finer culinary points of Scarlet Nantes versus Autumn King. It was only the fact that they talked about flavour and crunch that indicated these were carrots and not types of weapon, which seemed to be their other main topic of conversation. Jones and Evans looked around in puzzlement.

"The rabbits have skedaddled," I said, thinking they needed a bit of clarification.

"Phew, good, I don't like that big one with the scars. Bit of a psycho if you ask me. Like those Special Forces nutters," said Evans.

"We ARE Special Forces," said Jones and they generated their own argument, whilst Sergei sat on his haunches looking offended.

I was massaging my temples with one hand when what looked like half the British Army ran down the path.

"What the hell do you think you're up to?" shouted Knowles.

"Calm down. I just wanted to talk to Fine Jane without worrying if some trigger happy squaddie was going to put a bullet in my head."

"Who's he calling trigger happy," said Evans to Jones, their discussion abruptly ended by a 'zip it' motion from Knowles.

She glared at me, dialled a number and had an earnest conversation. The bit I caught was, "Sir, it might make things easier if we were to modify the standing orders? The Prof here isn't going to work well if he thinks we don't have his best interests at heart."

She ended the call and said, "Come on, we'll take you home."

"Fair enough, everyone bickering is starting to give me a headache."

"Yes," she replied, pointedly looking at Evans and Jones. "People are starting to act a little out of character."

I arrived home to find Smith in my house. Rather, he was sitting on the sofa, next to my wife, discussing new techniques for pruning roses.

Theresa rose and gave me a peck on the lips, wrinkled her nose and mouthed, "Why do you smell of fish?"

Smith said, "Ahh, Dr Voyle, I hope you don't mind me dropping in, there was something I wanted to talk to you about with respect to the college and it really wouldn't wait until tomorrow."

"It's all right Smith. Theresa can see entities from other dimensions. It appears they are a fact of life in this town."

"R...ight, OK, but perhaps we could discuss things at the college? There are still items that are confidential."

"Yes of course. Theresa, we'll be about half an hour."

"Nonsense," she said. "You wouldn't want to go plotting on an empty stomach now would you. Perhaps you'd care to join us for our meal Mr Smith? We're having omelette. The chips are in the oven and I can put some more French bread on? You could go and have your meeting later."

"That would be splendid," Smith said, before I could say how busy he must be and couldn't possibly accept.

Adam stood and stretched before hopping into the kitchen. We followed, and I helped Theresa with the food.

Smith sat at the table. He looked around and said, "Lovely place you've got here."

"It comes with the job. But we've done most of the decor ourselves. We've also made one or two changes. The kitchen's only a couple of years old."

"I see you've taken the advice on fire safety to heart," commented Smith, gesturing at the extinguisher and fire blanket strategically placed near the range.

"You can't be too careful Mr Smith," Theresa replied. "When I was a girl a family friend was a fireman and some of his stories were chilling. They made such an impression on me that I've been a bit of a safety nut ever since."

"We've got an extinguisher and smoke alarm in every room," I said.

"Really, how unusual." Smith seemed lost for words.

As the conversation was lagging, Theresa looked up from beating some eggs and added, "I suppose it's the result of having a physicist in the house as well."

"Can't be too careful," I continued, grating some cheese, "All of our furniture is the same as they use in high hazard environments. You've no idea how easy it is to cause a fire."

"I expect not. You certainly seem to be a very careful couple," Smith said.

"Sorry, this is taking longer than usual. It's because we're doing individual omelettes rather than sharing one between us," Theresa said over her shoulder as she folded the first one from the pan onto a plate.

"I hope I've not put you to any trouble," said Smith.

"Not at all, we love company, of any kind," I said, pointedly as Adam sat at the table and nibbled a lettuce.

It would be an understatement to say that things felt strange, knowing that Theresa and I could see Adam, but the rabbit's existence was a blind spot in Smith's perceptions.

As we sat down, I asked Theresa, "How was work today?"

"Oh, you have no idea, Angela didn't come in and I had to cover for her clients."

I still continued to eat because I was famished, but I had to ask, "Did she phone in sick?"

"No, we've had no contact at all and she isn't answering her phone. In fact she's not been seen for days." Theresa said.

Smith kept his voice casual. "It's probably flu, there's a lot of it going around. Maybe I could send someone to her house to see if she's OK? You've probably guessed by now that

I'm with the government. We're looking into what happened at the college. I have a few chaps who aren't doing much at the moment, and these bugs can be quite nasty if one gets dehydrated."

"That's very kind of you. John hasn't told me much about what happened at the college. Have you any idea what caused the accident?" Theresa asked.

I'd got so used to dealing with people who were involved that it came as a slight shock to realise that I hadn't shared the implications with her.

You had to hand it to Smith, he was smooth. "Indeed, there are some extremely unusual implications arising from the incident. I understand you've interacted with the entities that have taken a proprietorial interest in your husband. Speaking of which, I'm afraid I'll have to borrow him for half an hour or so. In the meantime, I'll detail some people to look in on Angela. No time like the present."

Of course, he was thinking the same as me. It could be something as innocent as flu. But it might not.

We finished the meal and Theresa wrote down Angela's address. Adam was coming with us, but I whispered that he should stay with Theresa. He looked uncomfortable, but agreed.

We left the house and Smith peered in at the window of a car and gave the occupants the address. They drove off. He turned to me.

"Would you care to explain what you've been doing today," he said.

"Well, I wanted to talk to the mermaid without you being there to antagonise anyone."

He snorted. "What did you find out from the aquatic entity?"

"Fine Jane told me that the effect from our work is quite localised. The dimensional instability seems to taper off a few miles from the epicentre of the field generation."

"Your laboratory?"

"Quite, but I also found out that she isn't adept at moving

between dimensions. Some people must just find themselves here, with no idea how they arrived in a different universe. We quite literally could have dimensional castaways wandering around."

"Possibly quite dangerous people," Smith mused.

"The other item of information that I've gleaned, is that the longer someone spends in a dimension, the more it affects them. This ties up with the observations from Wells that basic physical laws are different in his world."

"I don't really see how this is pertinent."

"Because it would mean that the longer an entity spent here, the more they would be affected by our environment. Effectively becoming more like us," I replied.

"But we'd already surmised that the vampires take their victims into another dimension in order to make the person edible," Smith said.

"It also means that if a person goes into vampire land, and survives, they will start to take on the characteristics of that dimension. We don't know what spending prolonged time in the vampire dimension will do to someone."

A man walking his dog hurried past us. I recognised him. One of the walkers who we'd met on the first visit to Fine Jane. That'll teach him to eavesdrop.

"I also want to ask you a favour. Could you organise a talk by the police on modern day slavery? I understand that a lot of women are trafficked and are forced into prostitution."

He looked at me, puzzled, "Why would you want that?"

"It's not for me. It's for Adam and Sergei, you remember Wells said that they were relatively naive. I thought they could do with having their horizons expanded."

He put his fists on his hips. I thought people only did that in nineteen thirties black and white films.

"You have a bloody cheek." There was a low growl behind us.

I made a placatory gesture, "It's Okay Sergei, we're just talking through something."

"You're conversing with one of those bloody rabbits again aren't you. Please, please don't tell me they're involved with people trafficking." He took a moment to compose himself. It was something people needed to do a lot recently.

"All right," Smith continued. "But I want you to provide some input to a video conference I have tomorrow. It's a cobra briefing."

"Cobra, like the snake?"

"Don't you ever watch the news? it just stands for Cabinet Office Briefing Room: C.O.B.R. It's not as high powered as it sounds. It's not even at ministerial level. I feel your insight could be useful," Smith said.

"OK." I replied, "I expect it'll just be a re-hash of the police briefing."

Which just goes to show how wrong you can be.

CHAPTER 24

Once again, I was in Smith's lair. By now the decor from a previous age conferred on me a calm, slightly nostalgic feeling. It was a reminder of a world where the monsters were on the other side of an iron curtain, not a quantum space away. Like all nostalgia, it was rubbish. This place had been set up to deal with precisely the situation we now faced.

A large flat screen TV sat, incongruously, on a pressed metal table and Smith fussed over a teleconference set up, itself now an anachronism in a world of laptop video calls.

We sat on ancient office chairs, non-adjustable tubular metal constructions dating from a time before ergonomics was considered for office workers.

The view on the screen showed an empty office with the plush blinds and faux wood veneer tables that characterised a more up to date bureaucratic environment. Presumably Smith's natural habitat, at least that's what I'd thought before I realised that he routinely armed himself.

Two men came into view and sat, arranging folders on the desk. They looked quizzically at their camera as people the world over do in video conferences. The effect was of them carefully scrutinising the rear of our television screen.

They settled down. One drew the microphone towards him.

"Hello, can you hear us?"

"Loud and clear. What's the weather like in London?" replied Smith.

"Clear and sunny. What about the benighted North." I could see this guy was going to get on my nerves in a very short period of time.

"So so. Bit windy," said Smith.

"Jolly good. As you've got someone with you it's probably best if you call us Andrew and David," instructed the one who'd identified himself as Andrew. He had a nervous habit of picking at the middle finger of his right hand.

"Is it just you two? I was expecting this to be handled at ministerial level," Smith said.

"No, at this stage we thought it better to maintain the management at Assistant Secretary grade. We've been looking at your reports and the stuff from the military. Have you got any closer to handing it over to the police?"

"Why would I want to do that?" I could hear the strain in Smith's voice.

Andrew said, "Well it's a bit of a rum do. But you're expending an awful lot of resources. Catching a serial killer is police business."

"I thought you said that you'd looked at my reports?"

"We have, but let's face it. Reading between the lines, you've obviously got some kind of theatrical magician or animal trainer on your hands. Certainly, the police seem to think so," Andrew said.

I was amazed that Smith kept his cool, in fact I rather admired him for it as he replied, "There isn't any "between the lines". The reports are factual. I've brought Doctor Voyle along to provide some scientific background."

"We're not sure that's necessary. Experts are all very well, but they do tend to lack the wider picture."

"What do you mean, 'wider picture'. For heaven's sake. You've seen the zoologist's report on the creature. There's video footage showing the animal attacking someone," Smith said.

"Yes, we prevented anyone seeing that film in case it caused them distress. We think the zoologist was mistaken. It's like the duck billed platypus. When the first preserved examples were brought from Australia, experts thought they were fakes. Bits of other animals sewn together. It's obvious your zoologist has been fooled by an elaborate hoax," Andrew said.

"But it turned out that the platypus was real. You've got your example the wrong way around. Don't you think that an experienced zoologist seeing the animal is perhaps better qualified than you to make a decision?"

I felt I could help, "Actually the platypus seems to have both mammalian and reptilian features. Which means that a hybrid, a bit like our creature, needn't be that farfetched. It's a bit of a hobby of mine," I added in a self-deprecating way.

Everyone else looked at me like I'd completely missed the point. Later in the conversation I realised that I had.

"What we have here is a definite threat to national security," Smith asserted.

"In your opinion."

"Yes. I want your support to run an excursion into another dimension with full military backup," Smith continued.

"We can't really support this can we, David?" Andrew turned to the civil servant who hadn't spoken yet.

The one called David spoke for the first time. "I think we should let it go ahead. Clive can take responsibility if this turns out to be an elaborate hoax."

So, they'd stitched Smith up like a kipper. Whatever happened, they had a fall guy.

I said, "A rift has opened up enabling beings from other dimensions to come here, some of them with ill intent, and you lot are playing power politics?"

Smith held up his hand to silence me and said, "That's that then. Thanks for using my name there Arthur. Great security."

"I say, that's a bit strong. I thought you trusted Doctor Voyle."

"I don't trust my mother that much. It's the reason you sent me. We've every reason to believe that at least one kind of hostile entity is crossing between dimensions. In fact, it's a much simpler interpretation of the evidence than the convoluted explanations you've contrived," argued Smith.

"Has anyone else disappeared?" asked the one called Andrew.

Smith continued, "The thing is, there are always people who disappear, more than you would think. But, it has to be said that there have been a few unusual cases where people have gone missing in this area. We have a source who has delineated the extent of unstable inter dimensional barriers. But we haven't had any bodies turn up."

I thought it quite canny that Smith had avoided saying that our source was a mermaid. These two were sceptical enough as it was.

I thought I could usefully add something. "I've been thinking about that. If you cross to another dimension, the reality of that world affects you in various ways. You start to adapt to it. Now, you've seen the video of the poor woman who was attacked. It seems she poisoned the creature that attacked her. We originally assumed that this would prevent the creatures from grabbing people. But this may be incorrect.

"Our theory is that the physics in our dimension is different enough to make the victim effectively poisonous to the vampire. However, we know from other sources that once one enters another dimension the physics of that dimension alters your body. For example, if someone came here from a dimension where there's telekinesis they would slowly lose that ability. The creatures could be using this effect to their advantage. They drag a victim into their dimension, leave them for a while so that the persons physics adapts to the natural laws of the vampires dimension. Then the person becomes edible. A bit like a crocodile will cache its victim until it has rotted enough to eat."

"So, the victims will lie waiting somewhere knowing what's going to happen to them?" Andrew asked in a horrified voice. I noticed that he wasn't behaving like someone who didn't believe what was going on.

Smith replied. "There could be another problem. We've talked to an expert from the local University and the venom resembles one that causes partial paralysis: you can keep breathing but lose a lot of motor coordination. Basically, you're paralysed but aware of everything that's happening."

"Just when I thought things couldn't get any worse. The reports indicated that these creatures didn't have much in the way of a brain. How could they work this out?" said Andrew.

"Who knows, maybe their brains work differently, maybe it's instinctive or maybe they had help," I replied.

"You mean some kind of mad animal trainer," said David. I could see this guy had something of an ultra-logical mind. It was his idea and he wasn't going to let it go.

"If you're lucky. If not, it would mean that we have several entities coming across the dimensional barrier."

"Well, Clive, keep an eye on things. I'm sure an expedition will sort it all out," said Andrew.

As they prepared to sign off, Smith added, "By the way. I like to keep a record of communications. As this is a video call, and you've restricted the number of participants, there's always the possibility that the notes might not record fully what's been said. So I've made a recording for the files. I'll forward it to your Perm Sec, so he knows that the expedition is a joint idea. Toodle pip."

With that, Smith cut the connection leaving a still of the enraged faces of his colleagues on the screen. He himself had a self-satisfied smirk.

CHAPTER 25

Smith surprised me. He's organised the visit to the police station within a week. It turned out they used the opportunity to brief some of their support staff. Wells and Tom accompanied me, so it didn't look like I was on my own. Obviously, Adam and Sergei were coming along, but they would do their invisible rabbit act. At least I hoped they would.

I drove our group to the local police station. Those of us who looked human signed in, and we were escorted to a briefing room laid out with chairs. There were talks from the police and, surprisingly, the Salvation Army. They covered a range of topics from modern day slavery through to the trafficking of women as sex workers.

By the time the talks were over, I was ashamed to be human. Wells and Tom looked sick. Adam was in front of me and his ears were lying almost flat on his head. I'd seen this reaction before. It was a sign of emotional distress. Sergei, on the other hand, looked quite unperturbed. Adam started talking to Sergei in a low voice. I could not overhear what they were saying but Sergei's growl carried across the room. Adam became more animated and the replies louder.

Interestingly, as the volume of the discussion between Adam and Sergei increased, it became difficult to ignore them. The other people in the room started struggling to hear the speaker. The effect was fascinating to watch. Every person in the room was trying really hard to ignore a vocal argument between two very large rabbits on the front row.

When the talks were finished, I thanked the Superintendent who had organised the evening. We introduced him to Tom, who I said was one of my students. Tom stuttered a bit conveying how upset he was. The Superintendent reassured him that the police and social services were working hard to abolish modern day slavery.

Once outside the police station, we walked up the street

before discussing events.

Wells said, "I know I keep saying this, but every time I think you people can't become any more depraved, I discover something even more disgusting. If this is where humanity originated, then I'm ashamed of my heritage. Do you really do that to your own species?"

Feeling I should leap to the defence of my own branch of homo sapiens, I replied, "Hold on a minute, these people are criminals. They're only a very small proportion of the population. You've seen how people help each other out in this world."

"It sounds to me like you've integrated this branch of criminality into your society and you're quite content to pretend you don't know about it," retorted Wells.

Tom interrupted us, "I think you should go and talk to the rabbits; they're getting a bit argumentative."

Worrying about what argumentative would mean to someone like Sergei, I followed the sound of raised voices until I came upon them.

Adam seemed to have taken on board the implications of what they'd been doing, but as I approached, Sergei was saying "Is nothing to do with us. We just move people around."

"Shame about those young girls though, isn't it," I said. Sergei shifted uncomfortably and grunted.

I continued, "I saw you playing with a couple of children in my garden. They seemed so innocent and carefree. Imagine if this happened to them. It could you know."

Sergei became very still. Then turned and loped off down the street.

Wells said, "Why did Sergei react like that?"

I told him how I'd seen the huge rabbit playing with children in what looked like a caring way.

Wells said, "I am not sure is was a good idea to put that idea in Sergei's head. These creatures have limited emotional experience. They can swing from one mood to another very quickly."

"I remember, when I was young. Someone could tell me something. Probably not an important fact. But I'd make mental connections and my whole world view changed in an instant." I replied.

"Well, I think you've just made an emotional connection in Sergei's head. He's probably feeling a level of empathy for humans that he hasn't had before," said Wells.

"Well, that's good isn't it? They'll stop what they're doing. I mean that's why I brought them to the meeting, so they could realise what they were getting into," I countered.

"Let's hope that Adam is a steadying influence. He seems more emotionally mature, although I'm not sure that's saying much," Wells replied.

"Of course, Adam will calm Sergei down," I said, although even to my ears it sounded like I was trying to convince myself.

"Yes, you're probably correct. In the meantime, those creatures that have such great control of their impulses have left you without a bodyguard," Wells said. "Would you like Tom to stay with you?"

"As a bodyguard?"

"Whilst I'm sure Tom will be able to stop you coming to harm, I was going to suggest that you could have him as a house guest whilst he settles into your society."

"Oh yes, I would love to sample your culture properly," Tom said.

"Are you sure? Do you realise how much things will change in your dimension whilst you're staying here?"

Wells replied, "I don't think you need to worry Doctor Voyle. Tom is thinking of settling here permanently. It's because ..." He paused as if searching for the right word.

"I'm an outcast from my society because of my total disregard for the safety of myself and others," Tom finished the sentence. He gave me a gentle disarming smile.

CHAPTER 26

Of course, randomly inviting people to stay without consulting Theresa was a high risk strategy. Fortunately, she was used to me bringing home the occasional waif and stray from the student fraternity. I texted her before we arrived. It gave Tom and I a bit of headroom.

"Hello, Tom is it? Nice to meet you. I've made up a bed," Theresa said.

"Thank you, Mrs Voyle. It's very kind of you to have me."

"Nonsense, anything to help out for a few days," Theresa said.

"Oh, I thought I was going to live here," Tom replied, looking at me for guidance.

Theresa's smile took on a forced quality and she gave me 'the look'. A gaze more eloquent than a half hour lecture on why I should avoid taking on permanent guests without consulting her.

"No need to worry. We'll sort you out with somewhere to live," I replied.

"As luck would have it, I work with a lot of people such as yourself. We'll help you to fit in. Are you escaping trouble in your society?" Theresa asked.

"Oh yes. I am. It's because I have a violent disregard for the safety of everyone around me."

At this point I felt that things were getting out of control. "Theresa, where Tom comes from, everyone is very risk averse."

"And when he adapts to our dimension?"

"He'll probably take up extreme sports. Until then crossing Lord Street will satisfy his hunger for excitement."

Tom's eyes gleamed. "I'm very excited about attending your husband's lectures. I understand his University is world famous."

This must have come from Wells. I made hand movements that I hoped were self-depreciatory without actually denying that the place was a famous academic institution.

Theresa looked at me archly. "Well, it's certainly quite an exciting place at the moment."

Tom nodded solemnly. "That would be all the vampires and soldiers and so on."

This time her look caused me to swallow, gulp really. I wondered if everyone else could hear it.

"On top of the talking rabbits. My, how exciting my husband's world is."

"It's not quite like that," I said, then stopped because it was exactly like that. "There were unexpected consequences to our work," I finished lamely.

Tom looked uncomfortable. "Sorry. I wish I hadn't said anything. I'd best not mention the people trafficking."

Theresa sighed. "I've made up a bed. Let's get something to eat."

"Can I help? I'm considered quite the chef where I come from," Tom offered.

This time it was Theresa's turn to smile. "Do come this way. It'll be nice to have a bit of help when it's my turn to cook."

I retreated to the lounge and switched the TV on. We'd got a couple of rump steaks for tea which I was looking forward to eating, perhaps with fried potatoes and some herb butter. I wondered how Theresa would pad them out to accommodate Tom. A few minutes later, I poked my head round the kitchen door to find Theresa with a glass of wine in hand, admiring Tom's telekinetic slicing of vegetables.

"I've just found out Tom doesn't eat meat. You don't mind going veggie while he stays with us, do you?" she said.

Funny, I'd never had her down as malicious up until now.

CHAPTER 27

Wells agreed to transport us to the dimension where the inimical lifeforms originated, or, as I liked to call it, vampire land. He let himself into our house causing Theresa to give a small shriek. Rushing from the kitchen, I came across him in the hall way with a surprised look on his face, mirroring that of Theresa, who was part way down the stairs.

The bread in the toaster had left a faint smell of burning.

"Hallo, Wells. There's a car picking us up in a minute," I said, to break the ice.

"Should I not have come into the house?"

"I suppose we must've left the door unlocked, it's an easy mistake."

"Oh no Doctor Voyle, I manipulated the lock. I hope I didn't cause any," he paused, "untoward reactions?"

"Not at all Mr Wells," said Theresa in a brittle voice.

I made a mental note to talk to Wells about the etiquette of home visits. Theresa had been scared witless. I rushed back to the kitchen. The bread had popped from the toaster, it hadn't burned after all. Buttering it, I munched as I made us all a nice, hopefully relaxing, cup of tea.

We drank from our best china. Theresa recovered her composure and commented on the news that a gang war had spread from Manchester to Southport. Wells was asking what a gang war consisted of when there was a reassuringly normal ring of the doorbell. Saved, Wells had a low opinion of us already, without having to explain organised crime..

One of Smith's blacked out obtrusive vehicles was parked out front and Evans was standing in the doorway.

"All set?" he said.

"Yup, let's go. There's just Wells and me. Adam will meet us there," I replied.

"What's going on?" asked Theresa.

"We're going to look over some old records," I said, as

Wells tutted at my blatant lie.

Theresa looked doubtful as she said goodbye. As we were driven off, I could see her standing in the doorway. She reminded me of the women waving farewell to troops going to the front.

Our destination was a disused factory on the outskirts of town. When they make a film of this, our vehicle will dramatically enter the building through wide aircraft hangar like doors. As it was, we helped lug some boxes across the car park and through some annoyingly narrow passageways.

Knowles and her people were clustered around trestle tables in the middle of a space once occupied by machinery. People were still bringing in large rucksacks and laying out the contents. Others were checking their weapons. A couple appeared to be applying makeup to each other. Knowles strode over to us. She was in military camouflage. Her face was painted in shades of green, and her hair was darkened and slicked back to her head. Ahh, hence the cosmetics. I looked around and realised I couldn't easily recognise people. I wondered if I'd be able to distinguish any I'd brassed off.

"Come over here and we'll kit you out," Knowles ordered.

She gestured to a series of black bags on the floor. I opened one and found everything from underwear to boots. Surprisingly, they fitted.

"I asked your wife what sizes you take," she said.

That explained why Theresa was upset.

"Did you tell her what we were doing?"

"Don't be ridiculous. I told her we'd got you on an outward bound exercise."

"I don't think she believed you."

"What else did you want me to say?"

"Never mind. Where shall I change?" I asked. Knowles snorted in answer and walked away.

I stripped off and put on the military outfit. Apparently, it was better than my walking gear. Wells did not move towards his kit.

He said, "I feel more comfortable in my tweeds."

There was a bang on the outside door and it was opened by one of the troops.

A group of people in laboratory coats set up extra trellis tables and arranged syringes, swabs and such like.

I wandered over.

"Roll up your sleeve please?" It was Witty Tee Shirt, today his chest was emblazoned with the logo: Statisticians Predict Shit Will Happen.

"Now ain't that the truth," I said.

He smiled at me and wielded a syringe. "Time for your inoculation. Don't want you getting any nasty bugs over there, do we?"

As I moved away, I could see the rest of the team lining up.

"This your idea, was it?" asked Knowles belligerently.

"Why do you assume that bad things are automatically associated with me?"

"Because they are Doctor Voyle, they just are."

Smith had come over by this time. He was in civvies I noticed.

"It's alright Lieutenant, this is just a precaution. We did cover it when we planned the operation. Have you had any opposition?"

"No, the only person on our side who's not having it is Pink. It's because she's allergic."

"Allergic to vaccines? How did she get in the army?" I queried.

Knowles squared up to me, "We're all volunteers, if she doesn't want to have the vaccine, she doesn't have to, so sod off."

I held up my hands in a placating gesture, "Sorry, just curious. She's put her life on the line for me, so I'm perfectly Okay with whatever she wants. Where is she? I can't recognise anyone with this war paint on."

"Over there somewhere," said Knowles, gesturing vaguely at the far end of the building.

Smith said, "Things are a bit tense, try and remember that

Voyle. These people will fight anyone on earth, and probably win. But **we are** ordering them to venture into the unknown."

He turned from me and addressed Knowles, "Lieutenant, could you brief me on your tactics?"

"Yes Sir. I've divided my people into two fire teams of four and a capture team with nets and some anaesthetic dart guns. We sourced them from a safari park. We've out-briefed. The fire teams will flank the capture team. Rations for four days. How are we going to attract them in?" finished Knowles.

It was my turn to contribute. "The creatures seem to be peculiarly attracted to me, possibly because of my exposure to the portals between worlds," I said.

"What, you're the bait? Won't your rabbit mate object to that, where is it anyway?"

"He's called Adam and I don't want him to know. As far as he's concerned, I'm the backup person to open portals in case Wells is incapacitated."

"Ahem, I am here you know," said Wells.

Smith and Knowles started as, to their perception, he suddenly appeared.

"I wish you wouldn't do that voodoo shit," said Knowles.

"Sorry, force of habit," Wells replied.

Just then there was another banging on the door and this time Adam came in carrying a bundle almost as big as he was. It clattered as it fell to the floor.

"What's that?" I asked.

Adam unwrapped the bundle to reveal a load of swords in their scabbards.

"I tell you I had to be very persuasive in regimental museums to get this lot. They're cutting edge technology," Adam said.

"Ha ha, are they all relatively modern?" asked Knowles. By this time her troops were beginning to gather round.

"Yep, all 1897 pattern infantry officers' swords except this one." Adam ran a paw along reverently along a curved scimitar, "This one is mine."

I raised my hand, "Why are you taking swords? You have enough firepower between you to start World War Three."

Wells said, "I'm afraid that was my idea. We don't know whether your weapons will work in the next dimension, so we're taking these as backup."

Knowles continued, "We've packed everything into modular rucksacks, so we're prepared for any environment from arctic to desert. As we find out what the condition are like, we can ditch the kit we don't need." She turned to her troops, "Right, let's get on with it. Sargent, form them up!"

A grizzled looking guy I hadn't seen before harried the troops, barking orders. They had to buddy up to don rucksacks which appeared as big as they were.

Smith looked us over. Wells and I were the only ones not carrying anything.

"Should I carry my share," I said to the trooper next to me.

She looked back at me with a rueful expression and shook her head, "No, Sir. With all due respect, you wouldn't be able to keep up. In Afghanistan we could hear the Taliban radio traffic. Our translator said they nicknamed us tortoises because of the size of the packs we carried. This should be a walk in the park compared to Afghanistan."

"I don't want to tell you your job, but I've seen one of these creatures. They seem to exhibit intelligence at a tactical level as well as cloaking themselves to our sight. Just to put the cherry on the cake, they're venomous."

She grinned and patted a short machine gun, with an ammunition box on the side, "Don't worry about that Prof, this holds 100 cartridges and fires at 600 rounds a minute. They're seven six two heavy duty NATO rounds and will turn anything that's alive into something that's very dead. And if it's already departed this world, it'll chew it up like dog food."

I noticed that Wells approached the Sergeant, who didn't seem to be going with us. They had a conversation and Wells nodded with satisfaction as a couple of soldiers next to him held up what looked like elongated soup cans with a pin and lever, like a hand grenade.

Knowles was in the middle of forming up when I asked her about it. "It's for Wells. Apparently it's part of his religious observances. The body has to be cremated immediately. So I've assigned a couple of my people as close protection for him. They've got thermite bombs to incinerate him in case he gets killed."

I was about to point out that if we lost Wells, we also lost our best chance of getting back home, but decided she had enough on her plate.

"Please be ready everyone," Wells said, and opened the portal. He held it open while we all walked through. Smith stayed back and disappeared as the entrance to our world closed. I waited whilst the nausea of trans-dimensional travel cleared.

Then I looked around in surprise.

CHAPTER 28

"Are you sure this is the right place?" Knowles asked Wells. We appeared to be in an English bucolic scene.

"Definitely. When a dimension has been opened, it leaves a trace, a feeling in the air? It's difficult to explain. But this is definitely where our problems lie. Doctor Voyle, imagine you are going through the process of opening a portal. See if the feeling associated with this place seems familiar."

"I think I can get it. The sense must be something that's on a mental level linked to the ability to open dimensions. It feels like running your finger over the cuts on a Yale key," I said.

"After you were attacked by the creature in Southport I visited the area. There was a feeling in the air like this. I'm as sure as I can be that we're in the right place."

"Now I know what I'm looking for, I realise the feeling pervades the lab," I said.

"It's just that this place doesn't look very evil," said Knowles.

"Also, why would a creature adapted to low visibility exist in an environment like this? All open spaces and sunlight."

As we conversed, Knowles made a series of complicated hand gestures to her troops. They sank down and formed what I assumed was a defensive perimeter. Wells and I were the only ones still standing. It left me feeling exposed, as well as a bit of a lemon.

She beckoned us over while Adam joined the perimeter guard. One of her troops opened a briefcase sized hard plastic case. He pulled out a screen, a radio control set and a small toy helicopter.

Knowles saw the look on my face. "Don't say it. This isn't a plaything but the latest development in drone technology." The soldier operating the system looked up and shook his head. "Unfortunately, the latest technology won't power up."

Wells said, "It could be that electrical equipment doesn't

work here."

Knowles activated some of the complicated looking sights on her rifle, then flipped down a pair of night vision goggles on her helmet. I guessed from the look on her face that Wells was correct. Nothing was working. She went around each of her troops then came back to us.

"All of our electrical kit is dead, not even the battery powered torches are working. Do you think the guns will fire?"

I took a packet of matches from my pocket and lit one. "It looks like chemical reactions work OK, so your guns should fire. They're basically Victorian technology with a few modern alloys."

"That's something then. We'll have to do this the old fashioned way," Knowles said, with a certain amount of relish.

She gave orders as everyone jettisoned their electrical gear and stacked it at the base of a nearby tree. A camouflaged figure pulled out something similar to one of the thermite bombs that Wells' protection team, or cremation service if you prefer, were carrying. I cowered as he pulled the plastic cap off, but it turned out to be an aerosol paint can. He sprayed a large red circle on the tree. Someone else climbed up into the branches with an agility I could only envy.

Knowles pulled out her compass. "At least that seems to be working." She raised her voice, "Take a bearing everyone. We'll need to orientate ourselves if it gets kinetic and we're separated."

Knowles explained to Wells and me that the red dot was so we could find our way back and return to the same place for, as she termed it, extraction. Or, as I called it, Wells saving our collective derrieres.

The one who climbed the tree reported that the landscape seemed to go on as far as he could see. Just fields, with no smoke to indicate cooking fires, although there was something that looked like habitation a couple of miles away.

The fields were bounded by overgrown hedges. There was a wooden five bar gate in one corner with a very clunky latch mechanism. Beyond the gate, a grassy track ran between the fields; it was rutted as if vehicles had run up and down it in the past.

"It must lead somewhere," said Knowles.

Not having much of an opinion, I just shrugged and Knowles gave orders via a series of gestures.

A fire team took the lead whilst another brought up the rear. Adam bounded off in front. Knowles didn't like this but conceded that he was more inconspicuous than a human. We advanced cautiously. After we'd passed a few fields, Wells tapped Knowles and I on the shoulder.

"Have you looked in these fields, either they are all lying fallow, or they haven't been worked for a long time. They're getting choked with brambles and there're silver birch trees," he said.

I looked through a hedge, which was so overgrown it was on the way to becoming a line of small trees. He was right. The land looked as if it had been abandoned. There were small saplings amongst the grass and brambles. We walked down the track until we came to the buildings our lookout had identified. The troops spread out again. I started to walk forward. Knowles grabbed me by the arm.

"Stay put. This is what we do for a living," she ordered and gestured to her troops. As though choreographed, the ones with the heavy weapons moved to each side of the building and set up their machine guns on bipods, trained on the doors and windows. Then a couple moved forward, taking cover behind piles of rotting hay and the remains of a wooden cart. They reached the wall of the building and flattened themselves against it.

Everyone else moved a bit closer whilst three of them faced back the way we had come. Their professionalism was starting to make me feel safer. One of the guys by the door nodded a countdown, then they put their rifles in a firing position and went through the entrance. There was a pause during which we all held our breath. Even Knowles was looking a tense.

Then a voice called out, "All clear," and the rest of us advanced.

When we got nearer the door way Wells said, "Excuse me, I'll pop in next, just to make sure that whoever called out is who we think it is."

"How's the telekinesis?" I asked.

"Better here than in your world, but can we have a discussion in a more relaxed environment?" Wells answered and entered.

He also called out that it was all clear and I moved forward. Knowles instructed the machine gunners to position themselves at the windows and everyone else to check the outbuildings.

The walls of the house were made from mud brick and about three feet thick. The windows were small and reinforced with substantial wooden shutters. Similarly, the door was roughhewn timber secured with bolts and a couple of crossbeams that slotted into the doorframe. At a guess I would say a charging bull would have trouble breaking it down, but there were fresh woodworm holes, so these barriers were past their heyday. The room itself had a homespun medieval vibe. There were rustic chairs and a table. The place smelt musty, like a house that hadn't been occupied for a few months.

There was a hearth with a chimney. Ashes, damp with condensation dripping from the metal grate, spilled onto the stone floor. I leaned in and looked up the chimney. Where it exited the roof, there were more bars.

I heard a sigh behind me. Knowles had her hand over her eyes.

"What?" I asked.

She shook her head. "Try not to stick your head where it can get chopped off, please? There could have been anything up that chimney, ranging from a booby trap to some beast waiting to chew your face off." Behind me I could hear someone snigger.

"Enough of that, Jones, remember he's a newbie and

doesn't know about fighting in buildings, or anything really. You're the child minder from now on."

Jones snorted in disgust.

"I can do it boss," said Pink.

"No, I need you on point," said Knowles.

Adam moved next to Jones and said, "Howdy buddy!" with his muzzle stretched in a grin. This seemed to make Jones' day. He turned away muttering curses under his breath.

I continued to look around. There were rudimentary clay pots and couple of metal pans on a roughhewn table. Some beds had been pushed up against the walls. The image that came to mind was rough but homely.

Wells was examining the door. "The wood is thick and reinforced with cross beams. It was built to keep something out. Everything around looks like it was designed for humans. So, we have the question, why has it all been abandoned?"

Knowles ordered, "OK, photograph everything and then we're moving on."

Someone answered, "Can't Boss, all our cameras are digital, so we left them with the other electrical stuff."

Knowles swore and asked Wells and I to take some notes.

Wells said, "It occurs to me that this is an easily defensible position. We can be sure that something is going to come for us at some point. This building looks like it was designed to keep it out."

Knowles said, "It didn't work very well. What happened to the inhabitants? Our operational objective is to find some of these creatures and prong them with darts. If we just sit here, we'll lose the initiative."

Raising her voice, she said, "Drop all unnecessary gear. Keep ammo and 2 days' rations. Hurry up; we need to keep moving."

Then she gathered her people together and we set off down a track.

We carried on for a couple of miles and saw little sign of life in the overgrown fields.

"Knowles, can you see any animals?" I asked.

"How do you mean?"

"There aren't any large animals. Nothing. No deer, cattle or horses. Just birds, or at least bird analogues, and small creatures that I can hear scurrying through the undergrowth."

"So?"

"It's just that I've realised everything we're seeing can either perch high in a tree or find a burrow."

"I think that what Doctor Voyle's trying to say is that nothing survives out in the open here. Which might include us," said Wells.

"Cheerful buggers," she huffed and rushed to check on everyone.

It was difficult to gauge time because of low cloud. Wells had a wind-up watch that was still working but, as he pointed out, we had no idea how long the day was.

At midday earth time, we took a break and ate ration packs, or as the troops called it, 'scran'. They were foil packs of tuna pasta which didn't taste too bad, apart from the plastic odour, but then I was so hungry I didn't care.

Knowles passed me a cereal bar as we marched.

"Are we heading anywhere?" I asked.

"Sooner or later, we'll come across these animals of yours, then we're going to kill or capture one of them and take it back with us. Simple really," said Knowles.

"Pink and the ginger bloke must have told you what they're like. We might not even see them until they're on us," I replied.

"I'm banking on Wells or the rabbit to tell us when the creatures are close. As you pointed out, we've enough firepower to finish World War Three. We'll be all right."

"Getting dark boss," one of her people said a couple of hours later. "Do you think they'll come out?"

Knowles looked around. "I hope so. The sooner we find one the sooner we get home. Right, I'll sort out watches." In answer to my indrawn breath she said, "Not you Doctor Voyle.

You need to get some rest." She turned back to the others, "Evans, get a hexi going for the MREs, Pink go with him to the stream over there. Make sure some F off big crocodile doesn't pull him in. I've got enough paperwork as it is."

Wells leaned over to me, "What did she say? I got the bit about crocodiles, but the rest is gibberish."

"I don't know," I replied, "But I'm going to the toilet."

I started to walk away when I was pulled up short by Jones.

"Where you goin'?"

"For a shit. Why, is there some strategic reason I can't? or does this military kit wipe my arse automatically?"

I realised I was being rude, but he was getting on my nerves. It wasn't my fault he got landed with the nerd.

"Well, this isn't the Lake District. Where you go, I go. The Lieutenant will have my balls if anything happens to you. After you've done your business, you can keep watch for me. I've heard what these animals are like and if the Boss ain't getting me balls, some poisonous carnivore isn't."

So we did. I might have been safe, but I don't think I was going to get used to military life anytime soon.

When we got back, most of the group were eating. The food was in foil pouches that had been heated up on a small portable stove.

Wells nudged me and pointed to the stove and his food pouch, "Hexamine stove and Meal Ready to Eat. I think I'm getting the hang of this. Look they've given me something called a bivvie bag to sleep in." He held up a plastic sleeping bag.

"What if they creep up on us?" I asked.

Jones pointed out that soldiers, hidden around us in pairs, were keeping watch.

I had just got my bivvie bag and worked out how to use it when darkness fell. Somewhere up in the clouds, the sun went behind a hill, or something, and it went pitch black. After a while my eyes adjusted. I could make out people and shapes of bushes.

"Can you see things," hissed Wells

"Yes, it's not a black out,"

"It's like the night time in your dimension."

"I just can't work out how the vampire creatures function. They're adapted to an environment where there's no visibility at all."

Wells said, "I can imagine that they, or something equally nasty, exists here because the farm buildings were built like fortresses, but this just doesn't seem like the natural environment of something that hunts solely by scent."

I fell into a doze, but kept waking. I thought nights were supposed to be quiet in the country. There was a constant rustle and something very annoying kept chirruping.

I was awoken by everyone else moving around. Jones came over with a cup of coffee, a toothbrush and toothpaste.

"Won't this leave a smell for the creatures to follow?" I asked. Jones shrugged and pointed out the importance of personal hygiene.

"Ah well," I said, around a mouthful of toothpaste, "off we go again."

CHAPTER 29

We walked for a whole day and found another abandoned farm similar to the first. Towards nightfall I noticed that the temperature was dropping.

I joined Knowles and Evans.

Knowles saw me and said, "Have you felt the change in the weather Doctor Voyle? Evans here was in a Navy meteorology unit prior to, unusually for the weather service, joining the SBS."

Evans said, "I think the weather's going to change dramatically. The temperature's falling like a stone here, but it'll be far lower on the higher ground surrounding us. If the cold air is rolling down the hills, it'll meet the relatively warm wet air down here and form a mist." He looked worried as he continued, "When I say mist, I mean quite a thick fog. If so, visibility could drop considerably and ..."

"Make a perfect environment for those creatures," I finished.

As if on cue, a dense fog rolled over the group. "Knowles, put your people on alert!" I called.

Adam had unslung his shotgun and Jones held his assault rifle in a firing position. Within seconds we had lost our view of the troops taking point.

"Knowles." I had to stop and swallow, suddenly my mouth was very dry. "This is it. Those creatures have evolved to hunt in this sort of environment. We'll have a bit of time while they track us down, but they will. We need to get in a defensible position."

"I thought you wanted us to get your darts into the hide of at least one of these creatures?" she said.

"Listen, this is their environment, we can't track them by infra-red and they can follow us by our scent. At least get your people to bunch up."

"If we move too close together, we make a bigger target," she retorted.

Just then there was a rattle of automatic gunfire. Sporadic shots sounded out and we could see gun flashes through the mist.

"Drop packs, defensive positions," Knowles shouted.

Then there was a chilling scream. I ran forward, which was probably the stupidest thing to do. The gunfire was in short controlled salvos, then came a longer sustained burst, as if someone had panicked and kept the trigger depressed.

The bullets passed overhead with a sound reminiscent of a sword cleaving the air. People describe it as a whizzing noise, but trust me, it sounds infinitely more solid. I found myself lying prone as more bullets passed overhead.

Knowles was shouting about using the grenades. Someone was listening because a fizzing cylinder bounced off my shoulder and started spewing a noxious aerosol of garlic into the air. I continued edging forward and realised that I had lost everyone except Adam, who hopped close to me.

We were lost, vague shapes ran through the mist, some human and some definitely not. A creature from nightmare launched itself at me, mouth wide and long fangs dripping venom. I froze and flinched at the bang of Adam discharging his shotgun. The blast completely removed the head of the creature, which still knocked me to the ground with the momentum of its charge. It lay on top of me spraying blood and twitching.

I heard a voice say, "Where's the Prof?"

Then Jones and Adam rolled the remains of the creature away and helped me up. We were all disorientated and didn't know if we'd been running towards the main group or away from them.

Jones pulled out a compass, shone a torch on it and said, "The others were on this bearing, come on."

Sure enough, we began to come across members of the main party. It wasn't encouraging. I stopped beside the prone body of one of Knowles' men. His gun was still warm, but he didn't move, and his eyes stared at nothing. I touched one of those staring eyes, he didn't react. When I stood up, I was on my own. The gunfire was less coordinated now. I tried to move in what I hoped was the correct direction. In the thick mist, I could pass a few feet away from Adam and Jones yet still miss them.

I came across what I took to be one of Knowles' people bent over a comrade, but as I got closer, I could see that her mouth was buried in his neck. She was so engrossed that I could back away unnoticed, which probably saved my life. You know in horror films when victim number 4 backs away from a monster and you shout at the screen "turn around!". Trust me, when you're that scared you don't, so I tripped over another body. This time it was one of the creatures which had been nearly sawn in half by a machine gun. Nearby I heard the boom of Adam's shotgun firing three shots, and then silence. Two figures approached from the mist and I froze.

It was Knowles and Evans. They'd both got their guns in slings. Instead they wielded the antiquated swords that Adam had purloined from various regimental museums.

"Are you alright?" asked Knowles.

"Yes, any idea what's happening?"

"No, we're dispersed so I'm going to try and regroup," she said and started to blow a whistle.

The loud shrill noise shredded my nerves as I imagined every vampire in the area homing in on the sound. From our left came the dull boom of a shotgun. There was a renewed rattle of automatic gunfire, but from further away this time.

Two more figures appeared from the gloom. Knowles and Evans crouched low either side of me and tucked in their heads. In the mist their camouflage made them almost invisible. I wondered why they'd left me standing on my own, until I realised that I was the bait for an ambush.

The figures came closer, but it was another couple of her team. One was a woman carrying a sword and supporting a man who was limping badly. Knowles and Evans stood up. Each group pointed their weapons at the other, until they realised they were on the same team.

One of the newcomers faced Knowles whilst Evans turned

outwards brandishing his sword.

"Report?" snapped Knowles.

"Sorry Boss, not much to say. We were with the forward group when the mist came down. The creatures came at us immediately. It was an ambush, they had us boxed in on both sides of the road. It wasn't just the creatures. There were people as well. I couldn't see them clearly, but they were definitely there. I don't know if there's anyone else left."

"Very good. Listen up everyone, we're pulling back to the farmhouse. You three, form a cordon. Come on."

The injured soldier leaned on me, I never did find out his name. I put his arm round my neck and took his weight as we set out. We made slow progress, but the creatures didn't attack us again.

"Hurry it up," said Knowles. All three of them started to walk faster. The injured guy also tried to speed up which caused me to stumble as I tried to help.

"Do we really need to pick up the pace like this?" I asked.

Knowles turned on me. "Listen Prof, back there those creatures might have lost their advantage when we screwed up their sense of smell by spraying the area with garlic. No doubt you're feeling pretty pleased with yourself as you suggested the idea. But we also doused ourselves with the stuff. Once we exit the immediate vicinity, we're leaving a garlicky trail of scent that leads to us like a Michelin guide leads to a French restaurant. Probably with a similar consequence. My people are taking on these things with medieval weapons and if they catch up with us, we are well and truly stuffed. Do I make myself clear!"

"I'll pick up the pace."

"You do that."

I got a tighter grip on the injured guy and we kept up with Knowles and the others. It seemed to take hours. The mist didn't let up and we relied on a compass for navigation. As we progressed, we only recognised particular features when we virtually tripped over them. A wall here, a gate there. Eventually we returned to the farm buildings we'd seen earlier.

With some relief, I lowered the injured soldier down onto a cot. As I stretched my back, the woman who'd helped him checked the dressing and stood up.

"Boss, we need to get him to a hospital, soon."

Knowles compressed her lips and nodded mutely as they barred the door and we settled down to wait.

CHAPTER 30

"Do the rest of them have compasses?" I asked Knowles.

"Of course, they should all be able to rendezvous with us here. I'm more worried about how we get back without Wells to help us. I don't want to be stranded in this hell hole." She gnawed her lower lip.

"If the worst comes to the worst I can try and get us back. Are we still trying to capture a creature?"

Knowles shook her head. "The aim now is to withdraw with as many survivors as possible."

"Sounds sensible," I agreed.

The troops had left most of their supplies here, presciently as it turned out. Smith put a billy can of water on a hexi.

The lookout shouted, "Someone coming!"

Knowles pointed at me and said, "You get the door. Evans on the window with a rifle. The rest of you with me."

I wiped sweaty palms on my trousers and grabbed the door handle. Knowles drew a pistol. The remainder of her team brandished swords.

One of them said to her, "That won't stop them Boss, that's why we use the swords."

I licked my lips, which were suddenly dry.

Evans said, "I can just about see them, moving slowly, Sorry Boss, the walls are too thick, they're out of my field of vision."

"Open the door partway but brace yourself to slam it shut," Knowles said to me.

I looked out. There seemed to be a soldier resting on something that was dragging him along. I drew a breath. It looked like he was being used as camouflage.

The soldier edged forward, his feet scuffing the ground. Knowles aimed her pistol. She hesitated, unwilling to shoot through one of her own men. He groaned in pain. There was a movement and two large ears popped up followed by the rest of Adam's head. "Any chance of some help here?"

They rushed forward to relieve Adam of his burden. He stood up and stretched, then said, "I thought it would get a bit hairy here, so I brought some items as insurance. Hold on while I set them up."

He flipped open a back pack and gingerly removed two green metal boxes. They were about the size of paperback books but curved. Hanging them on the external wall, the rabbit trailed a wire through the window which he plugged into a small box with a couple of buttons on it.

"Electrical items don't function," pointed out Knowles.

Adam tsked, replacing the wire with a piece of string, which he tied to a ring on the outside of the boxes.

Adam held up the end of the string, looked around and said directly to me, "Don't pull this under any circumstances."

"Why are you saying that to me?"

"Because you're the most likely person to do something stupid."

I opened my mouth, decided he had a point so whispered, "What is it?"

His muzzle cracked in that funny rabbit smirk and he said, "Claymore".

Bit gnomic I thought. But my attention was taken with the chap Adam had dragged for several miles. He had no obvious injuries, none of the lacerations we'd seen in people previously attacked. Looking closer I could see twin puncture wounds on his neck.

Knowles put me in charge of looking after the injured soldier. I guessed he was in a coma, but I'd no idea what to do. I covered him with a blanket and held his hand. A feeling of lassitude rolled over me.

Unbelievably, in the circumstances, I fell into a doze. Knowles kicked me awake.

"I told you to keep an eye on him! Try and hold it together Voyle." She looked more concerned than angry.

"I'm sorry. God, I can't believe I fell asleep. What's it like out there?"

"The mist seems a bit lighter, but the visibility hasn't improved much. Anyone in the open is still vulnerable. I'm worried that we've been separated from Wells. No offence Voyle, but he's the only one who can reliably get us back."

"I'm not going to argue with you on that one. Wells gave me some training, but I'm still a novice."

Someone handed me tea and an open sachet of rations with a spoon protruding from the packet. I took a mouthful, it was some muesli flavoured with dried apple. After one spoonful, I realised that I was ravenous and finished the pack before I took in my surroundings. The guy I was looking after was still unconscious. I wet his lips with a little water but got no reaction.

One of the people guarding a window said, "Don't worry Prof, I kept an eye on him while you were asleep."

"I'm sorry, I don't know what came over me."

"Stress, it takes some people like that."

"How long was I out for?"

"About six hours. We're calling it morning if that helps?" He smiled ruefully.

"Cheers, I'll see what I can do to lend a hand." I replied.

The others were positioned at the window and door, which was still bolted. It realised they'd been up all night taking four hour watches.

I knew what they were thinking. I was the only one here who could get the party back to our dimension. They wanted me rested and alert. Even so, they were praying that Wells would turn up. Frankly, so was I.

Hours passed, punctuated by cups of tea, which they seemed to have a bit of a mania about. That's British soldiery for you.

As the light faded, the lookout at the window shouted that someone was coming. Everyone crowded by the door as a figure approached. It was a woman in combat fatigues staggering slightly.

"OK everyone," said Knowles, "Same drill as last night. Voyle, brace the door. The rest of you on me. I want covering fire from the window. Put the rifle on automatic; these things are difficult to stop."

The figure drew closer. She showed no signs of injury but was weaving from side to side. As she came nearer, I noticed that she had dark hair in a long pony tail.

"What's regulation hair length?" I asked as Knowles, realising the danger, threw herself against me to shut the door.

We were too late, the woman accelerated and any doubts about which side she was on were dispelled as she cannoned forward. She was about five foot four and not heavily built, but hit the thick oaken construct like a battering ram. The door, with Knowles and I braced against it, half opened, and she slipped through, flying into the centre of the room.

At the same time there was a frantic swearing from the window and the lookout fired the rifle on automatic for three seconds, at which point the weapon ran out of ammunition. Those few moments were a long time in that situation. It was long enough for the woman to grab hold of Evans and fasten her mouth on his neck; long enough for Knowles and I to push the door shut and desperately try to grab the crossbeam. A mass of creatures with gapping maws rushed towards us and, in a split second of quiet clarity, I realised that we just weren't going to get it locked in time.

The creatures charge was hardly slowed by the rifle fire, but then Adam pulled his bit of string attached to the devices he'd called 'Claymore'. The two metal boxes detonated, producing a mass of shrapnel that scythed the pathway clear of life.

With ears ringing, Knowles and I got the door closed. She dropped the massive crossbeam into place. We put our backs to it as something massive crashed into the timbers. The door bowed, but held as dust jetted from the woodworm holes.

I turned around to see Knowles and the soldier with the

injured leg trying to prise the woman off Evans. Adam leapt away from the window and pushed his shotgun into the mass of writhing figures. There was a bang and the soldiers fell back, holding the limp form of Evans. His attacker writhed on the floor with a massive red hole in her chest from which blood welled, pooling on the packed earth. Now I could see clearly that her mouth opened at an impossible angle revealing serpent like fangs dripping clear venom. The mouth closed again, leaving the normal looking face of a young woman.

I then did something that, when I told them in the operation out-brief, caused them to stop taking notes and look at me with incredulity. In the farmhouse everyone held their breath. I admit it was ridiculously stupid.

I knelt next to her, leaned close and said, "It's going to be OK. I can take a message to your parents."

Her mouth opened a couple of times, but no sound came out and her eyes slowly closed. You see I'd seen her photo, placed before me in a police interview room. The vampires name was Natalie.

Suddenly everything we'd seen in this world made sense. I knew why the farmhouses were deserted? Why there were no people? But there was no time to explain because of the frenzied banging and crashing from outside. Knowles crossed the room in two strides, grabbed my arm and pulled me to my feet.

She said, "Look, there's no chance of the rest of the team getting to us, even if they've survived. You've got to get us back. Think you can do it?"

Her eyes widened in desperation as the door made an ominous cracking noise. "Now would be a good time."

Taking a deep breath, I tried to remember what I'd achieved with Wells. Closing my eyes I concentrated, shutting out the noise of the monsters battering at the door. I remembered the mental image of our dimension. The Yale key pattern of the physical laws that made our world. Got it! The centre of the room turned inside out forming a doorway to our world.

The guy with the injured leg limped through the portal, supported by his friend. Adam jumped to safety carrying the comatose soldier. Grunting with effort I took Evans weight.

"Go!" shouted Knowles, sighting her pistol at the door. A clawed hand punched through the wood.

"Go!" The door cracked and splintered.

I shuffled through the portal. My slow progress accelerated by the force of a small lieutenant running into my back.

As I fell towards home, the portal closed. I collapsed with a mixture of relief and the nausea.

I was kneeling on wet sand. My vision cleared, and I was starting to get a grip on the surroundings when my concentration was disturbed by the loud hammering sound of a helicopter. There was a tornado like wind as a big military machine landed next to us and armed troops fanned out. My God, those guys responded fast. How did they even know where we were? They ran past us, set up a firing line and proceeded to lay down covering fire. I turned in alarm at the thought that creatures had followed us through the portal. Maybe they'd opened their own?

Knowles was on her knees, laughing. "Well done, you got us back. We're safe."

Seeing my expression she put a hand on my shoulder. "It's all right, this is the Southport Air Show. We're going to be fine."

I raised my gaze and saw a huge crowd of people looking at us, held back by low fencing. Behind them were tents and an ice cream van. Disorientation overcame me, and I fell to one knee.

Pulling back her shoulders Knowles said, "Now, stop fannying about and pull yourself together. Come on, help me with the first aid."

Around us the crowds watched with rapt attention and licked their ice cream cones.

CHAPTER 31

I know what you're thinking. But a battle scarred combat unit appearing in the middle of the Southport Air Display was not the show stopper you might at first think. As far as the audience were concerned, we were part of the military demonstrations; as was the medical evacuation of the injured troops. Anyone who saw us suddenly appear put it down to theatrical trickery, whilst those who were more involved were sworn to secrecy. And, I suspect, interviewed by some scary people from the security services.

We all ended up at the hospital where the injured guys were being treated. Adam had formed an attachment to Evans. This was strange because before being trapped in the farmhouse, they'd most often met with a gun barrel separating them. Adam seemed torn between staying with me and accompanying Evans and looked relieved when I said I'd be OK. So, the rabbit followed his new friend.

The hospital staff triaged the team and those of us who were only tattered around the edges ended up in the hospital coffee shop. We had the place to ourselves; mind you, smelly wild-eyed people in military fatigues didn't do much for the ambiance.

I was wondering if the caffeine hit from a cappuccino was the best choice of beverage, when Knowles came in and sat down.

She looked at the drinks I'd bought for the team and asked, "How're you paying for that?"

"I took my credit card with me, why?"

She smirked and shook her head, "My people wouldn't think of taking identifying items into combat. Any chance of a drink?"

As I set a cup in front of her, I asked, "Did anyone else get out?"

She looked up, "The rest of the team were close to Wells

and fared better than us."

"How so?"

"It seems Wells' pacifist technique of putting up a telekinetic barrier enabled my people to re-group. Of course, they were a lot less concerned than him about avoiding violence and managed to put down some suppressive fire."

"I take it Wells' peacenik leanings didn't give him any qualms about that?"

"Funnily enough, they didn't. He seemed quite open minded about the use of massive firepower."

"Being assailed by vampiric monsters can affect one's sense of perspective. Were there any casualties?"

Knowles pressed her lips together, "We lost three people, missing, presumed dead. Some of our injured are suffering from lacerations and bites. At least one of those has life changing injuries."

"What about Evans and the guy we carried back?"

"They say that the people with puncture wounds are suffering from venom intoxication. They're bringing in specialists. The good news is that, unlike snake venom, there doesn't seem to be any tissue degradation. But they're suffering from paralysis and there seems to be some anti-clotting agent in the venom. It's like they've got a form of haemophilia."

"What happens now?" I asked.

"They'll take us to be out-briefed."

"Will it hurt?"

Knowles smiled, "Don't worry. It's just terminology. The intelligence bods will question us about what happened. They brief you on the way in. Then out-brief you when the operation is finished."

Foolishly, I breathed a sigh of relief.

As we finished our drinks a private in a nice clean uniform approached Knowles and said, "I've got the transport Ma'am."

Those of us who could walk were piled into a minibus and driven to Smith's lair in Birkdale.

We weren't allowed to wash or sleep, but waited to be

called to, what I made the mistake of calling, the interrogation room. Knowles pointed out that this was very definitely not interrogation, and I'd know the difference if I encountered it. We sat on hard plastic chairs. After an hour I came to hate that bilious green paint they use in government buildings to keep the inmates subdued.

When I was called, it was to find Smith accompanied by two people I'd seen before. They were Andrew and David. The stooges I'd encountered in the video conference.

Some of Knowles' people had gone into the room and returned unscathed, so I was unprepared for their attitude. Although meeting the gruesome twosome earlier should have given me a clue.

The first thing they didn't seem able to get their head around was that we'd been in vampire world for several days. Only a couple of minutes had passed here. To be fair to them, it came as a bit of a shock to me, even though my interactions with Wells had got me used to the idea of time progressing at different speeds in alternative dimensions.

"How did you get here so fast?" I asked.

"We'll ask the questions, if you don't mind," replied Andrew.

"No, I mean, if we only disappeared for a couple of minutes, how did you two get here?"

"There could be serious legal consequences if you refuse to answer questions. This operation is under military discipline," Andrew said, hardening his voice.

"What're you going to do to me? I'm a civilian."

My veneer of English politeness had worn thin. It must have been all that death and mutilation I'd encountered.

As Andrew drew in his breath, the quiet one, David, held up his hand.

"I can quite see Doctor Voyle's point of view. I think a bit of give and take might be called for. Doctor, we set out when Mr Smith informed us he was planning this ill-advised adventure. We're just trying to ascertain the sequence of events. Could you please give us, in as much detail as possible, a factual account of the events of the few minutes you spent in the, Ummm, for want of a better term, vampire dimension. That is to say, a few days from your subjective viewpoint."

As I did so, they made copious notes. I noticed that they didn't ask for any clarification. Was that some technique they'd been taught? Or were they just going through the motions?

When I'd finished, they sat back. Andrew inhaling through his nose and glancing at his colleague before continuing the questioning.

"Are you seriously trying to tell us that there are talking rabbits and people with telekinetic powers? Not to mention monsters and vampires? Wouldn't a simpler explanation be that you've been exposed to some hallucinogenic substance?"

"I wish it were, I truly do, because I've seen some terrible things in the last couple of days."

"We notice that there's no video footage. Doesn't that strike you as odd? Your narrative neatly explains the lack of verifiable evidence, but could it be the case that your story is tailored to fit around the facts?"

"What about the casualties?"

"Possibly some kind of overdose," Andrew said.

"I'll bet that's not what the medical reports come back with. They'll tell you the injuries are the same as received by people attacked in this dimension."

"We think a lot of that information might also have been misinterpreted," David said.

Smith had not been looking as uncomfortable as I would have expected.

"Smith, these idiots are unravelling your whole operation. Aren't you going to say anything?"

"Andrew and David are just doing their job. You'll find that their explanation of events has more holes than a sieve. Certainly, that's what the minister thinks. I assume your friends are with you? Perhaps it's time to show Andrew and David what we're dealing with." He called for Wells and Adam.

By this time, I was nearly falling off my chair with exhaustion. The door opened. Wells entered, accompanied by Adam.

The one called Andrew stood up and said, "We're interviewing Doctor Voyle and we shouldn't be disturbed, so get out..."

I had to say he had great presence, and it probably worked very well with the various sycophants and underlings he was used to dealing with. However, Andrew didn't get to say any more as Wells held up the palm of his hand and he fell back in his seat, pinned there. Adam had been doing his invisible rabbit act but must have come into view because Smith's companions gaped.

Adam helped me from my chair as, I'm ashamed to say, my legs started to give way. He and Wells held me as I made my way unsteadily to the door.

Smith smirked quietly to himself and said, "Oh no, Andrew, you've not been affected by a hallucinogen, have you? You too David? Both having the same hallucination? Oh dear me."

Adam showed his opinion by pausing to defecate on the floor. Quite eloquently, I thought.

CHAPTER 32

Knowles and the relatively uninjured remains of her team were drinking coffee and exchanging banter in the larger room, whilst waiting to see if the two stooges wanted to talk to them again.

I couldn't wait anymore, knowing they'd been deceived. They had to be told what we'd done. I called for attention.

"I'm sorry, I have to admit to something terrible. We briefed you that the operation was to bring a creature back to this dimension. Whilst that was true the government boffins also cooked up a genetically engineered canine Rhinovirus..."

"Rhinoceros virus?" a voice said.

"No, you idiot, common cold," said another

I continued, "Yes a modified common cold from dogs crossed with a virus from a dead creature. They put a gene sequence for garlic smell into it. Basically, the plan was to capture a creature, infect it and allow it to pass the disease to others of its kind."

Wells was looking at me with horror. I could feel my face reddening, but continued, "As the creatures find their prey almost solely by smell, the virus would knock out their olfactory apparatus. They wouldn't be able to hunt and, consequently, starve."

Another voice piped up from the soldiery, "You mean a bit like when Europeans brought smallpox to America and virtually wiped out all the native Americans. What? it was on television!" she added as everyone looked at her.

"If we could let Dr Voyle continue," said Knowles grimly.

"Thank you. As I was saying, we were going to infect a creature and release it. But there was a backup plan. They foresaw that the creatures might overwhelm the expedition so the injection you had was not a vaccine. It was a kind of virus. Well, it wasn't exactly a virus ..."

"Just call it a virus and get on with it," sighed Knowles.

"I'm sorry. There's no need to be alarmed. You won't be infected; our species are too different. But the virus will be in our bloodstreams for a few days until it's mopped up by our immune systems. During that time we're infective to the creatures. The people who were attacked will have passed on the virus to the creatures through their blood. I'm sorry. I didn't know they were going to give you the injection. It was just supposed to be me."

There was a short silence, then they carried on drinking their coffee. The buzz of conversation rose to its previous level.

Knowles said, "Don't look so bemused. We already knew."

"You mean you were quite happy to be used as bait? I asked.

"We've faced much worse odds than that. Don't think we didn't see your ridiculous attempts to wander off and get bitten. Going off to poo behind the bushes? Really? Anyway, not even Smith is stupid enough to send us in without a full operational briefing."

"It's my fault, I got Tom and Carole killed. I got all those girls killed." My voice started to break.

Smith had appeared in the room, wiping his shoe with a tissue. "But they didn't all get killed, did they? You repeatedly claimed that the vampire that attacked the group in the cottage was someone you'd met. Tomorrow I want you to look at the photos of the missing girls to confirm the identification."

"I recognised Natalie. Are we going to inform her family?"

Smith shook his head. "And say what? Don't be ridiculous! Go and have a shower. Someone will bring your clothes. You need to change before you go home."

Knowles smirked and said, "As far as your wife's concerned you went to your office this morning. How did you intend to explain three days growth of beard? Also, you smell like an old dog."

Smith said, "We also need to consider the implications of the time difference between dimensions. Our adversaries could use it against us. Well, good night. I'll see you bright eyed and bushy tailed in the morning. My colleagues will debrief the Lieutenant and return to London tomorrow."

Bright eyed and bushy tailed!? I was dead on my feet. Next to me, Knowles raised her voice, "OK everyone, kit to clean, I want a tally of weapons and ammo. Someone's going to play merry hell when they see what passes for an audit of our equipment. Chop, chop! Then it's out for a steak. The beers are on me."

"Woo!"

"Hope you got deep pockets Boss."

"Mine's extra rare."

Wells and Adam turned to me. Wells said, "You realise you've just committed genocide, don't you? Those creatures only hunt by smell. It won't just kill off the ones near where we were, it could wipe out the whole species. You could have destroyed the whole ecosystem. I'm horrified."

Adam just stared at me yet managed to convey deep disappointment.

They both took me by the arm and guided me to a communal bathroom, it was like being back at school. I hesitated, and Knowles shouted across the room, "Get yourself cleaned up. We'll be tidying for a bit."

Pink sidled over, but was called away and stomped off with ill grace.

Wells raised his eyebrows and said, "Bit of a fan there, you could have got your back scrubbed."

"Did you bring her back?"

"I thought you did?" Wells said.

"No, she must have been in your group."

"I suppose so. It's difficult to tell them apart with all that camouflage make up. Anyway, here's your army issue wash bag. Enjoy," said Wells.

Of course everything was khaki, washbag, towels. I was surprised that the soap and toothpaste were white.

Stepping from the shower I found my civilian clothes, folded with military precision.

Adam had acquired a car from somewhere and drove me home.

CHAPTER 33

The steps leading to my house seemed unfamiliar. Like I'd been away for months. Theresa hadn't arrived home so I made a hot drink. Probably the best cup of tea I'd ever tasted. I sat on the sofa to get a couple of moments' rest. I started as a hand was placed on my shoulder.

Theresa looked down at me, "You all right love? You were dead to the world. Another bad day?"

"Hmm? Sorry, I must've dropped off."

"He's not much better."

She gestured to Adam who was stretched out on the hearth and making little snuffling noises.

I stood up and hugged Theresa, burying my face in her hair. I could feel myself begin to cry. Theresa lifted my head and frowned with concern.

She rested her hand on my face. "Are you sure you're all right? If there was a problem, you would tell me, wouldn't you? You look absolutely dreadful!"

I wanted to say that since we'd parted this morning, I'd spent several days in a living nightmare.

I wiped the tears from my cheeks, "Yes, you know how it is. Rough day. I think I might be coming down with something."

Looking in the mirror I could see myself as she saw me. I might have washed and shaved but my eyes were sunken into a pallid face. Yup, I could pull off going down with something. I walked up the stairs to bed. Behind me Adam made a whimpering noise; like someone dreaming about being chased by monsters.

The next day I got up so late that Theresa had gone to work. Adam seemed his usual cheerful self, so all was well with the world. He still had his car, from wherever he'd hired it. We drove to Smith's lair, where we had trouble finding a parking spot. I always imagined these shadowy government types would have deep underground headquarters reached through iron gates. Not defunct Victorian hotels recycled as offices. Still, dreams are there to be shattered.

"How are you paying for that car?" I asked.

"Oh, I just borrowed it," said Adam as we walked to the rear entrance.

We hammered for a bit before one of Knowles' people let us in. As we entered, he bent down to pick up an envelope, then looked over our shoulders, scanning the road.

"Anything up?" I asked.

He shook his head. "Nothing really, it's just Smith keeps getting demands for payments on credit cards that no one knows anything about. We've recently had a couple of bailiffs round. It's not very secret service when there are debt collectors hammering on the door."

"How peculiar, maybe from a previous tenant?" I said.

Adam had a look of insouciance.

"No one's used the place since nineteen seventy three. Yet someone's been running up debts," said Smith from the corridor. He glared at the soldier, who, at that moment, seemed to be standing in for all of the untrustworthy military.

I edged past, being careful not to catch Adam's eye.

Wells was already there. Smith's colleagues were standing next to their luggage.

"Andrew and David are going back to London. They're just waiting for a taxi," Smith said.

"Borrow my car. You can leave it at the station," said Adam.

"What about the keys?" asked David, obviously uncomfortable about the necessity of acknowledging Adam's existence.

The rabbit looked nonplussed, "They make the car go, there is a sort of hole and you put the key in ..."

"Funny, where do you want us to leave the keys?"

"Leave them in the car,"

"Really, just leave them in the car?"

This was going on forever. "Balance the keys on the front

right hand tyre like you would if it were a hire car," I said, more to get rid of them than anything else.

Still looking a bemused at dealing with a talking rabbit, they took the keys and left. No "Hope you keep well", no "Good bye, keep in touch." A simple thank you would have been nice, but there you go.

We called a conference. Adam left for a few minutes, then re-joined us. We could discuss things properly now that the stuffed shirts had left.

Smith was about to start when Wells asked, "Lieutenant Knowles, how're your injured personnel?"

"They're all coming round. The guy who was mauled got bitten quite badly and he's still in hospital. The others are having some psychological issues,"

"Not really surprising is it? I mean, they were attacked by vampires. It's bound to put a bit of a damper next time your girlfriend does a bit of necking," I said.

Wells looked at me severely, "I think this is a bit more serious than that. We wish them a swift recovery, but I imagine that it will take time. Please send them our best wishes."

"You all acquitted yourselves admirably, even you Voyle," said Knowles.

"Nice to know I almost met your expectations."

Smith called a halt there and passed some photos in front of me. The images were of 6 or 7 young women. They were the usual kind of snaps you see on social media. Clipped to each set of photos was a sheet with some biographical details. I looked carefully at each one. Half way through I stopped. They were images of a pretty dark haired girl. She looked a bit severe in her passport photo, but there were a couple of other snaps where she was posing with friends, laughing and smiling. I recognised the girl. But last time I'd seen her was in a cottage in another dimension. Her face had been barely recognisable as her mouth was open at almost 90 degrees. She'd had long, venom dripping canines, whilst her sharp bottom teeth had pointed backwards. It was a mouth designed to hold prey until they had stopped struggling. I shuddered as I remembered.

"That's Natalie. You saw her, didn't you," said Smith.

"Yes, she was the…" I struggled to find the right word, "… the person who attacked us in the cottage."

Wells said, "I've noticed that people adopt the characteristics of any dimension they enter, so in my dimension Doctor Voyle developed limited telekinetic abilities. As you saw, he can move inter-dimensionally. So, if someone survived an attack by the vampire creatures, they could, to all intents and purposes, become infected. But only if they remained in the vampire world."

I chipped in, "This explains what we saw in the vampire dimension. Assuming the buildings we examined were occupied by humans, it suggests that the people in that dimension had found a way of living with the creatures. They built massive structures to keep the animals at bay. When the mists came they would hunker down and wait until the weather cleared. Then they would come out and continue their lives. They must have lived in harmony like that for hundreds of years."

"What do you think happened? Why were the buildings deserted?" asked Smith.

I continued, "The balance would be upset when human vampires appeared. They would pose as waifs and strays, perhaps begging to be allowed in as the mists came down. Then attacked the residents. I imagine that there are very few humans left alive in that environment."

"But these were massive physiological changes. This isn't just developing a mental ability; their entire physiology had altered," said Smith.

I said, "You're forgetting the time differential. These vampires have had decades to develop. In this dimension we re-appeared minutes after we'd left. But for us 3 or 4 days had passed. This is an extreme version of what happens in Wells' world."

Knowles said, "Hold on, that vampire looked just like

the young girl who went missing. If she'd been in the vampire dimension since her disappearance, then she should have aged. Subjectively, years would have passed."

I said, "It could be that she only spent some of her time in the vampire dimension. But there's something else. Some researchers have transfused blood from a young animal into an old one. The old animal then showed fewer signs of ageing. It's possible that the myth of vampires becoming immortal by drinking blood isn't just a story. The human vampires could've halted their aging process when they fed."

"What about the humans already there? Surely, over the centuries, there would've been instances where someone survived a bite and turned into a vampire?" said Knowles.

"You have a good point. We don't know what the relationship is between the vampire creatures and the ones who resemble humans. But something in that dimension must cause people to become vampires. It's unlikely to spontaneously occur," said Wells.

"Which means that someone could be deliberately converting people into vampires. I doubt those girls thought to themselves, 'Oooh, let's not go clubbing tonight, let's go and become haemovores.' Which leaves us with the question of who's been converting people and why," said Knowles.

"Whatever happened in that dimension had years to occur. The time differential will have seen to that. On a more practical level, if our virus is as effective as we hope, then the time differential will also mean that the creatures should've starved to death by now. It could be game over," I said.

"If the state of that farm is anything to go by the human vampires may well have exhausted their food source. If they've killed off all the indigenous humans, then they won't have any new blood. If they only feed on humans, they'll either starve or die of old age."

"So, problem solved," said Knowles.

"Possibly, but I've asked your C.O. if you can stay on for a while. However, I think we can lessen the intensity of your operation to protect Dr Voyle. Let's break for now and have some refreshments. Then you can start jotting down some records of your experiences. Could I have a quick word, Doctor Voyle?" said Smith.

I could never work out what the etiquette was between the honorific and me being just Voyle. Probably because I lacked a classical education.

Smith took me by the arm and led me to one side. "I'm sure there's no need for me to say this, but, you aren't going to do any more practical experiments, are you?"

"No, of course not," I replied, "all experiments on opening up dimensions are strictly on hold."

"This might surprise you, but I've dealt with scientists before. I don't mean put things on hold, I mean **do not** do any practical work."

"Well, naturally I wouldn't do any tinkering with dimensions. It would be completely irresponsible of me."

Smith sighed. "You know what I mean. I don't want you doing **any** practical work."

"Obviously, but there are aspects of the telekinetic powers shown by Wells that are interesting. And there's the becoming, to all intents and purposes, invisible; like Adam. If we knew more about how these worked, then we could get a handle on some of the abilities of the vampires. Surely it wouldn't do any harm to take a few measurements?"

"That's exactly what I'm talking about. No practical experiments! Nothing! Alles verboten! I'm not sure I can make myself any clearer. Do you understand me, Voyle?"

See what I mean about the honorific?

This seemed completely unreasonable. "We've taken out the vampires. There's no way that we can create any trouble by putting a few instruments around a person. Especially when they're already performing an activity they carry out anyway."

"That's how we got into this mess in the first place, if you remember?"

"But I can travel between dimensions myself?"

"That's something else that's got to stop. We might not be able to control what Wells does, but I'm damned if you're going to make the situation any worse. God knows who you're interacting with."

"What do you mean?"

"Nothing, just do as I say. I'll be watching."

He turned and went back to Knowles.

Wells, Adam and I left the building. As the stuffed shirts had the car we decided to walk to the town centre. Crossing the car park, I was surprised to see that the civil servants had not gone to the station in the car after all. They were standing by the vehicle with a short woman and two policemen. The woman was gesticulating excitedly. One of the police officers was taking notes whilst the other had the more outspoken of the government types in an arm lock.

"Adam," I said, cautiously, "When you said you borrowed the car, how did you borrow it."

"I took the keys. I was sure the lady wouldn't miss it, and I did get the car back before she returned. Those two should have driven off quicker."

"So," I sighed, "All's well that ends well. Probably best if we make ourselves scarce. It'll only muddle things if they start asking us questions."

"I'll just go back and tell Smith and the others what's happening," said Adam.

Wells and I started to walk along the street and were quickly hidden from view.

Shortly afterwards Adam caught up with us. "Mr Smith said that for security reasons they were going to lock the doors and pretend no one is in."

Wells said, "But there won't be anyone to corroborate anything those two government people say. They could be arrested or anything. If fact, one looked like he was causing a breach of the peace already."

I couldn't help but smile. "It doesn't look like those two have made many friends. Adam, you didn't do that on purpose did you?"

Adam affected an air of injured innocence, "Who? Me?"

I sighed, and strangely, felt myself relax a little. It was a nice sunny day. Walking back along the tree lined streets of Birkdale was going to be a pleasure.

Behind me I could hear raised voices. Yes, the day was definitely looking up.

CHAPTER 34

Wells accompanied Adam and I back to my house. Something had been bothering me.

"Wells, I hope you don't mind me asking, but you seem to cope with this better than us."

"What you have to remember is that to come here at all is regarded as reckless amongst my people. There's an air of unreality about this whole situation. It's a strange feeling but I've just realised that I'm proud to have rescued those soldiers. Don't tell my family, they'd be shocked."

"My lips are sealed."

"Doctor Voyle, you also did well, managing to open the portal to save the people with you. Do you think that your little campaign of genocide will solve the problem?"

"I'm not sure what you mean. Those creatures won't be able to hunt. They might die out. End of problem as far as I'm concerned."

"I wasn't making a moral point. You saw a human who'd become a vampire. How do you know they'll die out?"

"Maybe they'll starve with the other creatures?".

"Perhaps, but they might find other sources of food," Wells said.

"What like?" I asked, with a horrible suspicion I knew what he was going to say.

"If they can manipulate dimensions, then perhaps their feeding ground will be here." He turned to the rabbit. "Adam, will you stay with Dr Voyle for me?"

"Sure thing, Theresa is always good for a cuddle and some carrot sticks. To be frank we're getting rather fond of her."

I felt I ought to clear some things up with the rabbits, "She can see you. Do you realise that? Your 'Forget me as soon as I'm out of sight' trick doesn't work with her."

"I'm not bothered," said Adam.

Incorrigible. I turned to Wells.

"Care to pop in for a bite to eat?"

"I won't if you don't mind, I'd like to get back to see my family."

Wells walked away. I could see his stride lengthen. I did some mental calculations and realised that his family would be a couple of months older than when he came here a few days ago.

We went up the steps and let ourselves in. I had just settled down with a cup of tea, and put out some carrots for Adam, when Theresa got home. She was wearing her work skirt and jacket and came in gasping for a cuppa.

As I made the drink I said, "Adam's going to stay with us for a while. Is that OK."

"Sure," she said, stopping to scratch Adam behind the ears before trotting upstairs to change.

"We ought to make a room up for him." I shouted whilst waiting for the kettle to boil.

"What about Tom? He's already in the spare room."

"I could get him a ..." I stopped for a minute and turned to Adam, "How do you like to sleep?"

"Well, ideally I'd like a nice burrow somewhere but if you leave a blanket on the floor and the door open I'll be happy with the kitchen."

Theresa came down and I gave her a mug.

She said, "That's sorted then. I don't suppose you had a chance to get tea on?"

For the benefit of any Americans who come across this account, I should point out that in the North of England they refer to their evening meal as 'Tea' whilst in the South of England it's 'Dinner'. The midday meal is known, severally, as 'Dinner' and 'Lunch'. It's confusing for Brits, so just go with the flow.

"No, sorry, I'll put a frozen lasagne in the oven," I said.

"Sergei's coming back. Can he have a few carrots with us?" asked Adam.

"Of course, although I'd like to know what he's been up

to," I said.

Theresa cleared her throat. "In fact, I want to know what you've all have been up to. I think it's time we had that little chat, don't you?"

I made vague noises of confusion.

"You left yesterday and came back looking like you hadn't slept for days. Well, you've had a day to recover and now I want to know where you've been."

I drew a deep breath. "Adam and I did a bit of dimension hopping and time went a lot faster in the other dimension. In truth it was a bit hairy for a couple of days."

The door behind me opened. Theresa stared past my shoulder with a look of horror. Wondering what could upstage my account, I turned around and stared, dumbstruck.

Sergei was slouching in the doorway in as nonchalant a way as a 5 foot tall rabbit with Russian criminal tattoos can stand. Especially whilst wearing a multi-layered necklace of what looked like ears.

"Sergei, you're back!" said Adam excitedly.

CHAPTER 35

Like we didn't have enough to worry about.

Theresa said, "Are those things around your neck what I think they are?"

Sergei stood there, not saying anything.

Theresa sighed, "I can see you. I've always been able to see you. Are those ears round your neck?"

Sergei gestured at the disgusting things and said "Da," in a 'these are nothing unusual' manner. Who knows, where he came from, they might not be.

"Why're you wearing ears around your neck?" Theresa said.

"Shows I have ears to wear around neck."

"Sergei," I said. "Where did you get the ears from?"

"From people," as in, where else would they originate.

"This is like pulling teeth," growled Theresa

"These not good enough? Want teeth?"

"No Sergei, you are wearing a necklace of ears which indicates that you have cut them off people, who presumably needed them to hear with," said Theresa enunciating very clearly in a carefully controlled voice.

"Of course, otherwise is no point wearing them. Anyway people not need ears, because are all dead."

"Who is dead and how did they get to be that way?" I asked, feeling I needed to make a contribution.

"Perhaps I can help," said Adam. Turning to Theresa he continued, "We entered into a business deal or two with some rather nasty businessmen to bring some young ladies into the country. Your husband was kind enough to take us to a talk by your policemen. We learned that some terrible things happened to these ladies. As you can imagine we were very upset and wanted to make this clear to our former business associates."

"But I only wanted you to stop," I said.

"We have. Sergei has spent some considerable time and

effort winding up our affairs. Liquidating our business, so to speak," said Adam.

"Da, severed our links to bad people," added Sergei who was getting into the language of business.

"I think we're going to have to agree to disagree on this one," I ended, lamely.

Theresa walked over and, with a reckless attitude to danger, leaned down until she was nose to muzzle with Sergei.

"Get those filthy things from around your neck," she snarled through gritted teeth, "Adam, I want you to take them away from this house and you, Sergei, are coming with me to the bathroom because you stink of death."

"Da. Cause killed lots of people," replied Sergei proudly but he still removed the necklace and meekly followed Theresa into the bathroom.

Adam hopped off holding Sergei's macabre trophies at arm's length. "Bit of a dragon your wife," he said.

I went into the kitchen. The lasagne was bubbling nicely so I cut up some salad and set the dining room table for three. Tom appeared in the doorway.

"How much of that did you hear?"

"All of it," said Tom. "Mr Wells did say that he'd warned you about advancing their moral development too fast. You can't expect them to jump straight to law based values from their vengeance based honour system."

"Sergei has a concept of honour?"

"Let's call it an idiosyncratic value framework," Tom said.

"I see you've been doing all of the course work from your sociology module, but what does that mean to those of us who've not had the benefit of a classical education?"

"To put it another way; when you're dealing with the rabbits? I wouldn't wind them up," Tom replied.

Sergei came back from the bathroom smelling more floral than abattoir, just as Adam returned, minus human organs. Tom sat with us to eat, while the rabbits tucked into a sack of vegetables, then curled up on the blanket doing that strange digestive things rabbits do.

"Delicious," I said, as Tom poured Tabasco sauce over his plate and tucked in with gusto. Theresa got up and went into the kitchen for some more salad.

"Oh, I forgot to mention," said Tom, "After he's had his few days off, Mr Wells wants to go back to the vampire world. For us that would be tomorrow."

After that the meal really didn't taste as good.

CHAPTER 36

Wells showed up at about ten o clock. Theresa delayed going to work in order to meet him.

"Did Tom tell you about that other little expedition I was planning? There were a couple of loose ends I want to tidy up," Wells said

"You want me to go back there after that disaster?" I replied.

"It'll give you a chance to hone your interdimensional travelling abilities. Surely you'd like to see the fruits of your genocidal labours."

"What if it hasn't worked? We went with a load of armed special forces last time and were lucky to come out alive. This time we might not get two steps before we're massacred."

"We must go back. I think we might have been looking at this from the wrong perspective."

Theresa butted in, "He's not going. He told me everything. What can you possibly hope to discover? You won't find out if there are any of the creatures around until they attack you, and then it will be too late."

"Please Mrs Voyle, I'll stay close and shield your husband. I wouldn't ask unless I thought it was very, very important. Really, at the first sign of danger I'll throw a shield around the whole group and come straight back."

"OK," I said resignedly, "But we take both the rabbits with us. Do you want to come?"

I turned around, but Adam was already dragging a holdall into the room.

"This should do it," he said as Sergei drew a huge machete from the bag and nodded approvingly. Of course they wanted to come.

Wells thought it best to return to the building we'd camped in, I tried to call it a farm, but the word fortress kept springing to my mind. Our starting point would have to be on the beach.

We walked through the Winter Gardens, past the boating lake and crossed an area of salt marsh.

In the distance I could just see a vehicle trawling for shrimps. A bizarre looking contraption that appeared to be a cross between a boat and a truck. There was no other sign of life.

"Can we find where the portal opened. I wasn't paying much attention," I said.

"No problem," said Adam, "I lined up some land marks. Follow me."

So saying he walked looking back towards the town. Then he stopped. "Can you see the two buildings over there? We keep them aligned as we walk until another two at about 45 degrees line up. Then we're in the correct place."

"You had the presence of mind to triangulate our position, after we'd escaped from that hellhole by the skin of our teeth?" I was incredulous.

"Didn't seem much else to do while we waited for the ambulances."

Sergei was rubbing his front teeth. He really did take things too literally.

Adam stopped. "This is about where we came through. Shall Sergei and me go through first?"

Wells said, "It might be dangerous, so I could make the initial foray and set up a force field."

"Or Sergei and I could go through and chop up anything that looks unfriendly. Open the portal Voyley."

Where had he got that nickname? I felt forward, finding that key to fit in the vampire world shaped lock. This time it came easily. Got it, I opened the portal and Adam and Sergei stepped through. We waited a couple of seconds then Wells and I followed. The rabbits were looking bored. Of course the time differential meant that a couple of hours had passed whilst we'd sorted ourselves out.

"I hope no one saw us step through that portal," I said.

Wells replied, "You've still not grasped that people

rationalise what they see. If anyone had seen us apparently disappear, they'll assume it was some kind of optical illusion. Now, where are we?"

We scanned the area. I could just about make out the front of the building where we'd camped. Saplings had sprung up in the farmyard. Years had passed in this dimension. We moved forward, the rabbits slipping easily through the undergrowth; Adam faced forward whilst Sergei kept turning around to cover our rear. They moved silently. By comparison the rest of us seemed to make a nerve shredding racket.

Adam stopped and whispered, "I'll go and make sure no one is inside. Keep quiet, it'll give me the element of surprise."

"Okay, be careful." I hardly dared breath lest I give him away.

"Ready then, I'll creep up."

Wells nodded.

Adam sprung forward throwing a grenade through the door. Sergei gathered the three effete humans in his arms and bore us to the ground as there was a bang and shrapnel flew from the door and window openings.

Without waiting for the brown smoke to clear, Sergei and Adam loped inside and the rest of us followed.

I looked round, "Looks like a bomb's hit it," I said. Adam sniggered.

"I thought you were going to look inside," said Wells in an unusually testy voice.

"The soldiers taught me. It's called reconnaissance by fire. Lieutenant Knowles told me," said Adam then he turned to Sergei "Could you watch the door, please."

"I bet Knowles also told you not to do it, didn't she?" I said.

Adam put his paw to his mouth in an 'Oops there I go again' manner.

I continued, "What if a family had taken up residence? A mother, children."

Adam's ears flopped down on either side of his head.

Sergei said, "Not to do again."

Somewhat chastened, we looked round. The walls and ceiling were peppered with fresh chips from the shrapnel and the smell of cordite masked a musty uninhabited odour.

"Right," I said, "What are we looking for?"

Wells turned to us. "Doesn't it seem strange to you that humans and the vampire creatures could co-evolve? Surely the humans would have been wiped out before they could develop the technology to construct buildings like this?"

"But these buildings have been here for decades, possibly hundreds of years."

"Exactly, look in all of the nooks and crannies to see if there are any clues as to the origin of the people who lived here."

We systematically started to look through the building. There wasn't a lot to see. Due to the differential flow of time, the few days since we'd left had translated into years in this dimension. Soil had blown in through the door but the roof remained weatherproof. Whatever animal that occupied the small rodent ecological niche had burrowed into everything.

There were chests of drawers and small cupboards. It was more like archaeology than a search. Clothing disintegrated as we touched it.

I levered open a drawer and found a rotten leather pouch. Inside were ovals of brass covered in Verdigris. The surfaces were embossed with a pattern, which I rubbed with my finger. They were buttons.

Adam looked at one. "I've seen one of those before. They had buttons like that in the museum where I got the swords."

I started as, behind me, the door fell off a cupboard. Wells pulled out some rusting items. I looked closely. They were almost unrecognisable, but I could see the gleam from a cartridge case. They were the remains of rifles. The wooden parts of the weapons had rotted away. At the bottom of the cupboard we found plastic stocks and hand grips.

Wells said, "I think we have what we came for. Mr Smith has a bit of explaining to do."

"Why don't we get someone from the museum to identify

this stuff. It means people have been here before," I said.

"Someone coming," said Sergei.

"Let's not find out who or what it is. Come on, Mr Wells, as time is of the essence, could you facilitate our departure?"

"Really Doctor Voyle. You can overdo the calm in the face of danger thing you know. It can start to look like panic," Wells said.

"Open the bloody portal. Let's get out of here," I replied, almost hopping from foot to foot in frustration.

He waited a leisurely few seconds before opening a door to our world. I resisted the urge to push past everyone as we returned home. Wells checked the whole party had come though and sealed off vampire world.

"And sometimes you're just a Smart Alec," I said, almost collapsing with relief.

CHAPTER 37

I called Smith and told him I needed to contact Knowles to find out how her men were doing. We also needed to fulfil the promise to Fine Jane. I didn't tell him about our little expedition, which had taken virtually no time at all in this dimension. Even so, he huffed and puffed about helping the mermaid. I pointed out that we would probably need all the friends we could get in the excitingly dangerous new world we now inhabited.

Wells accompanied me to my office and we waited for Knowles to call. Instead she turned up in person with one of her soldiers. This was the older man who had non-commissioned officer written all over him. Knowles called him 'Sergeant,' and that was the only name I ever heard used. But then all of the Browns and Evans and Pinks were obviously pseudonyms, so Sergeant was a good a name as any I suppose.

We showed them the artefacts. Knowles passed the plastic stock and hand grip to the Sergeant.

He examined it carefully. "Looks like the butt of an L1A1. I've fired them, off and on, but they went out of service even before I joined."

"I thought they still used muskets when you joined Sergeant," said Knowles examining the rusted rifles. "This isn't an old L1A1. Do you mind if I get the cartridge out?"

"Help yourself," I said.

She picked up a hefty glass paperweight from my desk and gave the lump of rust a sharp rap. It cracked in two and she worked the cartridge loose.

"It's still live." She grabbed a tissue and rubbed the object. "Let's have a look. The base of every cartridge, bullet for you civvies, is marked with the type of round, hold on." Her eyebrows rose in surprise. "There's a turn up for the books, this is a three-o-three. They were used by the British Army in the early part of the twentieth century. Stuff like Lee Enfield rifles, Bren Guns, that kind of thing. It's a right little history of British

Army weapons you have here. Where did you get them?"

"We had a little trip to the farm we holed up in when we went to vampire world."

"Any sign of life?" Knowles asked.

"Sergei saw someone, but we didn't hang round to find out who it was," I replied.

"Was like old woman," said Sergei.

"With the rate time moves in that dimension compared to this, that could well have been a young woman when we were there," Wells said.

"But face was not human," added Sergei.

"Let's hope she stays there," said Knowles.

"OK, so we have a dimension where time moves more quickly than here. We know that humans have visited before us. In fact, at least as long ago as the nineteen forties. I think Smith has a bit of explaining to do," I summed up.

"We also know that they weren't wiped out by the vampire creatures. They had time to construct those buildings," Knowles said. "You'd better come with us and bring Smith up to date."

The rabbits were still toting their arsenals, so Wells and I insisted they dispense with them. They then made the perfectly valid point that the various items could fall into the wrong hands if they weren't secured, so stuffed them all into a holdall which Sergei slung across his back. He came over to me and put his arm companionably over my shoulders. It felt like a furry bag of cement. Determined that my knees wouldn't buckle, I turned to face him.

I'm a bit short sighted, so I could see every detail of his muzzle with the scar across it.

"Not to worry, if you get held up, one of us get back to look after wife."

"Thanks Sergei."

"Also she's bought in a load of carrots and lettuce for us," said Adam.

"You two are a bit mercenary, aren't you?"

"What's a mercenary?" asked Adam.

"It's a soldier who fights for money." said Knowles, before I could stop her opening an existential can of worms.

Adam came very upright, "We do not defend Mrs Theresa for money."

"I apologise, it's a turn of phrase and means that your affections can be swayed by whoever gives you carrots and tickles you behind the ears," I explained.

There was an awkward silence as the rabbits looked at each other.

"Fair enough," said Adam as they bustled out of the room.

Knowles had been speaking into a phone, but turned to us and said, "I've got some transport organised."

"I thought we would walk, it's only 10 minutes," I pointed out.

"The only people who can get us in and out of other dimensions are in this room. There's no way I'm allowing you to walk along the street. You make too good a target. Sod it, I'll get Smith to come to us."

This seemed a bit over the top as we had all just wandered around somewhere that had been rife with vampires, but she was the expert.

"Can I have a cup of tea?" said Tom, causing Knowles and her colleague to start. They obviously hadn't noticed he was there.

"I must try and learn this ability to blend in with the background that people from other dimensions seem to have. It could come in useful for departmental meetings," I said.

"Useful for a bit of a break when visiting the wife's family," added Knowles.

"Not an issue for me, Theresa doesn't seem to have any family."

"No one? Have they…?" She paused to find the right words, "… all passed on?"

"You know I never thought to ask. It was a friend who gave her away at our wedding."

HEIR OF MY INVENTION

"What, you never asked?" said Knowles. This was the most personal conversation I'd had with her and it wasn't a subject I felt comfortable with. Not least because I was wondering why I'd never asked?

I was grateful for the break when Tom came in from the departmental kitchen with a tray and handed out the tea.

We'd just finished the drinks when Smith and a couple more of Knowles' people came into the room. My office was now too crowded, so I took everyone to a lecture room that wasn't in use.

We placed the artefacts on a table at the front of the auditorium and waited.

Smith looked at us in a bemused fashion. "What are these?"

I decided that I would adopt the role of expositor as he was playing the 'what? Who? me?' like a children's cartoon character.

"This, I said, holding up the shoulder stock, "Is a British infantry weapon from the 1960s and 70s. This is a cartridge from a Lee Enfield rifle from pre 1960, possibly as far back as the First World War. Oh, I forgot about these." I handed Knowles and her sergeant the buttons. They got out a handkerchief and wiped them vigorously, looking closely.

Knowles held them up one by one, "Guards regiment, Queens regiment; this one," she continued, holding up a black one, "Is a Napoleonic era rifle regiment, it's made out of horn, see?" she said, proffering it. "A couple of these are contemporaneous with the gun parts you found. The horn button is 100 years earlier. So, apparently these items were retrieved from the vampire world by Messrs Wells and Voyle today. They're British military."

Smith shrugged, which seemed to annoy her.

She said, "They'll have kept the weapons because they needed the bloody things. But the uniform buttons meant something to these people. If you're a soldier, your uniform, especially your dress uniform is packed with meaning. Each unit has its own traditions which cements their **esprit de corps**. Basically, soldiers rely on each other and each unit has a history and traditions which help bond the regiment and the people in it."

One of her men cut in, "When they set up the RAF in 1918 they had to invent a uniform and parades and stuff."

The sergeant drew in his breath to silence the interruption, but Knowles placed the back of her hand close to his chest.

"That's all right Sergeant, this is germane to the discussion. Well, Mr Smith, did you send my men into a highly dangerous situation without enough information?"

I noted two things. First that her rough diamond manner had turned all home counties and second, that she had a tone of voice that might have given Sergei pause for thought about provoking her any further.

Smith took a deep breath, "When I came to the disused facility in Southport, I went through the records. There are reports of earlier incursions through a dimensional portal. There's no information about how they achieved this. I don't know about what they tried in the Victorian or Georgian era. The documents didn't go that far back."

"So what's been going on?" I asked.

Smith continued, "We've now made several incursions into the vampire world. It seems to be the dimension closest to us, and basically the easiest to get into. You remember the World War Two defence lines round Southport? The government were worried that the Germans were also experimenting with trans-dimensional travel. The concern was that an invasion force could come through a portal, perhaps following us back through the dimensional gateways we'd made."

"So they sent combat troops into vampire world?" asked Knowles.

"Indeed. Units were sent into, what we now know to be, the vampire dimension and were never heard from again. I now think that they just were unable to return to this world. It seems that the predecessors of Dr Voyle couldn't make stable portals."

"You could have asked us," said Tom.

"We wouldn't have helped. It's too dangerous," replied Wells.

Smith continued, "In the nineteen seventies, at the height of the Cold War, they tried again. Probably subject to the same imperatives as in the nineteen forties. In both cases we were facing what seemed to be an unstoppable enemy that was dedicated to the destruction of our way of life. We'd started exploring the other dimension and assumed that these monolithic aggressive entities would be further ahead than us."

"Were they?" I asked.

"Frankly, we don't know. It's possible that the existence of your tenured post and its history is just a lucky happenstance," Smith said.

Wells interjected. "We established our trading links in this town because it was easier to make the portals here. The experiments of Dr Voyle's predecessors must have weakened the barriers, so this was the first place we came to. It substantiates the theory that the experiments you carried out recently are starting to break down the barriers between dimensions."

"Do you think the barriers will ever repair themselves?" Smith asked.

"Perhaps, but that isn't the issue, is it," I said. "It explains why there were humans in that dimension. They were the remnants of ill-advised military expeditions in the past. With the time differential, those populations could have been there for hundreds of years. But the vampires have human DNA. They could be descended from the first people to enter that dimension."

"So what made them turn into the creatures?" asked Knowles.

"I don't know. Maybe it's something that happens intrinsically in that world, or perhaps they incorporated DNA into their genome from something in the diet. They could even have been bitten by an animal native to the dimension."

"It would explain why we didn't see any large animals. The creatures would have been an, what do you people call it, an invasive species," conjectured Wells.

I continued, "Those who didn't change would have built those substantial buildings for protection. Subsequent incursions found themselves fighting off the vampire creatures, took over the buildings, reinforced them and then found themselves in the same position."

"As we would have been, if you and Wells hadn't got us back," growled Knowles.

"Did anyone try to establish a colony?" Wells asked.

"Someone tried to establish a settlement at some point. There was a human population, so logically women must have been part of a colonisation effort. Probably in the eighteen hundreds, they were very keen on colonies back then," said Smith.

"But this might mean that there's a limited number of the vampire creatures because there couldn't have been many colonists," I said.

"So how come they got to eat your mate," said Knowles with characteristic subtlety.

I winced slightly, "It looks like our original thesis, that the experiments opened the portal and dropped Terry into their dimension, was correct.

"What worries me is that the pattern of recent attacks indicates some kind of planning. The creatures themselves don't have much in the way of intelligence, but they seem to have been following a plan. Someone is giving them orders."

"Like good little soldiers in fact," said Smith causing, it had to be said, a certain level of tension in the room and, if he but knew it, distracting us from a line of thought that would have saved a lot of heartache later on.

"The creatures could have some sort of collective intelligence. We've seen that Wells and the rabbits have mental control of objects and people's senses. Maybe the vampires creatures share their brain power." interjected Wells, helping to marginally defuse the situation.

I sipped my tea and changed the subject. "There **is** something I would like to do. We promised to get Fine Jane back to the sea. I don't think she can help us anymore where she is, so if we can think about how to move her, it would be useful."

"She helped us. We should honour the agreement," agreed Knowles.

"Absolutely not," said Smith, "She's far too valuable an asset."

"Sir, we can't go around breaking our deals with creatures from other dimensions. If we lose our credibility, we forfeit any hope of help in the future," Knowles objected.

Smith must have been tired because that is the only excuse I can think of for what he said next.

"Lieutenant, so far all you've managed to do is get several of your unit killed. A simple reconnaissance in the field, you turned into a shambles. Don't lecture me on what we can and cannot do."

I thought she was going to strike him. Her fists balled, and her Sergeant scowled like he was going to wade in. As it turned out, she didn't hit him. There was no necessity. A large furry paw shot out and punched Smith in the side of the head. He collapsed like a sack of potatoes. Sergei looked down at him with a certain professional pride.

Adam put a paw to Smith's neck. "He's not dead. Well done Sergei. You're really getting the hang of this morals business. He might not even have brain damage."

"Does not seem correct, still if Mrs Theresa says so, must be good," said Sergei shaking his head. He obviously had the old fashioned notion that when you put someone down, you should put them in the ground.

Knowles cocked her head to one side. "Just when his broken nose had healed. Still, I'm sure he'll be OK. Now, how do you want to get Fine Jane to the sea? Could I make a suggestion? Ideally I'd like to get one of the Royal Navy Reserve patrol boats to do the heavy lifting, but I suspect," she nodded her head towards Smith's prone form, "that we won't get much cooperation. So I think we should borrow a small vessel. Presumably we'll have to keep her wet, so we can put a bath of water in the boat."

She paused, "Sergeant could you put Mr Smith in the recovery position. We don't want him choking on his own tongue."

"Don't we Ma'am?"

"No."

The sergeant bent down and attended to Smith.

I had given this some thought, "I want to put Fine Jane in the water somewhere I can visit her. She might still have valuable information for us. It occurs to me there's no reason why other beings couldn't open portals under the water, and she could give us a heads up if that was happening. I was thinking of a small bay on the north coast of Anglesey. I've SCUBA dived there a couple of times. It's pretty isolated and isn't overlooked."

"Will we need a boat?" asked Knowles.

"No, it'll be difficult to transport her, but once we're on the beach your lads can carry her. We can just wade out and gently tip her in."

Knowles cheered a little, "That shouldn't be a problem for us. We can set up a bit of a beach barbeque as cover. It'll be good to get the survivors from our operation out into the fresh air. I'll organise a trailer and a large enough container to fit your mermaid in. We'll meet up tomorrow. One of my lads will collect you. Finished?"

The Sergeant had put Smith into a rough recovery position and evidently decided that he had mollycoddled him enough. He nodded his head and the military contingent started to file out of the room.

"Do you think he'll have concussion or anything?" I asked.

Adam stroked his chin, "Might do, best get him to Hospital."

Knowles sighed, "I suppose we'd better transport him to A and E. You three get off home. We'll deal with it. With a bit of luck he won't remember what happened. I'll concoct some cock and bull story to keep him off the scent. Sergeant! None of that now."

The Sergeant had stepped on to Smith's hand and was surreptitiously grinding it under his heel. "Sorry Boss, didn't see him there."

The non-military types took the opportunity to depart.

CHAPTER 38

I enrolled Tom at college. Well, to be more precise, I sneaked him in with the intention of making it official later. He'd already attended some lectures, so his continued presence didn't cause much in the way of comment. I said he was sampling college life and most people seemed to accept the excuse. The faculty head would probably have kicked up a stink if she knew. But, as no one liked her, it was the teaching staff's little secret.

The next day, I took him to Theresa's office. I'd never been in before; that is to say I'd met Theresa there, when we were dating, and had been to a couple of Christmas parties, but this was the first time I'd attended as a client.

There was a small waiting room with a paint job that reminded me uncomfortably of Smith's lair. It smelt of air freshener and someone had tried to brighten up the place with some flowers.

Tom and I were early so I got to see some of the clients. The first one was a man in his forties in a woollen shirt and tweeds. He had the look I'd seen in foundry workers when I'd lived in Sheffield. They had leathery skin and looked, there's no other way to describe it, fire proof. He sat on the plastic chair in front of the receptionist's desk and looked morosely around.

"Bit of a fire risk, those curtains," he said in the same tone of voice as you'd use to discuss the fabric pattern.

"Mrs Voyle will see you in a moment," replied the receptionist, without missing a beat.

"Could go up like a bonfire this place. Very combustible," he continued.

I couldn't believe it. He was having the sort of conversation one hears in films where villains are running an extortion racket. Of course, in films the criminals have a sort of purring menace whereas this guy spoke in a flat monotone.

"Glad to see you've got some fire extinguishers in. I'll

bring in some fire proof curtains if you like."

"That's alright. We've got fire retardant cladding. Go through now," said the receptionist.

As he left, she called us forward.

"Was that guy running a shake down?" I asked with some incredulity.

The receptionist looked up from filling out a form. She seemed remarkably unconcerned.

"Him? oh no, I suppose I can discuss his case. It is Doctor Voyle, isn't it?"

I nodded.

"Theresa tells me that I can discuss things with you as you've had experience of the sort of people who come to us. That gentleman just originates from a place where people can control fire. There was a lot of call for employees like him in the steel industry and such like. Since de-industrialisation they've had to re-train."

She leaned forward conspiratorially, "A lot of them went into the entertainment business, but he just didn't have the personality for it. Poor chap. We've just got him a new job welding railway tracks for Network Rail."

I nodded again. It seemed the only reasonable response.

Tom said, "It's awfully exciting isn't it?"

"Aww, is this your little waif and stray? Don't worry, we'll fix you up in no time," she said, leaning forward and patting Tom's hand.

"Has Theresa told you about Tom?" I asked.

"Oh yes, they've already had a case conference. I think someone is ready for you in room two. Feel free to accompany Tom," she said, pointing along a corridor.

Room two was furnished with a table and three chairs; one was already occupied by a lady with a file in front of her. I was immediately struck by how similar her clothes were to those worn by my wife. Organisational dress code I assumed.

She stood up and held out her hand, "Tom and John, gosh you almost rhyme! Pleased to meet you. Do take a seat."

It was so long since anyone, except Theresa, had called me by my first name that I looked over my shoulder.

She started with, "I'm sorry that Theresa wasn't able to see you this morning. However, she had a prior appointment with a client."

"The pyromaniac?" I said.

She straightened in her chair and replied, "We don't use pejorative terms here, John. Especially not for people with Hyper Flammability Disorder. I'd have expected you to show a bit more empathy."

"Because my wife works here? I apologise, it wasn't my intention to cause offence."

She nodded sharply and opened the folder saying. "I can't discuss other cases, but Theresa was uniquely qualified to deal with the other client because they come from similar locales."

"Excuse me, are you saying my wife is a dragon?"

"John! Please! I have warned you about the use of language that diminishes a person's self-worth. If you can't control yourself, I'm afraid I'll have to ask you to leave."

She paused for a moment as her mind processed our conversation.

"John, are you not aware of your wife's, ahh, origins?"

I sat and shook my head.

"Are you alright Doctor Voyle? You've gone a little pale," enquired Tom, in a worried voice.

I pulled myself together, anyone who can be that concerned for other people when he's making the greatest change in his life deserved my attention.

"That's not a problem. Can we discuss Tom please?"

"Yes, very well. I apologise. Now, Tom. I understand you're staying with Theresa and John for the moment. We'll continue with that arrangement until we have an opening in shared accommodation. Does that suit you John?"

I nodded. Who was I to argue with a fire god, or as I liked to think of her, my wife.

"Very well. Tom, we've enrolled you at the university

under a local authority scheme integrated into your pathway plan. Over the next couple of days we'll arrange for you to take some tests. They'll determine where you fit into the educational system and whether there are any gaps. Is everything clear so far?"

"Tom doesn't have a passport or any formal identification," I explained.

"We'll see to that. There's a long standing protocol for refugees from other worlds. We do get a steady, but limited, stream of people who, figuratively speaking, wash up on our shores."

"Does Smith know this?"

"Who? I'm sorry you'll have to discuss that with Theresa. Perhaps you could leave Tom here. Theresa will be free in a minute. Tom, can you find your own way home?"

"Oh what an adventure. I'm sure I will."

I returned to the waiting room. My world was a lot stranger than I'd thought.

"Are you feeling unwell? You look awfully pale," said the receptionist.

I wanted to say, "I've just found out that my wife is a dragon from another dimension, and I don't mean metaphorically. Of course I'm a bit pale."

What I actually said was, "I might have had some dodgy prawns last night, I'll be alright in a bit."

The man with Hyper Flammability Disorder exited. As he opened the door, he said to the receptionist, "Can you smell burning? I'm sure I can. Best get the wiring checked."

The receptionist compressed her lips, "Poor man. He's having a bit of trouble adjusting. Two cautions for extortion and he sets fire to things in his sleep if he's not careful."

"I bet he gets on with bar staff like a house on …" I stopped as she stared over the top of her glasses, "like someone who should worry less?" I finished lamely.

"Quite. I'm afraid Theresa's next client is coming in, so she won't be free today. Perhaps you could discuss things at home."

As the receptionist finished speaking, a tall woman in her thirties came in with five or six men of similar age, who were all approximately five feet in height. It was difficult to count them as they milled about. Meanwhile the woman tried to maintain order.

The waiting room seemed very quiet after they'd left.

I pointed after them and mouthed, "Snow White?"

The receptionist leaned forward and quietly said, "They come from a place where people live underground, like a sort of subterranean mining community. They have a high male mortality rate and have to practice polyandry. Being in a safe environment has come as a bit of a surprise. They're still adjusting."

"Thanks, I'll see you at the next Christmas party." I said.

"Oh yes! That'll be nice, bye!" she replied brightly.

I made my shell-shocked way back to the college.

CHAPTER 39

Tom caught my afternoon lesson. He had a meeting with the lecturer in New Age Studies at four. It wasn't that he was particularly behind in her subject, it's just that she had a small teaching load and doubled as the pastoral care tutor.

She thought Tom was a refugee from Afghanistan who'd been brought up in an English speaking household. To my mind it strained credulity, but I'd been around people from other dimensions for so long now that the characteristics of people from other worlds were obvious. For example, the slight mismatch between Tom's lip movements and what I perceived as language was as clear to me as the dubbing in a spaghetti western. She also seemed to be studiously ignoring his blond hair and fair skin. But who was I to be judgmental.

Nevertheless, as I set off home, I thought I was entitled to some explanations from my wife. Perhaps ask a few questions, such as when she thought it would have been a good time to tell me she was from another dimension and not, as I'd thought up to now, from Dorset.

Theresa opened the door to our living room to find me sitting in the middle of the sofa nursing a glass of whiskey. It was a carefully crafted scenario lifted from the confrontation scene in many a Hollywood production. She immediately spoilt my drama by walking over, seizing the glass and draining it.

"Phew, I needed that. Trying to get ex-miners to take to the hospitality industry isn't easy, let me tell you."

Completely put off my stride I said, "Miners?"

"Yes, you saw them. Group from a dimension where everyone lives underground. If you ask me they're halfway to forming a colonial organism, like mole rats."

"Oh, right." I saw I was being distracted. "When were you going to tell me?"

"Tell you what?"

"That you were, are, incendiarily challenged." If you

think you're so clever, you try avoiding negative language when you've just found out your wife is a dragon.

"But you knew I was from another dimension!"

"I certainly did not," I retorted.

"But I told you."

"You said you were from Dorset."

"What on earth makes you think I was from Dorset?"

"I distinctly remember you saying you were, and couldn't go back. I thought you'd fallen out with your family and didn't want to talk about it."

"No I didn't!"

"You did. It's the only time we discussed it and you said that your family were all from Daggons. I looked it up in the atlas. It's in East Dorset and ... Oh."

The fists on the hips said it all.

"Your family are all dragons. I'll go and make a cup of tea," I murmured.

As the kettle boiled it occurred to me that I couldn't really be blamed for mis-hearing. It's not like we'd ever discussed it again.

"All these years and you never suspected?" Theresa said behind me.

"I thought you'd had a bust up with your family. You can't blame me for mis-hearing. Up until recently I thought all of the work I'd done on mythology and quantum physics was harmless. It seemed pure luck that someone paid me to do it. I didn't think any of it was real."

"You're not very good at listening to other people are you," she sighed. "For our whole married life I thought you understood me, and you just hadn't noticed."

"I still love you. It's for who you are, not what you are."

"I know, but didn't you get any hints?" she said.

"I thought the whole fire awareness thing was some childhood trauma. I didn't like to bring it up. And you really are great at lighting barbeques," I said.

That got a smirk. Then, "You know I had trouble sleeping

for years. It was because I worried that I might loosen the molecular bonds of something near me and ignite it."

"Glad you didn't."

She hugged me, "Me too."

"You sleep well now. Presumably you've adapted to this dimension. Have you lost your abilities?"

"Always thinking about your work. If you'd listened properly all those years ago, we wouldn't be having this conversation. Life got easier over the years. It's a lot more difficult to cause fires now than when I first arrived."

"What about your office, how did that come about?"

"The same way many charities originate. There was a benefactor sometime in the early part of the twentieth century. Someone from another universe made good and wanted to help others like him. Thomas Alwether made a fortune in maritime insurance and set up a foundation," Theresa said.

"Thomas All Weather, did he control the weather?"

"Let's not go there. Come on. Tom will be home soon and I'm sure I heard Adam rummaging in the larder."

The door banged open and Adam hauled in a huge bunch of carrots, tops and all.

I set to defrosting a couple of portions of ragu, whilst Theresa put on spaghetti to boil.

There was a knock on the door. Realising that I hadn't given Tom a key, I crossed the hall holding the bowl with the garlic and herb seasoning for the meat base. Behind Tom was a girl I recognised as a student at the college. She wore a denim jacket over a jumper and had a long bob of light brown hair.

Tom said, "I've brought Marianne back. Can she eat with us?"

Handsome and vulnerable, gets them every time. Marianne peered diffidently around Tom.

"I hope I'm not causing you any trouble?" she said.

"Not at all," I replied. "Do come in. We were just preparing tea. You can sit with Tom in the living room and I'll bring you in a cuppa." The couple started to pass me in the corridor.

"Nice to meet you Marianne," I continued, "I hope you'll forgive me not shaking hands. I'm a bit messy from preparing food. Oh, I'm sorry, did I get some garlic on you?"

"It's alright, I'll sponge it out," the girl said walking to the kitchen.

Putting the safety catch on his pistol Adam said, "Smooth," in a voice Marianne couldn't hear.

CHAPTER 40

The meal went well. Tom walked Marianne home and was back within the hour.

"Do you think Tom can hear us?" Theresa whispered as we sat in bed, having made small talk with Tom and studiously avoided talking about girlfriends.

"I don't think so. Why do we care?"

"Because he's brought a girlfriend home. How long has he known her? We've no idea what she's like."

"Theresa, he's not our son. We're just giving him bed and board until he can find his feet."

"I know, but he's not used to our world. She might take advantage of him."

"There's nothing to take advantage of. He's basically a penniless refugee. Come on. Let's go to sleep," I said, turning the light off.

The next morning I entered the kitchen to find Tom with a suspiciously large breakfast in front of him. I recognised the signs, so it was no surprise that Theresa was grilling him about Marianne.

"So, how long have you known her?" Theresa was asking as I entered the room. I made a bee line for the coffee machine.

"Marianne's in her second year. She's helped me find my way around," Tom replied, taking nervous mouthfuls of his food.

I'd already imparted that information to Theresa, so she'd have to dig deeper.

"Where does she come from? Has she got a large family?"

Tom had developed the same expression a deer gets when it walks across a busy road at night.

"It's Saturday tomorrow, why don't we go for a walk. We can park on the road at Ainsdale. Ask Marianne, does she like hiking?" I said to give him a break.

"I don't know, but I'm sure she'd like to come along."

"Great, you'll need some boots, what shoe size are you?" I asked.

"I could visit my shoemaker," Tom said.

"Never mind, we don't do it like that here."

That got him out of the interrogation and, after trying on some footwear at a shop, a nice pair of walking boots.

On Saturday morning, Marianne came to the house and we drove to the car park near the Cheshire Lines footpath.

Knowles' people were, for once, discreet and unobtrusive. Marianne came prepared, so got a tick in my suitable daughter-in-law book, before I reminded myself that Tom was just a guest.

We had a great walk, only marred by one incident. Not having thought it through, I had no inkling of trouble until I came upon the sign for the Fine Jane pumping station.

"Cooeee!" we heard.

"Who's that?" said Theresa.

"I didn't hear anything." I lied

"Mister fish man! I'm down here. I can sense you're there you know."

Theresa said, "It's over the embankment, down by the water." She ran up the grassed bank and stood looking down, which elicited a yelp. I arrived to see Fine Jane thrashing her tail.

"What's the Dragon doing with you!" she screeched.

Theresa bridled, "Twenty years and they never let you forget."

"Can we all calm down a bit?" I said.

"Who are they talking to? I can't hear anyone," asked Marianne from behind us.

Tom replied, "That would be the m ..."

"Maintenance," I cut in, "Maintenance engineers. Softly spoken chaps, you two go on ahead, we'll catch you up."

Marianne nodded in understanding and, surprisingly, led Tom by the hand.

Initially taken aback, my attention was drawn to the rapidly deteriorating sub-species confrontation.

"What is wrong with you two?" I asked testily.

"She's going to boil me and eat me," wailed Fine Jane.

"Rubbish, that's just an old wives' tale. Have you ever seen one of us eat a mermaid?" Theresa said.

"Do you eat mermaids?" I asked.

"No of course I don't eat bloody mermaids. You can't get them at the fishmonger's. Have I ever tried to serve you up one?"

"She's not denying it!" wailed Fine Jane.

"Look, no one's eating anyone. All right!" I said.

There was the sound of running feet as Knowles' people arrived sporting shotguns, and not the kind you use for grouse shooting.

"It's alright lads. We've just had a bit of confusion here. Theresa, could you go and see that Tom and Marianne are OK?"

Theresa stomped off, muttering about brainless trollops.

"I'm sorry, Fine Jane. I didn't know you had issues with, ahh, people from other places."

"She's a dragon," Fine Jane said accusingly.

Cue sniggering from the soldiers, so she was deliberately making herself visible to them.

"Don't suppose you've got any fish on you?" she continued, having recovered her composure.

"Sorry, look, I've not forgotten you, but I've got a couple of things to sort out. I'll be back when I said."

"Okey dokey," she said, and sank.

The escort held back as I made up the pace. Theresa was sitting on a grassy verge looking over the flat reclaimed land.

"Where's Tom?" I asked, getting my breath back.

She put a finger to her lips. "Over there," she whispered.

"What are they doing?"

She turned her head as if to say, "stupid boy".

"I think Marianne thought we were putting on a little pantomime, so she could get Tom alone for a bit," she said.

"All right then. Let's start walking back. We can phone them in a while and pick them up at the bridge. Come on."

She stood up, and as we walked back, she put her hand in mine.

"Dragon lady!" I said.

She laughed and leaned in to me as we sauntered back up the track.

CHAPTER 41

Marianne and Tom became an item over the next month or so. She seemed a nice girl, so obviously Smith thought her highly suspicious and did some background checks. He collared me in my office.

"I've got the security report on Tom's girlfriend."

"And?" I countered.

"She's clean."

"So, there's no problem."

"Just what I'd expect from someone deep undercover. She's too clean."

"You realise you sound completely paranoid."

"That's why I'm still alive. I'm going to talk to her myself."

"Oh no, please, can't you just let them be?"

But Smith was not to be dissuaded and next thing I know he was approaching Marianne as she filed out of a lecture hall.

She came to see me that afternoon. "Who's Mr Smith?" she asked.

"What makes you think I know?"

"Because he arrived after that accident you had and every time he visits, it's you he's seen with. We might be students, but we're not blind."

"It was quite a serious accident. Mr Smith is from the Environment Agency. We lost someone you know."

"I'm sorry Doctor Voyle. It's just that strange things have happened since I started going out with Tom. People have been round to my parents' house asking questions. Then this Smith guy has been giving me the third degree. Is there something I should know?"

"No Marianne, not at all. We're just being a lot more careful since the accident."

"But it's nothing to do with Tom or me," she insisted.

"I know, trust me, it'll all become clear as time goes on," I said, hoping that things never became clear to her. Because if they did, she'd be in serious trouble.

But it was a bit much for her. As I walked along one of the first floor landings, I peered down and saw Tom looking shell-shocked as she tearfully shouted at him. He held out a hand imploringly as she ran away.

CHAPTER 42

A week later I got a phone call from Theresa.

"It's Tom, he's been hurt!"

"OK, take a deep breath and tell me what's happened."

"I've just had a call from the hospital. Tom's been admitted, and they won't give me details. It must be serious or the hospital would tell me what's happened."

"It might not be that bad. Remember we're not his family. I'll run home and we'll take the car."

I was seething. If he'd had an accident at college and someone hadn't told me, there was going to be hell to pay.

Fortunately I was working in my office, so I could drop everything.

Evans was on duty and wanted to know why I was in such a rush.

"Come with me. I'll get the car," he said

"There's no need."

"There is, Doctor Voyle. What if there's an ambush? That lad's your weak spot," Evans said.

I hadn't realised he was such a strategic thinker. He took the lead, updating Knowles by phone. We passed Marianne in the foyer as she and some friends milled about, waiting for their next lecture. She saw us running past and held out her arm to stop me.

"What's wrong?" she asked.

Against my better judgement, I told her where we were going. Her mouth set in a firm line and I waited for the put down.

"I'm coming," she declared, and our rapidly increasing party crossed the manicured gardens of Lord Street, where Jones picked us up.

On the way to Theresa's office Marianne asked, "Is he badly hurt?"

"I don't know, honestly. We've just had the call."

"Who are those two in the front?"

"Friends."

"Doctor Voyle, why don't you like me?"

"Whatever gives you that idea?" I said, taken aback.

"Because when we first met you deliberately threw garlic over me."

There was a snigger from the front of the vehicle.

"And you keep looking at me as if you don't trust me. Then there was that creepy Mr Smith who acted like he was accusing me of something, but didn't tell me what I was supposed to have done. That's why I broke up with Tom."

The 'creepy Mr Smith' got some quite loud chuckling from the front seats.

What could I say? I opened my mouth to speak, hoping to come up with a believable excuse, when I had an unlikely saviour.

"Voyle is in witness protection Miss," said Evans, "Not the full system, where they give you a new name and stuff. Just a secondary bodyguard. They call him 'Voyle the snout,' in the office."

That last bit was overegging the pudding. However, Evans was obviously enjoying himself. I thought I should elaborate the story.

"Yes, there was a group of academics indulging in," I searched for the right, or indeed any semi-plausible word, "plagiarism and I found out and dobbed them in."

"I didn't think that academics could be so dangerous?" Marinanne said, doubtfully.

Evans was hitting his stride, "Oh yes Miss. They can get dead bitchy, these professor types. Love throwing their weight around, don't you Prof?"

The necessity for further fabrication was ended as the car pulled up to the kerb outside Theresa's office, and she got in, showing surprise at the extra passenger.

We said nothing as the vehicle drove, in my opinion at too sedate a pace, to the Accident and Emergency department.

Theresa and Marianne were asking a receptionist about Tom, when the big double doors opened, and he walked out. The boy had a black eye and his arm was in a sling.

Theresa walked towards him with tears in her eyes but was overtaken by Marianne who enveloped Tom in a tight hug. As he gasped in pain she let go, and said something incoherent as tears and, less romantically, snot ran down her face.

"What happened?" asked Theresa.

"I'm alright, really. Some of the other students are into skateboarding so I went with them to the local park and I fell off. I've broken a collar bone but it's not serious."

"We just didn't know what had happened, it could have been anything," dribbled Marianne.

I handed her a handkerchief and motioned with my head that the rest of us should leave the couple alone.

We adjourned to the cafe and Evans joined us.

"Sorry Sir, but it's more than my job's worth to leave you alone."

"We appreciate you driving us over. It was very kind of you," Theresa said.

"Just glad to help out Ma'am. If you two can keep your noses clean, I'll report in."

"Voyle the snout, really?" I said as he walked off giving me a double thumbs up.

"I thought we'd lost him," Theresa said, then added, "Tom" as I looked at Evans. Her eyes were watering.

Like many childless women she had a whole world of love looking for an outlet.

"Tom's a grown man. He's got to make his own way in the world," I said.

"I know, it's just when you hear he's in hospital all the worst things go through your mind," Theresa replied.

"He's a risk taker. As he adapts to this world, he'll search out exciting activities. Skateboarding is a fad, it'll be replaced with something more dangerous. But it's his choice, not ours."

"How's your coffee?" she said, changing the subject.

"Awful, what about yours?"

"Bad. I should have had tea. You can't mess up tea. Except when you're not in Britain."

We laughed.

"Let's collect the love birds. God knows we could do with a happy ending somewhere round here," I said.

CHAPTER 43

That evening Theresa asked what I was up to the next day, I decided that the time for dissembling was over, so I said that we were going to liberate a mermaid who'd been cut off from the sea when they raised the level of the river Alt.

She gave me, what some would call, an old fashioned look.

The next day, come 6:30, we were awoken by the sound of a car horn outside. Knowles' people had obviously given up any pretence of covert activity. I got up and quickly decamped. Then rushed back upstairs and gave Theresa a kiss as she yawned and ran her hands through her hair. I think she was already back asleep by the time the front door closed. I threw my bag with wetsuit and fins into the back of the vehicle and we drove to the Fine Jane pumping station.

Several people were manhandling a trailer down to the water's edge overseen by Knowles. Resting in the trailer was a bath which filled through the plug hole as the contraption entered the water. One wet suited figure reached over and put the plug in.

I looked on, "Very high tech, Britain's enemies must tremble."

Knowles' mouth twitched at one corner, which is probably all she allowed herself in the way of humour.

"You get us the mermaid, and we'll do the rest." She paused with a moment of introspection. "I can't believe I just said that."

She continued, "Anyway, Smith thinks we're going to Wales for a bit of rest and recreation. I told him we're having a beach barbeque. Right Voyle, get down to the water's edge and do your mermaid whisperer thing".

I edged down the slipway and waited for a minute. I looked around to make sure there were no bystanders to see me making a prat of myself and said loudly but a bit self-consciously, "Fine Jane, Hallo? Fine Jane? Are you around?"

Nothing. I timed a couple of minutes on my watch, turned to Knowles and shrugged. When I looked back Fine Jane was bobbing jauntily in the water, smiling up at me.

"Do you wait until I turn away on purpose."

"I like seeing you jump. You've such a funny look on your face," she said.

"I've come to fulfil my part of the bargain. We're going to return you to the ocean. If you don't mind I want to take you somewhere I can come to visit you. It's a little bay where we can meet discreetly."

She clapped her hands with delight, "You're going to visit me, how wonderful." Then doubtfully, "Won't you drown?"

"I mean that I'll take you to a bit of the coast that we will both recognise. Then I can come to the edge of the sea and we can talk."

"Oh, I get it. How are you going to get me there?"

"Ah, well that's what this is for. We're going to put you in this bath, which is in the trailer, then we're going to tow the trailer to the sea, roll it in and you can swim out. Is there enough water in the bath?"

"Oh yes, plenty. I just need to keep wet."

"Will you need to breathe the water?"

She giggled, "I just live in water, I breathe air. I'm a mammal, like you."

I hoped no one saw my involuntary glance down at her chest, "Of course you are, right swim into the bath."

She obliged and sat there, for all the world like someone bathing at home, apart from the tendency of her tail to rise out of the water.

"OK lads, haul away!" ordered Knowles.

The mermaid squealed with delight and clapped her hands as the soldiers heaved on the rope. The trailer left the water and lurched up the slipway. Someone backed up the SUV and they hitched the tow bar.

"Now Fine Jane, I want you to listen to me. It's a sunny day. Will you get sunburn?"

"No. I'll be alright. At least I think I will be. If you see me waving stop and I can tell you what's wrong."

"Good. Now there's one other thing. Once we get underway, I want you to make yourself invisible or whatever you do to stop people seeing you. Can you do that for me?" I asked.

"Of course I can, you wonderful man, I'm going back to the sea, it's so exciting."

"But, you **will** make yourself so people can't see you?"

"Oh yes, of course."

Naturally she didn't.

We formed a small convoy. The towing vehicle and trailer being bracketed by a couple of other vehicles. We drove slowly to prevent the water, and the mermaid, slopping out of the bath. Fine Jane spent the whole time sitting perkily upright waving to the passers-by and people in other cars. We got quite a lot of cheering as we went through Liverpool because they weren't used to semi naked young ladies being driven through the town. We persuaded her to hunker down as we went through the Mersey Tunnel, what with the police and everyone looking on.

The rest of the journey was on faster roads, which meant fewer pedestrians, but more drivers who were going a lot quicker than us.

The trouble was that other road users, driving along in the half daze of a long journey, tended to veer crazily across the road when they looked up to see Fine Jane waving at them. We pulled over and tried to get her dressed in a jacket from one of Knowles' men, but she took it off almost immediately saying it was too hot. I suppose a lifetime of swimming around naked in ice cold water toughens you up a bit.

We drove along the A55 which joins Liverpool to Holyhead in the sacred isle of Anglesey. Fine Jane pointing excitedly to the panoramic views along the coast.

When the sea came into view, Fine Jane became ecstatic and started bouncing up and down in the bath. We were lucky that we didn't come across any traffic patrols. I'm not certain, but driving with someone having a bath in a trailer probably contravenes the highway code.

We crossed the Menai bridge, the modern two-storeyed one, top for the cars and bottom for the trains. Just after the bridge, we headed down smaller, and thankfully, less populated roads. We passed the old copper workings where the rocks are streaked with fantastical colours, but little grows. Fine Jane became subdued at this point. It was as if the post-industrial polluted landscape offended this creature of nature. She perked up again when we approached the isolated cove chosen for her release.

This was a popular place with tourists, but we'd arrived before the crowds, so had the bay to ourselves. We gathered round as the towing vehicle backed the trailer down towards the beach. Fortunately it was high tide, even so everyone took a breather before the next stage of the operation.

As I changed into my wetsuit, Knowles came over and helped zip up the garment.

"Why do these things have a zip on the back?" she said, standing on tiptoe to close up the top part of the suit.

"Possibly to encourage buddy diving. One of the biggest safety features for a diver is to have a companion, indeed it has saved my derriere on many an occasion."

"Yes, that makes sense," she said patting the Velcro protector in place.

"Although it could equally be that the manufacturers are misanthropes who enjoy making garments that only double jointed contortionists can get into," I finished, massaging a stiff shoulder.

Having made sure I was secure, Knowles said, "Are you sure you want to go into the water with her? We've got no idea how dangerous she is."

"I trust her," I replied, "she hasn't hurt anyone, that we know of. There were never any unusual deaths in those drainage canals. It'll be OK."

"I'm not happy about this. Up to now you've had some

kind of protection. If you go into the water with her, we won't be able to help."

"Up until now your help has included trying to kill me at the merest hint of a security breach. Although your guy Pink did try to save me from her colleague."

Knowles looked at the ground, "We owe you. You got half of the team out of that hell hole. That counts for a lot."

"I couldn't get them all out, it was lucky Wells was there or it would have been a massacre," I said.

Knowles said, "Don't forget it was me that removed us from the safety of the farm house. In combat situations you make decisions. Sometimes they're wrong and people die."

"I'm sorry I didn't mean to upset you."

"It's one of the reasons that people don't like to talk about wartime experiences. Sometimes survivor guilt is justified." Her voice had a trace of bitterness.

Then she looked me in the eye, "Like I said, we owe you. I'll try and keep the same team on this operation. After what you did for us, my people will protect you with their lives. So for god's sake don't go into the water with that porpoise with tits," she pleaded.

"I must go in the water with her, we have to show mutual trust at some point. Come on." I looked around. "I'm glad your lads have got the barbeque on. I'm going to be freezing when I get out of the sea."

I gathered my fins, mask and snorkel and made my way down to the water's edge. Wading out, I huffed and puffed as the cold water made its way into the suit.

They pushed the trailer into the water up to the axles, lowered the tail gate and pushed the bath out so that it sank. This enabled Fine Jane to sinuously slide out and sink below the surface.

I waded further out and floated so I could put my fins on. On the north side of Anglesey, we were protected from the westerly winds by the Welsh coast, so the water of the cove was flat calm. I edged further out. Fine Jane had disappeared below the surface. I turned towards the team on the beach.

"Do you think she's alright?" I shouted.

As I looked back out to sea she broke the water and did a back flip that created a massive splash. She then broke surface and walked backwards on her tail before diving again. Behind me there was a massive cheer.

Knowles shouted, "I think that would be a yes."

I turned over and finned straight out to the middle of the cove. The visibility was good, and I could see the sandy bottom about four metres below me. Fine Jane shot past, more fish like now that she was in her element. An atavistic spasm passed through my chest, left over in our minds from when we were small ape like creatures near the bottom of the food chain. I consciously let my breath out and relaxed. She returned and turned to look up at me.

I'd never seen Fine Jane in her natural habitat before. Here in the sea her dolphin like tail looked completely natural. It was I, flapping about with bits of plastic on my feet, who was out of place. Her blond hair floated round her face like a halo. The elegant marine creature effect was slightly spoilt by her excitedly waving with both arms. She flipped over, seemed to search the sand, then one of her arms shot out. There was a small sandstorm and her hand came back holding a plaice that had been hiding just under the surface.

Fine Jane surfaced and floated next to me as she tucked in with a look of bliss on her face.

"I wanted to speak to you here, so you would know where to meet me," I said as she finished the fish and licked her fingers. "I'll return here every second half moon, what we call a Neap tide, at high water. Will you come and speak to me?"

"Of course I will, you wonderful man," she answered, grabbing my face with both hands and kissing me on the lips with her raw fish tasting mouth. She then turned and dived below the surface. I'd started to shiver, so made my way back to the shore.

As I walked up the beach carrying my mask and fins, I saw

that Knowles' people had taken their cover of a beach barbeque very seriously. Someone had got a Bluetooth speaker playing, somewhat surprisingly, seventies disco. They had a couple of portable barbeques set up that were just getting to cooking heat. Knowles came over with my clothes and a towel.

One of her men came down to the beach from the path that led to the hill overlooking the cove. He had a gun slip over his shoulder which he put in a lockable compartment in an S.U.V. The man nodded to me and I realised that Knowles had kept me covered as best she could. He had been up there looking at us through a scope on a high velocity rifle.

"Was that for me?"

"Not anymore," said Knowles, "My guys know they owe you. But if fish girl had tried anything she would have been sporting an extra earhole. High velocity rounds like that will kill something a couple of metres under the water."

Evans came over. He handed me a cup of tea, "Thought you would like this, sir. The water's always a bit parky in this country."

I wondered when I had earned that "Sir".

"Nice to see you again, I'm sorry, I don't know your first name?"

Knowles coughed meaningfully as Evans opened his mouth.

"Just call me Evans," he said

"How are you feeling?" I asked. The scars on his neck were nearly healed.

"Fine Sir, never better."

"Could you put the steaks on the barbeque please, Evans," Knowles ordered.

Knowles turned away, so she was ostensibly looking out to sea, and said, "Watch this."

Evans picked up a large tray of steaks, pulled off the cover and walked to the barbeque. He carefully placed the steaks on the hot grill. As they started to sizzle he looked at the tray that had held the meat and absentmindedly put it to his lips to drink the blood that had accumulated as the meat defrosted.

He then realised what he'd done and looked around guiltily. Everyone was pretending not to see him, but they weren't making a very good job of it.

Evans turned to me with a look something like panic. I walked over and put my hand on his shoulder.

"I'm sorry Evans," I said, "It looks like you've turned into a Frenchman."

There was a couple of seconds of shocked silence that was broken by a muffled sniggering. Then there was uproar, "Bonjour Monsieur," "Hold on I'll find some snails," "Hon he hon he hon", and so forth.

Evans flipped the steaks, then shrugged, slipped one off the barbeque onto a plate and tucked in, chewing happily with blood dripping down his chin.

Knowles took me to one side, "Thanks, he'll be OK. He's a lot better than he was, but he's got this thing about blood. It's like the psychological scars are slower to heal than the physical ones."

"Aren't they always. What about the others?"

She shook her head, "The medics aren't sure they'll ever be able to leave a secure facility. It was similar to contracting a disease. The effects were like those legends about people being turned into vampires. Evans is lucky."

"They might recover. People seem to adapt to the dimension they're occupying. This is their own world, so perhaps the vampire effect will wear off," I tried to reassure her.

"Maybe," Knowles said, kicking a pebble before joining the party.

Someone came over with a plate of food for me and a glass of red wine. I realised it was the girl who put so much faith in her machine gun.

"Here you are, Sir," she said with a smile.

"Thanks, I suppose everyone needs a bit of a party. I can't see Pink, I haven't seen her since the debrief, Is she OK?"

"Oh yeah, she was fine, but she was very off colour

this morning. Obviously caught some kind of bug." She saw me looking at her, "No, seriously, she has a perfectly normal stomach bug. Bit of relief, someone having a normal illness, if you see what I mean."

"So your little machine gun pulled you through did it?"

She shuddered. "I don't want to talk about it. It was a nasty business. I was in the group that Wells extracted. If it hadn't been for his force field shit, we wouldn't have made it. There seemed to be loads of them vampire buggers, moved like bloody lightening they did. I ended up lying doggo and cutting the murderous sods in half after they'd passed me. Look, like I said, I don't want to talk about it. Let's go and join the rest."

We wandered over and finished our meal. Someone poured a bucket of water on the barbeque and I helped pull the trailer back up to the SUV.

The journey back was relatively slow, and I was feeling relaxed. There hadn't been another disappearance for weeks. This would correspond to years in the vampire world. So it looked like our little attempt at genocide had paid off. I'm not saying I was proud of it. But if you pushed me, I would have to admit that there was an element of retribution for Terry and Carole.

Those of us not driving passed round some cans of lager and I was feeling a little tipsy by the time they dropped me off at home.

Theresa met me in the hall way, "You're looking happier than I've seen you for a while. Have you been out drinking?"

I pulled myself up to my full height, "I may have had the odd drink but I, my dear, have been re-wilding a Mermaid."

Chuckling she sat me on the sofa next to Tom who was watching a game show on TV.

"Of course you have," she said.

CHAPTER 44

I sat in my office writing smug little papers of the 'Sociological implications of witch trials in Medieval England' variety. These articles had absolutely nothing whatsoever to do with the scientific basis of magic.

This was because Smith had called in on me earlier. He'd sat down on a laboratory stool and looked at the circuit diagrams on my computer.

"What're you doing?"

"What, this? I'm just going through designs Terry drew up for his apparatus. I'm wondering what aspect of the device could have interacted with other dimensions. An initial observation would suggest that there was nothing in the design that could act at a quantum level."

"So why did it?" said Smith in a level voice. That tone should have warned me that he wouldn't approve. Indeed, we could have avoided a tragedy if I'd thought about how the situation would appear to an outside observer.

"It's because we weren't thinking about things in the right way. People have done experiments with teleportation and passing information faster than the speed of light. Have you heard about that?" I said.

"Funnily enough I haven't," said Smith. "You'd have thought it would have made a bigger splash in the press if they'd got a teleportation device. Did Transport for London suppress the research or something?"

"No," I laughed, "It's a big thing in physics but they've only achieved the phenomenon with light waves and atoms. It's usually in the broadsheets as a paragraph on page twenty."

"And?"

"The point being that all the experiments we carry out have effects at the quantum level. If you look at physics the various theories address observed phenomena. So, Newton's mathematics explained the movement of the planets and so on.

Later observations of subatomic particles and so forth needed different mathematics to describe them. Hence the theories of Einstein. Now, with the experiments with teleportation we're having to develop alternative concepts to encompass these new phenomena."

"I may have had a classical education, but you've already said that Terry's work was acting at the quantum level."

"Yes, but the actual experiments were really supposed to be at Newton's level of knowledge. The scrying scope must operate at a deeper level of physics than our current theories can cope with. I mean, the existence of other dimensions, let alone disruption of the barriers separating worlds, are beyond our present understanding. I thought that I would try and work out where the destabilising force came from in the scrying scope."

"How would you know?" Smith said.

"If I isolated different elements of the etchings John Dee made in the scrying scope, then I'd be able to safely determine the cascade pathway that occurred at the quantum level."

"What would you do then?"

"I'd be able to find some way of sealing up the barriers."

"How do you know that you wouldn't make matters worse?"

"Because I'd separate work on each element. The risk would be minimal."

"No Doctor Voyle, it wouldn't. We've talked about this. It was experiments like these that got us into the current situation. The only reason I can see that anyone would want to carry out this work is to recreate the original experiments to make interdimensional travel easier."

"I say, that's a bit unfair," I answered, feeling unjustly accused. "I wouldn't do anything to make matters worse!"

"Not intentionally. But then I'm sure Terry didn't intend to tear open a dimensional barrier and drop himself into the jaws of a ravening monster. I'm not taking the risk. I've got a couple of people from the National Physics Laboratory arriving to dismantle the equipment. Until then, I've instructed the building maintenance people to cut off the power to your labs. I'm serious. This work stops now."

He turned on his heels and left.

But you can't keep a good physicist down. A few months ago, I'd have quietly gone along with his instructions, but I wanted to know more. Also, I'd told Smith I wouldn't conduct any experiments using the scrying scope. I didn't mention anything about other phenomena and I had a willing subject, Tom.

My interest was piqued when I set up a Geiger Counter on a lab bench. I was going to open a lead lined container holding a reference gamma ray source. OK, pause a moment. We aren't talking about people in hazmat suits and breathing apparatus. This was one of low level sources of the kind you find in any secondary school. They give out a certain amount of radiation that you can use to calibrate your detectors.

In this case the device was ticking away recording the normal background radiation. When I got a bit lazy.

"Tom could you pass me that wooden box on the table next to you?"

"Of course," he answered and, without thinking, lifted the container using his powers of telekinesis.

As it bobbed through the air, the ticking noise emitted by the Geiger Counter subsided, then resumed when Tom had finished the task. I opened the lid to lift out the source with a pair of tongs. Yes, I know I said it was safe, but I'm not completely stupid.

"Ooh, that's bright," Tom said, squinting at the dull metal sphere.

I put it back in the lead lined box. "What about now?"

Tom looked at me quizzically. "Well, you've switched it off, obviously."

"I think I've been very stupid," I said.

"I wouldn't say that Doctor Voyle, one or two of the other students speak very highly of you."

"When we first met you stopped a couple of people from

entering Wells' apartment. Why did you do that?"

"As I said at the time, they were armed."

"How did you know Jones and Evans were carrying guns?"

"Because I could see them."

"But they were wearing coats."

"Yes but I could see the guns under the coats. I'm sorry Doctor Voyle but I don't understand what you're getting at."

At that moment Evans came into the room with some mugs of tea.

He looked at the set up. "Have you been doing experiments?"

"I know I'm not supposed to, but I've discovered that Tom can see in the X-ray part of the spectrum." Seeing a look of incomprehension on Evans face I continued, "It means he perceives the world in a totally different way to you or I."

"I'm not completely stupid Prof, you're telling me he can see through things like an X-ray machine."

I nodded.

"I'm going to have to tell Smith about this."

"Can't you just tell Lieutenant Knowles?"

Evans compressed his lips. "All right, Smith would probably do his nut anyway. He's acting a bit weird." Evans turned his head to look at Tom. "It makes you wonder how he sees Marianne?"

"Maybe she has good bone structure?" I answered.

CHAPTER 45

That evening we had a visitor. Sergei insisted on opening the door as I stood behind him. It was Knowles; she raised an eyebrow.

"Either Wells has been teaching you tricks, or someone I can't see just let me in."

"That would be Sergei. Cup of tea?"

As we settled at the dining table, Knowles kept looking around.

"Don't worry. We're alone," I said.

"Good. What were you doing today?"

"I wanted to do some research on Tom's telekinetic powers."

"Smith told you not to do that. Give me a good reason not to pass on Evans' report to him."

"I don't think Smith is behaving in a completely rational manner. It was bad enough when he laid into you, but now he won't let me do anything to try and ameliorate the situation. Have there been any more disappearances?"

Knowles took a thoughtful sip. "No one has been reported missing since we came back. It's like Smith doesn't want to believe we've solved the problem. But he's still the person I report to. I'll let it go this once, but please don't put my people in an awkward situation like that again."

"Fair enough. Maybe he'll loosen up with time."

"Doctor Voyle, there's something I want to ask you that's of a personal nature."

"Sounds a bit scary."

"Is there anything going on between you and Pink? Your personal life is your own, but I need to know if anything might affect the ability of my people to do their jobs."

"No, nothing. I've not spoken to her that much, but I was extremely grateful that she stopped me from being shot. I suppose she might have a soft spot for me. Understandable really."

"It's not a laughing matter. She's trying to get on every personal protection rota. I've deliberately kept her away from you."

"I don't think you need to do that. If I can cope with vampires, I think I can subtly discourage her amorous advances. Picking your nose usually does it." I demonstrated.

"I see what you mean." Knowles looked at her cup and continued, "Suddenly I don't feel like finishing this. Thanks for the chat. I've got a couple of guys lined up to go with you to see Fine Jane tomorrow."

"That's good. Is Smith happy with the situation?"

Knowles frowned. "That's the problem. He doesn't seem too bothered. He goes mad about you doing experiments but is blasé about you consorting with denizens of the deep. He's been distant ever since the operation to disseminate that virus. At times he's downright hostile. I suppose that's the way of civil servants. They have pressures we don't know about. He'll probably calm down as long as there aren't any more incidents. Good night."

She left the house and strode off, pausing to confer with my bodyguards before leaving.

I realised I'd started to think of the soldiers as bodyguards.

I was picked up the following morning, bright and early to catch the tide. We drove to the bay in Wales where we'd released Fine Jane. I'd timed this with the phase of the moon and high tide, so there was a window of a couple of days when we could meet each other. I couldn't arrange anything within a narrower time frame as mermaids aren't renowned for the accuracy of their calendars, but were pretty spot on with tides and currents.

I didn't want to bother with SCUBA gear, so donned my dry suit, which would keep me comfortably warm for at least an hour, maybe longer if I was active. I decided to stick to swimming on the surface. The bubbles coming out of a SCUBA apparatus scare fish so might spook Fine Jane.

I got my snorkel and waded out, putting my fins on when

I was knee deep, then starting to swim when I was still well within standing depth. Knowles' men, Evans and the marksman who had covered me on the first trip, watched from the shore. Mr Marksman moved up onto the headland, no doubt suitably beweaponed should there be any surprises.

There weren't any. Not if you were expecting to meet a mermaid that is. I finned into the middle of the bay. After a while, a porpoise like shape shot under me. A couple of minutes later, it came back. This time it slowed, and I could see it was Fine Jane. She stopped underneath me and was lying on her back smiling upwards. She then rose beguilingly and surfaced next to me. Putting her arms round me, she gave me a big sisterly smack of a kiss on the forehead.

Which I was grateful for because she smelt like a seal colony, a malodorous rotting fish smell. I held one hand palm upwards in the direction of the headland, to indicate that I wasn't being attacked.

"How is it, being back in the sea?" I asked.

"Absolutely wonderful, really, there's so much food. I've really got quite fat; do I look fat?" she said coquettishly.

"No Fine Jane, you look in the peak of health. I'm really pleased that getting back in the sea was everything you were expecting."

"It's been lovely. You've no idea how boring it was stuck in that canal day after day."

"Have you seen any other people like you? Have you family?" I was, if you will forgive the pun, fishing for information.

"Yes, oh yes, there are dolphins that are playful and seals that can be such pets."

Having dived near a seal colony, I knew that they could also be playful. I once saw a diver roll themselves in a ball before being pushed along the sea bed by mischievous seals. But that was not what I really meant.

"What about other mermaids and the such like?"

"I've not seen any, but the dolphins say that there could be some people like me further north."

"Wait a minute, you can talk to dolphins?"

"Oh yes, they're not very clever but you can get some information out of them, such as where the best shoals of fish are to be found. Things have changed a lot since I was last out here. Did you know there are big boats that have nets that go out a very long way? I had no idea the seas were so dangerous now. So, I stay close to the shore." She nodded gravely.

Of course. Fine Jane would not have known about factory ships. If she got caught in one of their large trawls that hoovered up the ocean, she'd drown.

"Oh, I almost forgot," she said, "I've brought you some presents." She dived down and came up to deposit some lumps of rock in one hand and a huge lobster in the other.

"I hear you like these, so I got you some. Look a bit useless to me but you landies are funny. Well, bye bye," she said, dived down, and was gone.

I lay on my back and finned slowly to the shore. With both hands full, I sort of beached myself and tossed the strangely heavy stones and the lobster above the water line. I then took off my fins whilst preventing waves from breaking over my head, not as easy as it sounds.

I stood and walked up the beach to Evans. He looked nonplussed at my presents. Retreating to the car parked along the road, I changed between two open car doors.

I'd had the forethought to bring a portable gas cooker and large pan together with some bread and other accoutrements. The original plan was to cook some frankfurters, but a bit of lobster would slip down a treat.

I carried the stuff back down to the beach. Mr Marksman had returned, and Evans was examining the rocks Fine Jane had given me.

"What's this Sir?"

"Hold on," I said, "First things first." I ran down to the sea, filled the pan and set it on the cooker. I got Mr Marksman cutting up some bread and slicing tomatoes. Then I turned to Evans.

"Right, lunch is sorted. What did she give me?"

I looked closely at the rock. It was heavier than you'd expect. I thought about it for a bit, then rapped it on the short wall that ran along the beach. It cracked and inside was a yellow metallic gleam. I tapped it some more and saw that it was a gold coin. I explained to Evans and Mr Marksman that when things have been in the sea for a long time, barnacles, sand and other stuff form round them to form a rock like casing.

They seemed more interested in the fact the coins were gold. I said that we would do this by the book. We'd say we found them on the shore and report them to the Receiver of Wreck. If no one claimed them, they were ours and we could do with them what we wanted.

"Are you going to share them with us, Sir?" asked Mr Marksman.

"Sure, why not." I must admit I was a bit taken aback. What were they getting at?

Evans chipped in, "It wouldn't occur to him not to. Just like it he didn't think of zapping himself home when it got hot in Vampire land." He turned to me, "A lot of people wouldn't have stayed with us. As soon as it kicked off, you could've just opened a portal and stepped through."

I could feel myself blushing and I rapidly needed to change the subject. "Lobsters ready, come on let's eat. Today we feast!" Fresh cooked lobster, fresh air, it just didn't get any better.

Whilst Mr Marksman, went for a pee, I asked Evans how he was feeling.

He said, "I still get it. Like I'm dead thirsty and only that salty metallic taste will do. It's getting better. But I think I'll always want to have my meat raw. Early on I swear I could hear voices calling me. Like there was a place somewhere I belonged, that would be like a family. Similar to being in the Forces, if you get my meaning. Like a camaraderie. I haven't told anyone. They might give me a biff chit or bin me altogether."

"Err,"

"Put me on permanent sick or discharge me, Sir."

"OK, well I'm not telling anyone. But that thing about hearing voices. It might be some kind of telepathic communication. Anyway, whatever the buggers were, they're leaving us alone now, so even if there are some survivors from the plague we unleashed, they're keeping themselves to themselves."

And that was another clue I should have picked up on.

With that, we cleared up and made our way back. Needless to say, they broke out some beers on the journey home.

They dropped me off at about six. I walked up to the front door, which opened as I fumbled for my keys. Theresa stood and looked at me.

"Don't tell me, you've been hanging out with the 'mermaid' again," she said making little quotation mark gestures with her fingers. I sniggered, she sighed and stood to one side, closing the door as I stepped through into the living room and collapsed onto the sofa.

I made another trip to the cove a month later. I learnt that there was a certain amount of competition to be my escort, funny that.

Fine Jane didn't turn up that time, or the next. I worried that she'd got caught in a trawl net or been hit by a boat's propeller. But, she was free and literally in her element. Even with the risks she was better off than being trapped in a drainage canal. As Fine Jane was not noted for her reliability; it was entirely possible that she'd just found something more exciting to do.

CHAPTER 46

The classes at the college ran like clockwork. Having said that, it's difficult to talk about vampires in the abstract when one has chased you down the street. But what can I tell you, it's a living.

As ordered, my research moved away from the relationship between magic and interdimensional physics.

I now studied the Tudor era to establish a cladogram, or family tree, of mythical creatures across different cultures. Of course, if we ever had any more trouble with vampires or the such like it would provide useful background knowledge. In the meantime, it was harmless and occupied my time and talents.

I sat for hours in my office musing over esoteric academic publications. I liked my office at the college. It was a nice, no nonsense room. A bit narrow because of the old fashioned steel filing cabinets that lined one wall, apart from the space near the window, where I had my desk. Perched precariously above my computer were bookshelves of learned journals. As a natural slob the journals had, over time, also claimed the tops of the filing cabinets.

The window looked out onto a covered courtyard. This meant my desk got indirect light and the office never became too hot. The wall behind me, facing my document archives, had pin boards with schedules for the courses I taught. I'd snuck a small fridge into the remaining space, atop which sat a kettle, mugs and instant coffee, in fact all the comforts of home.

I sat at the desk one evening a few weeks after the last attempt to contact Fine Jane. It was past 6 pm, so I could get on with some work. There were none of those pesky students clamouring for attention. I know what you're thinking. Hideous creatures had dragged one of my colleagues into a parallel dimension where he had suffered a grisly death. And here I was, sitting alone, at night, in the very building where it had happened.

However much this might sound like the brainless act of victim number three in a particularly bad horror film, all was not what it seemed. I still had an escort provided by Knowles' people, who, at that very moment were sitting in the staff room doing a spectacularly bad impression of visiting researchers from Imperial College.

In fact the troops ran a rota. So I appeared to have a staff of twelve. This was the subject of some envy amongst my colleagues. That these staff appeared after the terrible death of one of the people who worked for me, and the unexplained disappearance of another, only added to the gossip.

Knowles' people did the best they could to blend in but, bless them, they always stayed between me and any exit. Then tagged along whenever I left. Needless to say, my faithful watch dogs were heavily armed. Attempts by the regular staff members to strike up conversations had ceased when one of the 'visiting academics', I think it was Brown, had reached up to retrieve a jar of coffee. As he did so, the lecturer in New Age studies had seen his automatic pistol in a shoulder holster. After her bangles had stopped clattering, and she'd drunk a reviving cup of camomile tea, she spent quite a lot of time trying to get him in bed, with some success if rumours were to be believed. Just goes to show, opposites do attract.

My colleagues would have been even more suspicious if they'd been able to see my two lagomorphine friends who also roamed the building. I mean that they did see them. Quite often they brought large amounts of salad for lunch but fed it to the rabbits. Afterwards they could remember the nice, what was it, dog or cat or something that had somehow sneaked into the room. They'd remember stroking some animal, but they just couldn't quite remember what it was.

Adam was particularly adept at this. Sergei could make a stab at it, but he always had an aura of menace about him. People would talk about that 'scary Rottweiler'.

So, this particular evening my watch dogs were Pink, who, I think, had something of a soft spot for me. Her buddy was the guy who seemed to specialise in marksmanship, and who I nicknamed in my head Mr Marksman even though his real moniker was Dave. Adam was off on some, no doubt nefarious, errand of his own, which left me with Sergei. As Sergei tended to err on the side of caution when it came to deploying excessive violence, the problem was more one of overprotectiveness rather than me being in danger.

Pink and Mr Marksman were in the staff room, which was deserted at this time of day. Sergei was no doubt curled up somewhere.

I was just getting down to marking some essays when something made me look towards the door. Smith was standing there staring at me.

"I'm sorry," I said, "I didn't notice you. Here, have a seat." I stood up to move one of the chairs in his direction, but he held up a hand.

"It's alright Dr Voyle. I won't keep you long. I just wanted to talk to you about a couple of things. I've sent Knowles' people home. I told them I'd keep an eye on you. We shouldn't be disturbed."

"Of course. That's not a problem." I looked at my watch. "Tom and Theresa should be here at any minute. I wouldn't worry about Knowles' people not being around. They've been a bit light touch recently anyway. There's not really a need for them."

Smith glanced at his watch, "I'll also be leaving shortly. Since your little expedition to vampire world, we've not had any more disappearances. Certainly not of the young ladies that the vampire creatures seemed to favour. There will always be some people who just disappear for various reasons. But those numbers are actually fairly constant, so we'd notice if they fluctuated."

"They've not …?"

He smiled. "No Doctor Voyle. They haven't, therefore, we must assume that the vampire creatures have stopped their activities. Possibly due to the virus you were so instrumental in unleashing. I must say, I wanted to ask you about that. The accounts we got back from the expedition, including yours, were very clear. There seemed to be the vampire creatures themselves, but also some vampires that were more like a human. You had the hypothesis that people were affected by the dimension and became like vampires when they were there for any length of time. Have I got that right?"

I said, "Not exactly. We saw that the people who survived the attack of a creature almost immediately showed signs of, what I'm going to call an infection. Evans still has a sort of strange liking for blood, but it only manifests itself in his preference for very rare meat. I use the term infected, but we don't know if it's a bacterium, a virus or some sort of protein cascade like you get with bovine encephalopathy. Anyway, my theory is that once bitten, the resulting infection caused the transition to vampirism. In fact, I have another theory about the people who were there from earlier excursions into the dimension."

"Really, do tell."

"It seems to me that they must have established a pretty stable colony for some time. When you think about it, they built vampire proof buildings and had some kind of self-sustaining agricultural community. You know it would have been fascinating to see what kind of society developed in a group of people isolated from our world, but with the social mores of previous generations."

"Please Dr Voyle, get to the point," Wells said.

"Sorry," I continued, "It occurred to me that something upset the balance and gave the vampire creatures an edge. In fact, I was wondering whether there could be a whole second species of vampire. What if there were some other vampires that could work out a strategy to overcome the defences of the settlers and that's why we found the settlement abandoned and...."

I stopped speaking because he had drawn an automatic pistol from inside his jacket. It had a black cylinder attached to the barrel.

"Actually, I agree with you," he said, pointing the gun at me. "This is a silenced weapon. No one will hear when I shoot you. It's unusual in the Civil Service to be trained to use these, but then I'm not mainstream Civil Service. Far from it in fact. I must admit, I never did very well at marksmanship but then at this range I can hardly miss. So please, let's not make this any messier than it has to be."

"What, I mean, what are you doing?" I was aghast, as you might expect. I kept my hands in view but slowly moved my arm so I could reach for the mobile phone in my pocket.

Smith looked more relaxed than I had seen him for a long time. As if he had finally made a decision, one that I didn't think I was going to like.

CHAPTER 47

Shifting his weight so he could heft the weapon more easily, Smith said, "Please don't try and phone anyone, and don't waste my time with a display of innocence.

"You see it occurred to me that the sudden cessation of disappearances was a bit too good to be true, even taking into account the time differential between the dimensions. I looked at the records and, sure enough, we didn't have any more people reported as missing. Then I thought to myself, what about the people who'd already disappeared from society. The ones below the radar. What about the homeless and street sleepers who aren't on any records. So, I dug a bit deeper and you know what I found?" He raised his eyebrows.

Numbly, I shook my head.

"I'll save you the suspense. I discovered that there had been a sudden fall off in the number of people sleeping rough. The homeless shelters had fewer people coming to them. Would you believe that the local politicians and social services are congratulating themselves on bringing the number of homeless people down. Seriously, they think their policies and initiatives have been a great success. But we know better, don't we Voyle? We know that the vampires have just switched over to a different type of person to prey on."

I could feel the sweat starting to make my armpits feel damp. Smith had obviously lost his reason.

"What makes you think that I had anything to do with it? Why me?" I asked.

"I must admit you covered your tracks well. But who else? You're the only survivor of the team that carried out the original experiments. Maybe you'd already had a few trips to other dimensions before Terry disappeared. I wonder when you happened upon the vampire world?"

"That's ridiculous," I countered. "I didn't know anything was happening until Terry died."

"It was when people started to disappear. Especially young ladies. Fancy yourself with a little harem, did you? You disgusting piece of filth." He'd gritted his teeth at this point, the muzzle of the pistol tracking up my chest. He made a visible effort to calm down.

"There's no evidence that I'm any different to you. For heaven's sake Smith. You know me."

"I'll tell you what I know. I've ascertained from Wells that you can detect when someone from another dimension is near. Also, you're immune from the perception effects of the rabbits."

"But that's due to the influence of the equipment Terry constructed."

"Yes, the equipment that was used to explore other dimensions. We've only got your word that you weren't exploring other worlds. The only people who could corroborate your story are dead."

"We don't know that Carole's dead."

Smith ignored me. "I've done a bit of thinking myself. You see it was obvious that someone was feeding information to our enemies. I've gone through the reports from Knowles' people and guess what? You were always at the centre of things. The vampire creatures attacked the expedition in numbers. Someone had to organise that. Who better than you? Have you converted a few others? Perhaps they are the second type of vampire you were talking about. Some of the soldiers' reported they'd seen people attacking them, as well as the creatures. Presumably you'd organised the ambush in Vampire World before you even went through Mr Wells' portal. Then lo and behold, when things get sticky you can miraculously conduct interdimensional travel."

"But Wells had given me training."

"And I bet you took to it like a duck to water. You must've been zipping in and out of dimensions like nobody's business. Given the time differential you could get up to all sorts of nefarious activities in other worlds and no one would even know you'd been away. My guess is that you initially found yourself in the vampire dimension and got converted somehow. How am I doing so far?"

"It's nonsense. Put the gun down. We've all been under a lot of stress."

But the black muzzle of the weapon was still aimed at my midriff.

Smith continued with his theory. He didn't seem to care if I was listening. "Then what, did you suddenly realise that you could achieve immortality by drinking blood? Then the idea of a harem of blond female vampires at your bidding was quite seductive, wasn't it? I think you grabbed them and took them into a portal to convert them."

"No, I'm not a vampire. Get Knowles' people to put me in irons or something and test me," I pleaded.

Smith laughed, "Not a chance. You cleverly got that bunch on your side when you so successfully, some would say unbelievably, managed to save them. I can see them fawning over you and calling you 'sir', but it cuts no ice with me. Besides which, as soon as I took my eyes off you, it would be seconds before you dimension hopped. If you try that now I won't hesitate to shoot you."

He hefted the weapon. "Don't rely on your powers of recuperation to save you. This pistol has hollow point ammunition packed with lead azide. The bullets explode on impact. You're not going to hop anywhere. One bullet in your chest and it will probably take out your spine as well as your heart and lungs."

"But you haven't shot me yet. You're not sure are you?"

I realised I was begging for my life. I'd always imagined myself sneering disdainfully in the face of certain death, but the whole unfairness of it was affecting me badly. Least ways, that's what I told myself, no one likes to realise they are a coward like everyone else.

Smith continued, "I'm sure about your guilt. The reason I haven't shot is because something's bothering me. Why were you so cooperative about the virus that killed off the

vampire creatures? What happened? Were they some kind
of competition? You see I have another little theory. I think
you kidnapped those young women and converted them to
vampires. Then the more animalistic vampires were competing
for resources, weren't they? Somehow you'd made them
biddable, but once you had your harem they were just in the
way. By the way, I especially liked the bit of theatre when one
chased you down the street. What a stroke of luck you getting
away like that."

I couldn't deny that what Smith was saying sounded
plausible, but managed to object, "There's something else you
want to know, isn't there?"

"Clever boy, yes, I want to know who's collaborating
with you. Where are they and how can we find them. We can
dispense with the bit where you declare your innocence forcing
me to resort to extreme measures. Let's cut to the chase, just to
save time. I'm going to shoot you in the leg then work my way
up your body. I imagine that when I've blasted your pelvis apart,
you'll tell me everything I need to know."

I looked over his shoulder and saw Pink sliding silently
into the room. Thank God she'd ignored his instructions.
Holding a finger to her lips, she started to edge across the floor.

Realising I had to keep his attention, I met Smith's eyes
and desperately tried not to look over his shoulder as Pink
gingerly walked up to him.

"But there was always someone with me. Even when
Knowles' people weren't in the vicinity, there were the rabbits," I
replied.

She was just a few paces behind him now.

Smith smiled. "Of course, the rabbits. Not exactly the
most reliable of witnesses now, are they?"

As he spoke, Pink reached from behind and grabbed his
wrist, pulling the pistol to one side. Her other arm snaked
round his neck and compressed his wind pipe. All that military
physical training payed off as he was overpowered. Even so, she
must have been unusually strong to immobilise someone as big

as Smith.

She hit his arm against a table. The pistol fired with a muted bang and the bullet buried itself in a filing cabinet. Pink grimaced with effort and slammed his hand against the edge of the table twice more, a second round embedding itself in the filing cabinet. The noise of the bullet tearing through the sheet metal was louder than the silenced gun. No one would have heard him kill me. I shuddered.

Finally the gun fell to the floor. Smith turned red and I waited for him to become unconscious, so we could tie him up. Pink transferred her grip to his head and pulled it to one side. His feet scrabbled against the floor as the pressure on his windpipe slowed the blood supply to his brain.

"You OK?" Pink asked.

"Yes, thank you so much," I replied almost collapsing with relief.

In an almost conversational tone she nodded to the cabinet. "Done much damage to your files?" she said.

I realised she was trying to stop me from freaking out.

"The third year comparative physics students will need to print out their essays again," I said, beginning to relax.

She smiled, "Right, better get on then."

So saying, Pink opened her mouth and sank her long needle like canine teeth into Smith's neck.

CHAPTER 48

Smith struggled against Pink's iron grip, but as the venom took effect, his movements became less coordinated.

After only a second or two I recovered from the shock and figured that this would be a good time to slink past them and light out for the hills as fast as my legs would carry me. But as I moved forward, two girls entered the room from either side of the doorway.

They were dressed in diaphanous white robes as seen in every vampire film since nineteen fifty. I moved back towards the rear of the room, by the window. They had detached smiles that reminded me of the Mona Lisa and looked at me with polite interest. Much as one might look at the lobsters in the water tank of a French supermarket. The office was narrow. I could probably have pushed past Pink but these two completely blocked the only door.

Then, just to put the cherry on the icing on the cake, Carole came into the room, yes, disappeared, presumed dead Carole.

Smith had stopped struggling. His eyes were moving but the rest of him was paralysed. I once saw a lizard in the jaws of a snake whilst walking on a country track in Croatia. That lizard had the same look of helpless horror that I now saw in Smith's eyes. Somehow it didn't seem appropriate to say, "I told you so," but don't think I wasn't tempted.

Pink lifted her mouth from his neck and I could actually see her fangs retract as blood dribbled down her chin.

"Hi, I don't want to feed until he's been in the other dimension for a bit. Gives me stomach ache," said Pink brightly. "Still, we're glad you're here. You really have no idea how much we've been looking forward to getting you on your own." She winked.

Carole walked forward. Gesturing down at Smith she said, "It's a shame he's not unconscious because it must be painful for him to know how close he was to being right. I expect some things are starting to make sense to you now, right? I recruited Pink quite early. The bait was the development of powers of recuperation and extended recovery time in my dimension."

"Because?" I enquired.

Carole sighed, "Because of the time differential, try and keep up. Without the ability to recover she'd have been drummed out of the service, having her ears cut off and all. By the way, do tell me if this is a bit much for your limited intellect."

I swallowed and said in a croaking voice, "We did see the trophies, the ears, but everyone was so matter of fact that we assumed Sergei had got them from someone else."

Pink sniggered, "Funny how people can ignore facts when they don't fit in with their preconceptions."

Carole settled into her gloating like a TV villain. It was up to me to be her nemesis; the only problem was that I couldn't see any way out.

She continued, "Smith should have worked it out of course, but it's amazing that even with contradictory information, people will stick with what they want to believe. I guess he never liked you and wanted you to be guilty."

Turning to Pink I asked, "What about when you saved me from a vampire creature?"

She replied, "Smith was right, pure drama. I would run and grab you as the creature bore down, a flash of light and alas poor Pink, died attempting to save Doctor Voyle from being eaten. When in fact, we'd be tucking into you with a bit of a side salad. Then those coppers got in the way, literally got in the way, and I had to think on my feet. Suddenly brave Pink is the only one who won't kill poor Dr Voyle, oh diddums," she pouted with mock sympathy.

"Could you control the vampire creatures?" I asked playing for time, hoping someone would come along.

Carole interjected, "Yes, I could. But Smith was right about that as well. They became a liability once I'd got my little commune going. In fact, the only thing Smith got wrong was deciding you were the mastermind. As if you could mastermind anything."

I said, "Those animal vampires weren't what you think. They're what happens when you get infected and stay in the vampire dimension. Were there any humans left when you got there?"

"Yes, quite a thriving colony, some of them could trace their ancestry back to the Napoleonic era, back here that is. Whenever the mist came, they would hunker down in their bunkers. Now you mention it, they did say that there were originally no vampire creatures. They appeared out of nowhere. You have an interesting thesis to explain their testimony, but I don't give a shit," said Carole.

"So when did the creatures appear? Did the colonists ever describe human like vampires such as yourself?"

"I don't know," she said mockingly, "because we didn't get a chance to ask them. We fed on most of the colonists using the same trick that nearly worked on you. Getting them to open a door by appearing as some lost waif and stray. They should have known better, no one can survive out in the mist with the creatures there. But that's humans for you. They couldn't just keep the door locked and stopper their ears, oh no, they had to go ahead and open the door and then, hey presto, vampire smorgasbord."

I noticed she referred to humans as a different species.

"If Pink was already a vampire by the time I met the rabbits, then all this must have started much earlier than I thought," I said.

Carole smiled, "Well done, give that man a banana. Terry didn't just happen to fall into what you call Vampire World. We'd worked out how to travel between dimensions and been carrying out our own exploration programme. Terry's luck ran out, but I was bitten and got away."

"How? Those creatures are halfway to being indestructible."

"Actually, I opened a portal and closed it halfway up the creature's body as it attacked me. It chopped the bugger in half. Those things were tough, but being guillotined slows even the meanest predator."

"You could have come to me, your supervisor, anyone!"

"I was considering talking to someone. Not you, obviously, you're useless. But then I got thirsty, however much water I drank. It took me a while to determine what was making me feel like that. I spent quite a while working it out. I was actually starting to show signs of aging before I realised what was going on."

"I thought you looked a bit peaky at the police meeting. I didn't realise it was because you'd aged. I assume you're better now?"

"Don't try and distract me Voyle. Anyway, to continue, I started to drag people into the vampire dimension to feed on them. I did that to get a bit of privacy, but as it turned out, I was lucky again as they got to marinade in the other dimension for a bit and weren't poisonous to me. Then I noticed a weird thing. I didn't get any older."

"We'd worked that out."

"Oh you had, really, how clever. Well I looked it up myself. I reckon that my metabolism changed, and I get some youth enhancing proteins direct from the blood of my prey."

So now humans were 'prey'. This wasn't getting any better.

Carole put her thumbs where a suit's lapels would be and assumed a professorial air, "You realise this means I transport proteins directly into my blood stream. My first boyfriend was studying digestion. He'll be incredibly interested. Just before I rip his throat out," she snarled.

Pink smirked, "See, it's not just you."

Behind her, the other vampires were showing signs of getting bored. One opened her mouth in a ninety degree gape. The vampires' teeth were long, sharp and pointed backwards. The whole effect was reptilian.

Carole had not finished with her gloating, "You know I reckon I am over 100 years old. Well, in my timeframe. Just think how much I've learned."

Like I gave a shit. "When did you start converting other people?" I asked.

"I started almost immediately, as you surmised. You see I got lonely, so I thought I'd create a little sisterhood."

"Did they all want to become vampires?"

"No, of course not. But it was similar to becoming a drug addict. Some tried to go back, but then realised they needed me and their sisters to get their blood fix."

Maybe I could talk my way out of this. "Look Carole, you can't go on like this. Those vampire creatures were what was left of the original colonists who got bitten. This vampirism is an ongoing process. If you stay in that dimension you'll follow the same path. You'll steadily become more animalistic until there's no human left. Look at your sisters. I bet they've spent more time in the vampire dimension than you. Look at them."

It was the first time I'd seen Carole appear uncomfortable.

I pressed on, "I bet they don't talk much now, do they? They've spent so much time in Vampire world that they're further along the road to becoming animals than you,"

Carole cautiously looked behind her, no doubt thinking I had some trick up my sleeve. One of the girls had finished yawning. She was looking at Smith and dribbled, spoiling the whole ethereal gothic look. The other was losing interest and was looking to the side like a bored dog. As she turned her face I could see that her nose and jaws had started to elongate.

I realised that I knew one of them. Not well, just as much as you would a spouse's colleague at an office Christmas party.

"Hey, Angela," I said loudly.

The vampire swung her head round. Even that movement wasn't like a human's; it was too rapid, like a dog responding to its owner's voice. She looked at me for a second, then lost interest and went back to staring at the meal lying on the floor.

Carole turned back to me, "You know you could have a

point. The thing is, I've been following you for a reason. It's not that I fancy you, except as a quick snack. I want you to experience the constant thirst. I want you to experience the loss of your mind as my friends have done, because this is all your fault. If you hadn't started these experiments, we would never have been drawn in. Terry would still be alive, and I'd be living a nice quiet domestic life with him."

This struck me as a bit unfair and, unwisely, I said, "But it's not my fault. I didn't even know that you'd started doing interdimensional travel."

She screamed at me, "We were explorers and it was your fault that this happened, and you're going to find out what it's like."

Her compatriots were stirring uneasily. They'd obviously been trained to follow orders, but, like any dog, were unsettled by their owner getting upset. Besides which they were looking at me with naked hunger and were becoming impatient.

Carole started to advance on me when who should appear in the doorway but Sergei. I'd never been so happy to see a psychopathic lagomorph in my life.

I have to give Sergei his due, he didn't even break stride. He must have recognised Pink, thought to himself, "That's funny, I recognise her and she's overly enhanced in the auricle department" and launched into action.

The rabbit threw himself down the room. He bowled aside the two vampires and hit Pink in the small of the back, gathering Carole in another arm. His favourite little combination knife and knuckleduster in one paw.

Both of his victims feet left the floor and his momentum carried them along the length of the room, still accelerating, until they hit the window and crashed through the frame, falling two storeys to the floor of the atrium below.

The two remaining vampires looked nonplussed for a moment. I backed towards the window. They turned to Smith and started to squabble over him. It was obvious now how much they'd degenerated into an animal state. They hissed and bared their teeth at each other and then the dominant one, knelt down next to Smith. She ripped his shirt apart and started to feed, dribbling clear fluid.

As she sank her teeth into him, Smith barely twitched but his eyes were fixed on mine.

The less dominant one looked at me and opened her mouth. I could see my fate unfolding on the floor. The window ledge was pressing into my back, so I couldn't retreat up any further. The vampire extended her arms. It was reminiscent of the pose Pink had adopted in the ambush on West Street. So this was it.

The vampire advancing towards me hesitated as the one feeding started to gag.

They needed to drag their prey into the vampire dimension. Once there, the change in physics that caused people to transform gradually into vampires also altered the humans they brought through such that they became edible.

These two had lost so much intellect that they couldn't work out the need to take their prey to the other dimension. I say this now, after I have had a period to analyse what happened. At the time I was paralysed with fear.

Just then a voice called out in the corridor. "Doctor Voyle, are you in the office. Theresa will be along in a minute ..." It was Tom.

The vampire who had been advancing towards me stopped and turned. She immediately jumped at him. He didn't have a chance to defend himself as she wrapped her arms round him and fixed her mouth on his neck.

I took the opportunity to scoop up Smith's gun and ran over. The one feeding on Smith was retching and ignored me. Tom was making gasping noises and I put the pistol to the head of the vampire attacking him and pulled the trigger. The gun jumped, and a small hole appeared in the vampire's head. The skull didn't explode like in the films. I guess the bullet detonated in the skull and mushed the brain, or what was left of it. The vampire slumped, lifeless.

Tom was still conscious, "Leave me. Theresa is out there somewhere. Find her, make sure she's safe."

"What about you?" I asked.

"I'm fine. Go!" he replied and lay on his back, panting.

I ran along the corridor and down the stairs. No sign of Theresa. What if Carole and Pink were still about? I fumbled my mobile phone out of my pocket and pressed the panic button. Nothing seemed to happen, but a couple of seconds later the screen lit up. I put the phone to my ear. Slowing down a little, I told the person answered where I was, and that help was needed, fast. Then I continued towards the ground floor, nervously looked back up the stairs, in case the remaining vampire was recovering.

I reached the courtyard. Sergei was a bundle of fur, not moving. I found Carole painfully pulling herself across the terrazzo floor, leaving a trail of blood like a slug leaves slime. Presumably the fruits of Sergei's artfully wielded knife as they fell the two stories from my office window.

Standing over Carole I asked, "Why didn't you go to the vampire dimension? We're on ground level here. You wouldn't have fallen."

She turned painfully to look up at me, with tears in her eyes, "I can't go back, I'd end up like them." She nodded towards the second floor where the remains of her comrades lay. You don't understand. We were such great friends after I converted them. It was as if becoming like me had given them freedom. They didn't want to return home. They seemed to enjoy the life of the vampire."

"Yes, well, I suppose all that power and immortality would make you question your perspectives on life, I said.

Carole coughed and continued, "Then they started to change even more. You're right, they began to lose their mental capacity. I had to spend time here with Pink, but they were in vampire world for decades more than me. Every time I went back, they were less communicative. A bit less quick on the uptake until they were little more than faithful dogs. No better than the creatures I managed to train. Then I realised that it was a state of being that waited for all of us."

"Except you kept dragging people into your vampire dimension so you and your girl scout group could have a wholesome time draining their blood."

"Be fair, we left the carcasses for the creatures. We called them doggies." The matter of fact way she said put a shiver down my spine.

But there was still hope. "Look the troops will be here in a moment. We can rehabilitate you. It might take a while."

She looked sad, "You idiot. Terry always said you weren't the sharpest tool in the box. I can't stay here, and I can't go back there. If they get to me, I'm going to end up as some kind of lab rat."

She looked at me imploringly and I raised Smith's gun, hoping the safety catch was off and pointed it at her head. I hesitated, my hand shook as I mentally prepared myself. Then, she smiled, and I realised that I'd made a fatal mistake.

With snakelike speed, her hand whipped out and grabbed the silencer, twisting the barrel towards the floor. To my left, there was movement in the twilit shadows of the hall.

Pink loped towards me with what might have been a smile on her face, it being difficult to tell from her befanged gaping maw. It was too late to let go of the gun and scarper. Her lope sped up to a run, she would bowl me over in her signature lethal, almost intimate, embrace. So, I defended myself in the only way I could. I opened a portal in front of her. An entrance to the very first dimension I'd found when practicing with Wells. Pink didn't even utter a scream as she ran headlong into a furnace. I let go of the dimension and the portal closed, leaving charred flooring and cinders.

I wrenched the gun back as Carole cried out in loss and agony. Incongruously, a smoke activated alarm system, in a calm female voice, told anyone willing to listen that they should leave the building by the nearest exit.

A few steps away Carole looked up with defeat in her eyes.

She tried to drag herself a few feet, but the damage Sergei had done was too much even for her hyped up metabolism to cope with.

CHAPTER 49

There was one thing I could do to make some amends. Steeling myself I raised the pistol again and pointed it at Carole's head. Then the doors burst open as the cavalry arrived. Knowles led the way holding a machine pistol. Her people piled in behind her and spread out, guns at the ready. The image of them toting automatic weapons whilst wearing civvies was strangely jarring.

Knowles surveyed the wreckage and immediately assessed the situation and pointed the machine gun at me.

"Don't do it Voyle. Turn around, put the gun on the floor and move away from it," she barked.

I did as I was told. One of her team retrieved the gun and made it safe whilst another covered me with her rifle.

This was going to take a bit of explaining. Knowles was stressed and had almost completely lost her 'one of the lads, salt of the earth' demeanour,

"What on earth's happened? Where's Pink, and who is this? It's all right put your bloody hands down and turn around. What are we dealing with? Quick."

I felt almost too tired to speak, "Upstairs there are a couple of vampire creatures. They fed on Smith after he attempted to kill me. Tom tried to stop them, and he's been bitten and is badly injured. The body there," I gestured to the charred remains, "is Pink. This person is Carole, my colleague who disappeared, and be careful she's a vampire."

As if to prove my point, Carole opened her mouth to display as fine a set of fangs as seen outside of the reptile house of a zoo.

I continued, "Sergei is over there and saved me from Pink, who was also a vampire and who I incinerated."

" OK, details later, Sergeant, take a combat detail up to Doctor Voyle's office at the double, but be careful. Try to leave as small a footprint as possible but kill those creatures. Don't take any chances. You know how deadly they are."

To the rest of the team she said, "You three, follow the sergeant and call in some help for Tom. You two help us carry the rabbit to the duty vet, if there is such a thing. You," she said pointing to another hapless individual, "get your phone out and look up an open all hours veterinary practice."

A couple of her men were nervously covering Carole with their machine guns but keeping a respectful distance. One was throwing up.

The sergeant said, "Sorry boss, he's never smelt an incinerated body before."

Knowles rolled her eyes in an 'all around me are incompetents' way and continued to shout orders. "The rest of you, clear up anything incriminating."

That seemed a bit of a tall order, "There are bullets and everything" I said as I chanced my arm and stroked Sergei's head, hoping he didn't come around and switch into attack mode.

Knowles looked around, "Don't worry, we'll clear up the cartridge cases and cook up some story. You know, you were out with one of my people who was a prospective student and she went into your office, shot herself out of boredom and fell through the window. It's farfetched but it'll sound plausible to anyone who knows you."

Despite my scowl she continued, "Carole will just disappear, and I am sure someone somewhere will be overjoyed to study her."

Just then there was a sustained volley of automatic fire from my room. Bits of plaster and brick dropped from above us. The windows opposite shattered as dozens of bullets passed through them and buried themselves in the plasterwork of the atrium.

Knowles sighed and pinched the bridge of her nose in a way that I was starting to realise was a character trait.

"Not exactly light touch, but after our little escapade in Vampire land they're not taking any chances. OK, we might have to work on the story a bit. Voyle, go with Sergei and make sure the vet doesn't ask too many questions. Like, 'Why is this giant rabbit talking to me.' Go on, we'll clear up here. I'll get Tom to a hospital and send someone round to Wells' place. We'll keep knocking on the door until he answers."

One of the soldiers came in and whispered to Knowles.

"Say her husband has taken the big rabbit to the vet's. Don't look at me like that, just go and do it." He hurried off.

Her phone rang, she answered and turned to me, "That's one of the guys I sent upstairs. Tom's in a bad way but they've called an ambulance."

I drew breath to state that I should accompany him, but Knowles knew what I was about to say.

"There's nothing more you can do to help Tom. But the big rabbit definitely needs you. Don't worry about your wife. We don't want her seeing all this. We'll sort it all out. You can explain to her when you get home."

Knowles was right. I needed to help Sergei. The two who'd been designated as my little helpers came back with an internal door that they'd ripped off its hinges. They used this as a makeshift stretcher for Sergei.

He was lying with his leg at a strange angle. As a trio we slid him onto the door whilst trying to avoid moving his leg. We left the college as fire engines and a police car drew up, but didn't attract their attention.

Tony, the vet who'd treated Adam, had the misfortune to be working late as we rocked up to his practice.

I pressed the buzzer and came to the door. His face changed when he saw me.

"Not you again. I'm sorry, we've closed, there's a duty vets in Ormskirk and I am sure they will...Oh God, here we go," he finished as the soldiers pushed past me and manoeuvred the makeshift stretcher through the door.

"Look," I said, "This is an emergency and we really need to get this rabbit seen to."

"Rabbit? It's huge, I thought it was some kind of big dog."

"Don't say that you'll upset him. He's very sensitive," said one of Knowles' men.

They asked where to go and the vet directed them into the surgery without arguing, wisely in my opinion. They laid the door on the examining table and gently moved Sergei onto the stainless steel surface. The rabbit was still woozy and I suspected concussion. I told the vet of my suspicions.

"OK, let's have a look. Hmmm." He manipulated Sergei's leg gently and the rabbit winced, "I think this is a simple fracture. We have a couple of options. The first is amputation and..."

He stopped again as I straightened, and Knowles' men moved forward. They had a relaxed aura of menace that made me uneasy, and they were on my side.

"Okaay," said the vet warily, "The other is an operation to pin the bone. I would suggest putting the leg in a cast, but I am not sure how that would work with a rabbit of this size. My recommendation is definitely to operate. Now let's have another look. Hmmm, concussion as well you say. That can be quite difficult to diagnose in an animal."

I tapped Sergei gently on the shoulder and held up three fingers in front of his muzzle, "How many fingers am I holding up?"

Sergei lifted his head and groaned, "Oww, three. No operation, put leg in plaster, will be OK." His head sank back to the table.

"Oh God, another talking rabbit," said the vet, "That rabbit just spoke, didn't it? No. Don't tell me. Rabbits can't speak. My patients don't usually voice an opinion on their treatment options."

"Happened before, is not a problem. Set leg, will be no problem," Sergei growled.

The vet visibly braced himself, "OK, we'll try the leg first. Let's manipulate the limb and put it in plaster. Ahh, I'm not going to use anaesthetic. I've no idea how he's going to react to it and I wouldn't want to have any accidents. Will he be, ahh, mercurial?"

"Don't worry, he'll be fine. He's extremely tough. In fact, he prides himself on it," I said.

The vet set up his equipment and plaster of Paris. He pulled on Sergei's leg, causing him to tense up and growl in a most un-rabbit like manner. The vet braced himself and pulled again, beginning to sweat, and got the limb in position, then wrapped it in what looked like crepe paper and set it in plaster.

He finished and stopped to draw breath.

"I can't do a lot about the concussion, but give him one of these and keep an eye on him," he said, giving me a pack of pills. "Give him lots of rest."

"What are the pills?" I asked.

"Paracetamol and codeine. Frankly, they're mine, but given his size I think he can cope with a human dosage. Come to think about it, he can probably also cope with an explanation about how to take them. My patients usually rely on their owners. Not sure about the toxicology but then he's not a normal rabbit, is he? If there are any adverse reactions, come back to me. We'll X-ray the leg in a week or so."

"Thanks, we'll pop back when you said and see about getting the plaster off. Isn't that right Sergei?" I said.

"Da, no problem," the rabbit replied.

"Yeah, we'll come back with him, just to make sure you understand," said one of Knowles' men with, what seemed, an unnecessary air of intimidation, given Tony was having to cope with a major change to his world view.

I gave the soldier an exasperated look, then thanked Tony again and said he should send the bill to me at the college.

Tony asked if he was likely to encounter any more unusual patients. I said that we did have a mermaid, but she'd gone missing. He laughed nervously, then sobered up as he realised I wasn't joking.

One of the Unit's SUVs had pulled up outside and we gently manhandled Sergei into it. We drove carefully to the makeshift barracks that Knowles and her people were using.

On the way, I phoned Theresa and told her I was going to be late because Sergei had been in an accident. I assured her that we'd taken him to the vet's and he was in good hands.

We ensconced Sergei on a bunk and someone went off to brew tea. I sat on a threadbare sofa that they'd dragged up from the nether regions of the building.

Evans appeared with the brew. "Have this sir and then you could get yourself cleaned up. I'll send one of the lads to your house to get some fresh clothes. Probably best if we ditch these."

I stood and looked in a mirror. I was like one of those people you see being escorted from bombed buildings in Second World War footage. No wonder Tony had been uneasy.

"Aren't you helping the others?" I asked him.

"No Sir, I'd come too close to ending up like that myself. Lieutenant Knowles thought it best I come back here. You can doss down on one of our bunks. We'll call you when there's any news."

I did as he suggested and immediately drifted off into a dreamless sleep.

CHAPTER 50

I was shaken awake by Knowles. She was holding a mug of tea and looking down at me.

She said, "Stay calm. You're safe. Don't feel guilty about zonking out. Your adrenal hormones have been in overdrive. It's common to keel over as soon as the action is finished. We retrieved your phone and I got the gist of what happened from a recording. Smart move on your part to activate it."

I didn't like to say I'd been trying to phone for help and tapped half the icons on the screen.

"What time is it?" I asked.

"Morning. Don't worry," she replied looking at my expression, "We contacted Theresa. We said there'd been an incident and you couldn't get away. Get yourself cleaned up. You know the drill by now."

"Thanks."

She continued, "Do we still need to worry about the vampire creatures?"

"I don't think so. The vampires needed Carole, or the one masquerading as Pink, for transport between dimensions. From what I could see the girls that had been converted to vampires were so far gone that they were losing the ability for higher thought."

"But could they have learnt the technique for inter-dimensional travel?"

I shrugged listlessly.

She hid her irritation, but her voice rose a notch to get my full attention. "Voyle, do we need to worry?"

"Sorry, let me think. I learnt how to open portals by studying Wells as he practiced the technique. I could be wrong, but those poor girls probably can't summon up the mental capacity to jump between dimensions. That's assuming they had the opportunity to observe what happened when they were transported by Carole. What about Tom?" I asked.

Knowles put a hand on my arm, "I'm sorry, he didn't make it. He was pronounced D.O.A. at the hospital. But he'd died earlier. Don't look at me like that, I've seen a lot of corpses. One vampire was clinging on to life, but my people took no chances. You heard the gunfire."

"What about Carole, once she recovers a bit, she'll jump to the vampire dimension or somewhere else."

Knowles looked me straight in the eye and said, "She won't. She attacked one of my people and I had to shoot her dead."

"But she was seriously injured. Sergei must have gone to town on her with that nasty knife thing of his. She was in no fit state to do much."

Knowles continued to stare me in the eye and enunciated carefully, "The report will state that she attacked someone, and I put her down. Do you understand. There is no way she could be imprisoned, so it's for the best. I repeat, do you understand?"

I understood.

CHAPTER 51

I thought it best to inform Wells as soon as possible so immediately made my way to his lair. One of Knowles' men was standing next to the front door.

"Has anyone come in or out?" I asked.

"No sir, not seen anyone." Even outdoors, I could smell the smoke on his clothes.

"OK, you take a break. If Wells comes along I'll talk to him." I didn't like to tell the guy that Wells was standing next to him with a quizzical look on his face.

When we were alone Wells said, "Thank goodness you've come along; I was beginning to get a bit concerned about that young man. He stood outside all night. I thought I'd keep him company at sun up, even if he didn't know I was there. What's happening? Have those military idiots decided that I'm a threat to national security or something equally absurd?"

This was going to be difficult. "Look, there's something I need to tell you. It's Tom."

"Has he decided to settle down in this dimension? I have to say I'm not surprised. To be honest he has a wild streak."

I interrupted, "No, just listen. He's been killed. He walked in as I was about to be attacked by a vampire and the creature got him. He was dead before he got to the hospital."

The colour drained from Wells' face. "Tom, dead?" He looked aghast. "So where's the body? Have you brought him here?"

OK, I wasn't expecting this. "No, we don't just cart dead people around. He's at the hospital. Someone will have to officially identify the body. We can do some paperwork and get him released. Then you can take him back to his family. I don't know how I'm going to tell Theresa."

"When did he die?" Wells asked.

"Last night."

"We have to get to him. I have to see him. Oh, you people

just don't understand. What are you waiting for? Come on! Take me to him!" Wells shouted.

The trauma was obviously getting to him, so I said, "I don't know what your rituals are or how you prepare your dead. But when the hospital release the body, we can bring him back here."

"No, no, we have to go and get him. It will have started. Come on let's go." He'd raised his voice. The passers-by were beginning to stare.

I put both hands on his shoulders and tried to calm him down. Then he gave me a look of such intensity that I was brought up short. There was a moment of silence; then he spoke to me slowly and carefully.

"We need to go and get Tom now. This is urgent. You are about to learn something about us, but we have to get to him before it is too late." He gritted his teeth. "Now get me to this hospital place, fast."

"OK," I answered, "No problem. I'll see if Knowles' people have got a car."

"Good, come on then."

I led him to the coffee bar where the soldier I'd stood down was paying for his drink. "I'm sorry, no time for coffee. We need to get to the hospital really quickly. Have you got a car?"

He didn't hesitate. He put the coffee cup on the counter and started to walk towards the door saying, "Follow me, it's parked on the front."

Wells threw a coin onto the counter, grabbed a big handful of chocolate bars and followed him.

The coin was shiny and yellow.

I said to the couple behind the bar, "My advice is to pay for the chocolate yourselves and share the money from selling that coin."

I turned and ran to join the other two as they walked purposefully across the Remembrance Garden, crossed the road and up onto the Promenade.

The driver gunned the engine and set off before we were

properly inside, thus narrowly missing tearing a fender off the next car.

"Who's injured?" he asked.

"I'm not sure, but Mr Wells needs to get to the mortuary so there must be a good reason," I answered, as we went through the traffic lights by driving on the wrong side of the road, the drivers of the oncoming traffic benefitting from emergency braking practice.

"I'm not sure we are in quite that much of a hurry. Do you know where you're going?" I asked as the vehicle accelerated to 50 miles an hour before swerving round an estate car doing a snail like 30.

The driver executed a hand brake turn and replied, "Do you really think we're so amateurish as to be on a job like this and not know the location of the nearest A and E?"

"Please do hurry, we may already be too late," Wells said, as we turned into Eastbank Street, barely slowing as we ran a red light.

I was starting to feel sick because we were slaloming along Scarisbrick New Road, which is long and straight, enabling the driver could get up a good turn of speed.

After what seemed ages, but in reality, was about 5 minutes, we skidded into the waiting area in front of the hospital. The driver was immediately on his phone, presumably to quiet the jangled nerves of the police switchboard operators as they were inundated with calls from members of the public.

I didn't stop to listen as I was following Wells through the hospital entrance. He stopped, looking lost, so I took over and led us towards the mortuary, following the signs helpfully put up by the hospital administrators. The low activity suite, as it was euphemistically named, was down a flight of stairs then along a corridor.

"Are you sure this is the right way?" Wells asked anxiously.

There was no need to answer as we heard shouting from further along the passageway. Hurrying along we burst into the mortuary, ignoring the 'Staff Only' signs. Tom was walking round the room in full zombie apocalypse mode. Everything was there, the lurching gait, the lopsided shoulders. He was pushing surgical trolleys to one side as he made his aimless way around the room. A couple of staff were trying to restrain him.

"Oh no, please no." Wells' shoulders slumped. "We're too late."

I tried to remember what I knew about zombies. "Do we shoot him in the head?" I whispered.

Wells looked at me with the most confusion and incomprehension I'd ever seen on his face.

"What?" he said.

"Hasn't he got an insatiable desire for living human flesh?"

"You people. You really are very strange," he said shaking his head sadly. He walked up to Tom, unwrapping a chocolate bar. Tom seized the candy and started to push it into his mouth, making a mess as he wasn't quite capable of chewing. The two people who were trying to restrain him stepped back and stared at us.

Wells unwrapped another bar and put his arm round Tom's shoulders.

"Come along old chap," Wells said. A tear rolled down his cheek.

Wells closed his eyes for a second. A portal opened, and he guided Tom through it to his own dimension. As they were about to disappear Wells turned to me and said, "Wait here for me, I'll just take him to his parents. I don't know what I'm going to tell them." The portal closed.

It happened so fast that the other people in the room didn't really register their disappearance. I assumed my best expression of insouciance and hoped they thought they must have been mistaken and not seen a couple of people vanish into thin air.

I turned and intently studied the poster telling me that I needed to examine my testicles. So how long would Wells be? I tried to estimate the time differential between his world and this. It wasn't as extreme as the one between here and vampire world, but it was still significantly different. I guessed it wouldn't be too long a wait. The mortuary people rushed off to get help.

Just then there was a glimmer of light in the air next to me. The white luminescence spread to surround the opening of a portal as Wells stepped through.

By this time, several people were arriving. Before they could get their bearings, I grabbed Wells by the arm and headed for the exit.

He wouldn't let me speak until we got outside. "Is that it, is it over?" I asked

"Never mind that." Wells turned to our driver. "Could you take us back to my apartment please?"

"I think you can cancel the backup. Everything's alright," I assured the driver.

We got into the car and set off at a more sedate pace as the driver tried to phone in a situation report.

We were dropped off outside of Wells' building. The passageway down the side of the edifice was a bit drab compared to the facade. Wells let us in and we went upstairs into his Art Deco living room. We sat down, and Wells poured a couple of glasses of pale spirit.

"You must be exhausted," I said.

"Why do you say that?"

"You're not using telekinesis to pour the drink. What do you have to tell me?"

"What do you think happened today?"

"I'm guessing your people have found some way to cheat death. A bit like your telekinesis. How long will it take Tom to recover?"

Wells put the drink down on the table beside me and went and looked out of the window.

"No one can cheat death, Dr Voyle. Tom's not coming back. I took him back to his family, so they could perform the death rites. We use cremation you know," he said turning to look at me.

"What do you mean? Didn't Tom make it?"

Wells sighed, "When he was cremated he was in exactly the same state as when you helped me to collect him."

I was horrified. "You mean you cremated him alive?"

Wells frowned, "No Dr Voyle, he was dead. When we die, it's the same as when someone dies here. Then the body comes back, a mindless creature. Dead but not dead, if you see what I mean. In my world it's very important that the rites of death and cremation take place before the body re-animates."

He sat on the edge of his chair and rested his elbows on his knees. "I had to take him back to his parents. When the cremation is too long after death, the family bind the body as best they can, but it is still moving as the funeral pyre is lit. You see now why we have such a morbid fear of sudden death? We feel loss just like anyone else. Imagine having to cremate a loved one who is still moving."

I sat still and listened. There really didn't seem a lot to say.

"You see now why we're pacifists, imagine the aftermath of a battle. Hundreds if not thousands of re-animated corpses, wandering across the countryside. Families trying to find their loved ones in the midst of carnage. We very quickly learned to avoid sudden death. Violence is one of the main taboos of our society. Risk taking is frowned upon. The thought of what you think of as extreme sports is a complete anathema. Hence no ocean voyages, no flying, etc."

Wells continued, "Tom's family blamed me. They were right really, even though he was a bit of a wild one, he was in my care." Wells ran his hand over his face. He was pale with fatigue.

I tried to comfort him. "But when Tom was here, he was so excited all of the time. He was, from the perspective of your society, living life on the edge. Surely he crammed more into his short life than most people where you come from."

Wells sighed, "I know you're trying to make me feel better, but you're using the logic of your world, not mine. If my family knew I'd accompanied you on that expedition to the vampire world, they would probably disown me. I would bring shame on myself. The reputation of my children would be ruined. They'd probably have trouble finding someone to marry. Suitors would worry that the madness of risk taking was inherited."

"So, you don't really have a very advanced attitude to mental illness?"

"Not from the point of view of your society. I don't agree with it, it is just how it is. In many ways I love being here. Would you believe that after interacting with you, I find my own society claustrophobic? I love being with my family, but I always want to come back here. I've read about your Victorian society. Compared to the way my world is run, your Victorians were positively bohemian."

"So, you're not going to be replaced anytime soon?"

"No, but I'll need to find a new apprentice. I'll keep my nose to the ground when I am home. I'll look for a whiff of scandal. Someone a bit wild who climbs trees and swims in the sea." He looked at me suddenly. "What are you going to tell your wife?"

"She'll be gutted. Tom was one of the family. But I can't tell her what happened to him. I'll tell her he died, but leave out the rest of it. We'll have to brief the government people."

"I suppose so. I don't want to really."

"Why not? I shouldn't think they'll be judgemental."

"It's not that. It's the capacity of you people to turn anything into a weapon. I'd always worry that you'd use it against the populous in my dimension."

I couldn't argue with that. He was probably right. I finished my drink.

"Do you want to come around to my house? Theresa would like to see you and it's not a good time for you to be alone."

Wells smiled sadly. "Thank you Doctor Voyle, that's very kind, but I'd rather be by myself. Go back to your wife. Make sure she's all right."

I let myself out of the apartment and walked slowly down the street to have a conversation I was dreading.

CHAPTER 52

I looked at my watch, Theresa would have left for work. I made my way to her offices. As I entered, the receptionist raised her head, took in my expression, and lifted the handset of the phone on her desk. She didn't get to speak as the door to Theresa's office opened.

She came out saying, "Something's wrong. I can feel it. What's going on?"

Seeing me, she stopped dead, the blood draining from her face. I walked closer.

"I'm sorry. There was nothing I could do," I said.

Her eyes filled with tears.

"It's Tom. There was," I drew breath, "There was an incident at the college. Tom died. It was quick, he couldn't have felt a thing."

She put a stop to my lies with a sharp slap across the face. Then another, before she collapsed sobbing. I helped her to one of the plastic institutional chairs lining the waiting room.

Someone brought her a cup of tea and a worried looking client was shown from her room. When we were alone, Theresa stopped crying for long enough to ask, "It wasn't an accident, was it?"

"No, the creatures we've been battling got into the building. Tom died saving me."

It was, I like to think, a white lie.

"I was supposed to be with him but a client ran late. Can we go to the funeral?"

"I'm sorry, it's too late. Time runs faster in Wells' world."

"I see. You seem to be very calm?"

"Yes, I'm fine."

I followed her gaze. My hand was shaking, the tea nearly slopping over the edge of the cup.

"Come on," she said, "Let's get you home."

Funny, I thought, as she put her arm round me, I'm

supposed to be helping her.

"And where are those bloody rabbits when you need them?" she said.

When we arrived home, Theresa was shocked to see Sergei on the living room couch with his limbs in plaster. His escort was still there.

"Sorry Ma'am, we wanted to wait until you got back. The rabbit let us in."

Adam hopped over and squatted next to his friend. The escort took in Theresa's tear-stained face and said, "I'll put the kettle on. It's been a long night. Shame about Mr Smith. Get yourself in the shower sir, you'll feel a lot better."

Theresa started, "Smith as well?"

I nodded. "It's a long story, and probably covered by the Official Secrets Act. But I think it's all over."

A couple of days later, I was at home with Theresa, catching up on some gardening when my phone rang.

"How did it go with Tom?" Knowles asked. We then indulged in one of those conversations where each person knows what really happened, but both are surrounded by people who mustn't know the truth.

"It was Okay. They have some kind of ritual in his world where they have to bury you quick."

"Religions are funny things. You upset the mortuary staff by running off with him," Knowles said.

"Did you hear anything? Is there going to be any fallout?"

"Not to worry, there are reports of a disturbance, must have been you and Wells making off with a body," said Knowles carefully.

"Yeah, probably."

"By the way, the new government guy is arriving next week. I'll arrange a meeting, so we can brief him."

"Sounds good, what's his name?"

"Smith."

CHAPTER 53

Of course, life goes on. It's perhaps the biggest emotional lesson we learn. You lose someone close, but meals still have to be cooked and clothes laundered. Even when you're grieving you have to go to work. After a short while, people start laughing and joking around you.

Theresa and I managed to resume a more normal life. The rabbits seldom came around, although we still sometimes find Adam sitting in our lounge. I've never worked out how he gets in, and he won't tell me. Calls it a trade secret. Knowles' team were redeployed.

We saw Evans again. He'd left the army and visited us with Adam and Sergei. Theresa was delighted to see them and invited them all in for tea.

"You should have told me you were coming. I'd have got some cakes in, and some different varieties of lettuce," she said to the trio.

We sat in the kitchen and she pulled some items together.

"Are you working as a team now?" she asked them.

Evans said, "We've formed a security firm. I'd got a bit fed up with all the military bull to be honest."

"I'd kind of noticed that you'd started to answer Knowles back. I can't imagine the military taking it well," I said.

"Knowles started the company," said Adam.

"She would've come with us, but they had a job over in Mesopotamia," said Evans

"Does that still exist?" Theresa asked.

"No, that's rather the point. We were wondering if Doctor Voyle would like to help out in an advisory capacity."

"I'm not sure I'd really ..." I began, then realised that Evans had a slightly frightened look on his face.

I turned and swear I saw smoke coming from Theresa's nostrils. But it must have been my imagination.

"In any case," Evans said quickly, "we knew he wouldn't

want to, so we just dropped in for a chat."

"We also work for the company," said Adam.

"Do the British Army use civilian contractors?" I asked.

"Them too," he said.

Evans shifted uncomfortably in his chair, "The boss will have my guts for garters," he said looking pointedly at the rabbit. "He means we're sometimes employed by non-state parties."

Theresa and I just looked at them.

Evans turned red, "We also do some pro bono work on modern day slavery. What you might call direct action."

There was the characteristic low growl that was Sergei's equivalent of a polite 'ahem'.

"Help people who can't help selves," he said, and that seemed to finish that part of the conversation.

"By the way, is Evans really your name?" I asked.

"I've got used to it."

"How's your condition?" asked Theresa.

"Well under control, thank you Ma'am. As time passes, it gets less. I just have a preference for underdone meat now."

"That's nice," she said brightly.

"Me and Sergei still like carrots."

"Of course you do, dear. Here, have another," offered Theresa.

CHAPTER 54

Theresa still helps people and I've continued teaching at the college. The main difference is that I no longer do any practical research. The new government man, imaginatively called Smith, saw to that. The college principal was upset as I was one of the few lecturers who attracted research funding, but Smith was quite eloquent about the need to curtail my work, including some blatant threats. Which was fine by me, I'd reached the limit of what I was prepared to do.

The new Smith was taller than his predecessor and balding but with the same air of tension. Presumably it came with the job. He met me in the makeshift office space the college had constructed for me, out of plywood. It was on the ground floor, next to the toilets. I think I might have blotted my copy book as far as the principal was concerned. Burning the place down was one thing, not getting money in was something else.

"Nice place they've made for you," Smith said over the noise of the students going between lectures. He had the trace of a London accent softened, I guessed, by moving around the world.

"Yes, they had to find me somewhere after the explosion in the laboratory."

"Not a bad cover story, your messing about with solvents, even though I do say so myself. Funny, all those bullets from World War Two they found embedded in the walls," Smith mused.

"Frankly, I'm just glad to be in employment."

"Well, you know there's a countrywide shortage of comparative physicists."

"Was it you that kept me in a job?" I said.

"Let's just say that I prefer to have the errant Doctor Voyle where I can keep an eye on him."

"Are you staying up here?" I asked.

"There doesn't seem to be any sign that the weakness

between dimensions will repair itself anytime soon. And I want to have you around in an advisory capacity in case there are any more incidents." He emphasised the last word.

"Do you believe what happened? All of the guys your predecessor spoke to in London seemed dead set on explaining it all away."

"Hmm, they've all been reassigned. It was more jockeying for position in the Government hierarchy than anything else. They had a story that the minister wanted to hear. However, when it all came out the naysayers ended up with egg on their faces. I have to say that the testimony of Knowles and her people was pretty persuasive."

"What about my report?"

Smith said, "I thought it was useful, but to be honest other people's information was given more credence."

"I hope you don't want to start up any work. I'm not sure I can go through that again," I said.

"It's thought best to leave well alone and hope other resources aren't required. I've explained it all to your principle." He looked at the walls of my office. "I'm not sure he took it that well."

"Other resources being the army?"

"Just so. However, there are one or two loose ends that might need attending to from time to time," Smith said.

I had a sinking feeling. "Like what?"

"A little bird told me that there are rumours circulating around the fish farms in Scotland."

"What's that got to do with me?"

"The rumours concern a mermaid."

"Ahh, I see. Do you want me to pack?"

The End

AFTERWORD

I would like to thank Patty, who has been my mentor, and Hillary who proofread the manuscript.
Southport is a real place. It is a resort and commuter town just north of Liverpool in the United Kingdom. It has an air of faded grandeur dating from the 1920s when it was described as the Montpellier of the North.

I have taken the liberty of giving the town a fictitious University. There was a College on Lord Street, but it is now a vibrant community space with a museum and theatre. I recommend a visit.

The Fine Jane pumping station is situated on the Cheshire Lines footpath. It can be accessed as described in this novel. I advise against entering into conversation with any mermaids you may encounter.

Printed in Great Britain
by Amazon

36004507R00165